"I am leaving now."

⁓∘∘⁓

She pulled at her gown to straighten it, although he had done nothing to mar it. Likely that would have changed within the span of five minutes if she hadn't broken away. She glared at him with all the censure and haughtiness of the highest duchess in the Empire.

Nicholas stared at her. "You are leaving?" he repeated stupidly.

She nodded once. "I will return tomorrow, though. And I expect you will have some information for me regarding your own search for my brother by then. Good evening, *my lord.*"

Nicholas flinched as she left the room and slammed the door behind her. He stared at the place she had stood. In his thirty years on this earth, he had been with many women. His reaction to them and theirs to him had varied, of course, but none of them had ever kissed him and pulled away first. None of them had ever looked at him like his touch was akin to acid.

None of them had ever been so unmoved by his prowess as Jane Fenton. And he had never been so driven to prove to a woman that he could make her tremble.

HER NOTORIOUS VISCOUNT

Jenna Petersen

AVON

An Imprint of HarperCollinsPublishers

AVON BOOKS
An Imprint of HarperCollins*Publishers*
10 East 53rd Street
New York, New York 10022-5299

Copyright © 2009 by Jesse Petersen
ISBN 978-0-06-147081-3
www.avonromance.com

First Avon Books paperback printing: April 2009

Avon Trademark Reg. U.S. Pat. Off. and in Other Countries, Marca Registrada, Hecho en U.S.A.
HarperCollins® is a registered trademark of HarperCollins Publishers.

Printed in the U.S.A.

10 9 8 7 6 5 4 3 2 1

This book is for all the MMA fighters who have entertained me with their limitless talent and inspiring heart in the octagon. And to Michael, who is forever patiently correcting my stance. Eventually I'll throw a jab the right way, babe, I promise.

HER NOTORIOUS
VISCOUNT

Prologue

November 1815

Nicholas Stoneworth raised his head reluctantly and tried to determine if the pounding that echoed in the room around him was part of a dream or reality. Since it mirrored the painful throbbing of his alcohol-laden haze, he decided it was, unfortunately, real.

With a groan, he pushed away the arm of his companion, a delightful flame-haired barmaid named . . . Anna? Annabelle? Arabelle?

Well, whatever her name was, when her arm flopped off his naked belly she didn't stir, just sank a little further into the warmth of his bed.

Getting to his feet, Nicholas searched around for a dressing gown as the winter chill slapped his skin. The fire had been the least of his worries the night before when he and . . . Alexandra . . . no . . . Amelia? When he and his *paramour* came stumbling into his room.

Now his small chamber was chilled and he was paying the price.

And still the pounding at his door went on, making his head ache and his stomach turn from the alcohol he had consumed hours before.

"I'm coming, goddamn it!" he bellowed as he tied his robe around his waist negligently and strode down the short hallway.

Nearly ripping the door off its rusty hinges, he threw it open.

"What?" he bellowed into the face of his best friend and fellow pugilist, Ronan "Rage" Riley.

Normally Rage was smart enough not to rouse him before afternoon. The two men had grown to be almost like brothers after all their years in the underground, participating in the fights that had made Nicholas both revered and reviled in varying levels of Society.

Rage's dark hair was sticking up at odd angles, and the strange, almost pained look on his face stopped Nicholas in his tracks. He stared at his friend for a long, silent moment, watching as Rage's eyes softened with pity.

His stomach sank. This visit was not going to end well.

"What is it?" Nicholas asked again, this time his voice softer. "Tell me."

Rage opened his mouth and shut it, almost as if he couldn't find the right words. Then he shook his head and merely said, "Stone, your brother is dead."

Nicholas staggered back, the force of his best friend's blunt statement hitting him in the gut like a sucker punch. If he had been nauseous before, the feeling now grew until it was overpowering. His headache faded into the background of a far deeper, more powerful pain. One that overwhelmed him until he couldn't see anything, couldn't hear anything, couldn't *think* about anything except the echo of his friend's voice.

Your brother is dead. Your brother is dead. Your brother is dead.

Although he didn't recall moving, Nicholas found himself on his knees on the uncomfortable wooden floor. When he lifted his hands they were clenched in fists and shaking. His breath came in broken, sick heaves.

He looked up at Rage, wishing he could call him a liar. Wishing he could punch him and make his friend take back those four horrible words. But he couldn't. He knew Rage too well. His best friend wouldn't tell him such a thing unless he had evidence that it was a fact.

And that meant that Nicholas's life had just been altered in every way imaginable.

Chapter 1

April 1816

Jane Fenton watched as another group of giggling, simpering young women spun by her in the arms of the current group of eligible bucks and titled lords. She held back a sigh and tried to keep her toes from tapping to the beat of the country jig, beneath her plain, serviceable gown.

How quickly things changed. Just two years ago, *she* had been one of those silly girls, enjoying her Season with all the hopes in the world for the future.

"Jane," the Countess Ridgefield said at her side. Her employer lifted the gold-rimmed spectacles she kept on a chain around her neck and scanned the crowd. "Do you see anyone of my acquaintance?"

Jane stifled a smile at the picture Lady Ridgefield made. The feather Jane had placed in her employer's hair earlier in the evening had begun to list downward, sticking out at an odd angle to the side of her head. Her spectacles, which she really should have been wearing all the time, although she argued that point with Jane incessantly, were crooked and gave Lady Ridgefield a madcap appearance that lightened Jane's heavy heart considerably.

Although flighty, Lady Ridgefield was one of the kindest women Jane had ever met. She knew full well she was lucky to have obtained a position as her lady's companion. Other young women of her acquaintance had not been so fortunate in their employers.

Rising to her tiptoes, Jane scanned the crowd.

"Lady Williamston is over by the punch bowl," she said, then lowered her voice to indulge in Lady Ridgefield's love of gossip. "Likely putting whiskey in her cup from that secret stash she keeps in her reticule."

Her employer giggled like a school miss. "Anyone else?"

Jane continued to whisper little details of the attendees around the room, adding her own commentary to the descriptions until Lady Ridgefield's cheeks were pink with pleasure.

"Whom would you like to speak to first?" Jane asked with a pull of dread in her chest.

Once they were with the other ladies of her employer's rank, she would be forgotten again, despite the fact that many of the women had once been friends of her mother and father. This constant reminder of what she'd lost was never easy for Jane, no matter how she prepared herself for the inevitable.

"There is a commotion over there," Lady Ridgefield said with a wave of her fan. "What is happening, Jane? I cannot see!"

Jane turned toward the entrance to the ballroom. As silly as she was, Lady Ridgefield could be quite observant when it came to matters of Society. Indeed, an unnatural crowd had formed at the entrance to the ballroom. Someone very important must have entered. How pleased Lady Ridgefield would be if Wellington or even the prince himself joined their party tonight. It would keep her employer happy for months, which Jane had come to see as a lofty life goal.

Finally the crowd parted, almost as if Moses himself were moving them aside. But it wasn't a biblical figure who stepped away from the fray. No, indeed, the man who sauntered into the ballroom did not look like the kind to *read* a Bible, let alone belong in one.

Rather, he looked like sin.

Jane sucked in her breath despite herself. The stranger was tall, very tall. More than half a head bigger than any of the men who surrounded him.

But it was more than his superior height that drew her attention. He had a presence about him. A strength that was reflected both in the lean lines of his body and the way he moved.

He was dressed . . . oddly. His coat was a few seasons behind the fashion and his shirt looked a little faded. Plus the items were ill-fitted, too tight in some places and far too loose in others.

Certainly he was aware of the scrutiny of those around him. One would have to be daft not to see and feel it. And it wasn't friendly interest, either. Shock, anger, even disgust were reflected on the faces in the crowd.

Jane looked at the interloper more closely, surprised by the ire he inspired. There was something familiar about him, but she didn't think they had ever met.

"It is a man," Jane murmured since Lady Ridgefield had now begun tugging on the woolen sleeve of her ugly gown. "I do not know who he is. I feel like I've seen him before, but . . ."

She trailed off. He was getting closer now, and for some odd reason her heart began to pound.

"I know who it may be!" Lady Ridgefield whispered. "Oh, I had heard he might be making a return to Society, but I never thought he'd dare come here tonight!"

"Who is he?" Jane asked, ever more distracted the nearer the man came.

His eyes, God, they were beautiful. Bright, almost painful blue against his tanned skin and dark, close-cropped hair. She started when she realized one of them was faintly blackened, as if he had recently been in a fight.

And then he turned his gaze on her. Those eyes that had so surprised and captivated her moved over her in one sweep. If Jane's heart had pounded before, now it felt as though it stopped completely. As though time had frozen as this man looked at her.

But then he moved on, dismissing her just as everyone dismissed her.

Jane sighed.

"Yes, indeed," Lady Ridgefield crowed as she lowered her spectacles and grasped Jane's arm in a death grip. She was practically vibrating with excitement. "That *is* him! His name is Viscount Nicholas Stoneworth. He just inherited the title from his poor late brother—"

"Anthony Stoneworth," Jane finished, her gaze rushing to the man who now had a name to go along with his harsh, handsome face.

A name that explained why Nicholas Stoneworth seemed so familiar. He had been Anthony Stoneworth's twin brother, and Jane had seen the late viscount dozens of times. Perhaps she had even danced with him before she fell into her current situation. The other man had always seemed gentlemanly and kind enough.

But the expression in Nicholas's eyes was far from kind. And there was nothing gentlemanly about him. He resembled a tiger who had been caged for exhibit. Dangerous and feral.

"The poor viscount died just six months ago and it's been a terrible ordeal for the family," Lady Ridgefield continued conspiratorially.

Jane flinched. "Death is always difficult, especially of so young and healthy a man. It was a riding accident, wasn't it? And he had children?"

"Daughters," Lady Ridgefield said with a sad nod. "Hardly out of the cradle, both of them. But the ordeal comes almost as much from Nicholas Stoneworth himself, as from the tragedy of his brother's death. After all, he dissolved into the underground years ago, doing Lord knows what, but some people say he owned a gambling den, fathered a hundred bastard children, even that he was involved in . . . *pugilism.*"

Well, that would certainly explain the black eye. Jane's gaze flashed to the man a third time. He had a drink in his hand now and was glowering at anyone who dared come within an arm's length of him. No one seemed willing to test the parameter he had established.

Yes, he looked like he belonged in the London underground. Jane held her breath. She had never yet met anyone who had *real* connections to that dark and dangerous world, no matter how hard she searched. Yet here someone had been dropped almost into her very lap! Perhaps it was providence.

"The underground?" she repeated, knowing that her employer would not be able to keep herself from gossiping.

"Yes. I don't know the particulars of why they quarreled, but he was all but disinherited by his father. Yet, what could they do when Anthony died? Nicholas Stoneworth is legal heir to the Bledsoe title since his brother didn't have sons." Lady Ridgefield sighed. "It is a truly terrible thing in every way. And I always liked the boy as a child."

Jane wanted to ask more, but Lady Ridgefield was already moving across the ballroom. "Come now, we must find Griselda! I *know* she will have something to say about this."

Jane followed Lady Ridgefield blindly into the crowd toward her pack of friends across the room. But her mind was not on her employer's gossip or even on anticipating Lady Ridgefield's every need.

Instead, Jane could only think of Nicholas Stoneworth, and how he might be the key to everything her heart desired.

Nicholas Stoneworth glowered at the room around him. He hated being here, he hated the crowd, and he hated this blasted cravat that felt like a noose around his neck. Mostly he hated looking into the mirror before he departed the town home he had let in London and seeing his brother's face staring back at him. For a moment it had been quite startling, and the maids would probably be picking shards of glass out of the Oriental carpet for months to come.

But he was here, by God. And he intended to drink as much as he could. In fact, as he snatched a third glass of whiskey off the tray of a ridiculously liveried serving boy, he intended to do so until he wouldn't hear the whispers and see the stares of those around him.

Being on display wasn't the problem. When he was in a boxing ring, he never minded the gaping masses that talked about him and cried out catcalls when he passed. Truth be told, he reveled in the power his impeccable record gave him.

No, it was the discomfort of not *belonging* where he was that troubled him. Everyone around him was judging him, just as his father had always judged him. They were all comparing him to his brother.

And he would never do anything but come up miserably short.

"Nicholas."

He froze, drink midway to his lips, and stared with unseeing eyes at the wall across the room from him. That voice. Although they had spoken a few times in the past strained months since Anthony's death, it was still a shock each time he heard it.

His father.

Slowly, Nicholas turned and faced the man whom he had never pleased in thirty years. He flinched. He wasn't yet accustomed to how much older his father looked since Nicholas had left the family. The past six months had made him older still. His dark hair was lightened by gray and his eyes, the same blue eyes Nicholas and his brother had inherited, had lost some of their luster.

With practiced calm, Nicholas smirked. "Hello, my lord. Fancy meeting you here."

His father's jaw twitched as if his teeth were set, but he didn't explode as Nicholas expected he would like to. Of course, that had nothing to do with a desire to control his infamous temper or an attempt at peace. It was more about maintaining appearances. Here in the ballroom, where everyone was either blatantly or secretly watching the exchange between estranged father and son, the marquis could not say whatever was truly on his mind.

"I did not realize you would be in attendance," his father choked out.

Nicholas tilted his head. "I got an invitation from Lord Glormoker—"

"Glouchester," his father corrected on a barely perceptible sigh.

"—and I assumed there would be alcohol," Nicholas continued with a smile, though he felt little good humor at the utter disappointment on his father's face. The old man had stopped trying to hide it long ago. "So I came. Although I wouldn't count this"—he downed the watery drink in one swig—"as spirits of any kind."

Though when he drank enough of them in short succession, they did help him obtain the desired haze. After another five or ten, he might be happily numb and survive the evening.

His father stepped forward and leaned in. "You are making a spectacle of yourself."

"How so?" he drawled in response.

The marquis clenched his fists at his sides. "Those clothes are a disgrace. You have two days' worth of stubble on your cheeks, you are drinking like a sailor, and is that a black eye I see?"

Another thin smile lifted Nicholas's lips. He'd gotten that black eye sparring with Rage in the parlor of his town home two days before. Three of the poor servants had promptly resigned out of sheer terror, but the exercise had relieved Nicholas's feeling of being trapped, at least for a while.

"I see you find this funny," his father said in disgust, stepping away. "You care very little about your reputation, or the reputation of this family."

Nicholas shrugged, years of bitterness welling up in him as he stared into the eyes so like his own. "And? Do you really expect more from me?"

"Not expect," his father said as he turned away and strode back into the crowd in a few long, angry steps. "Only hoped. A fool's hope."

Nicholas stared at his father's back as it moved away from him. Farther in the distance, he saw his mother watching him. Her face was crumpled and soft with pained emotion.

And suddenly the fun he'd had tweaking his father, the moment of pleasure he'd taken in living up to every expectation the old man held, disappeared. Leaving behind shame, disgust, and grief. Grief for his brother. Grief for what should have been, but would never be.

So he set his empty glass down and left the ballroom.

Jane watched surreptitiously as Viscount Nicholas Stoneworth and his father had it out in front of a large portion of the Upper Ten Thousand. Most of the people around her weren't even surreptitious. They stared openly, practically drooling as the little family drama played out across the room.

She couldn't help but feel sorry for them both. Although she couldn't hear the soft words the men exchanged, it was plain from their expressions that there was a great deal of painful emotion between them. It actually put her to mind of her own brother and father, the way they had exchanged words in the weeks before Marcus vanished, never to be seen again.

She had never understood what *they* fought about, either. When her mother died years and years before, the three of them had formed a tight, cohesive unit, bonding together in their grief. For a long time they had been happy.

But then that had unraveled. Slowly at first. An argument here, an emotional outburst there. Soon it had grown out of control, like a racer's phaeton on a sharp turn.

But still, when Jane looked across the room at Nicholas Stoneworth and his father, she couldn't understand how in God's name they could fight as they were. Especially so soon after such a tragic family event. Anthony Stoneworth's death should have brought them together, allowed them to overcome their petty differences.

If the new viscount couldn't even do that for his own family . . . could he truly help *her*?

Well, there was only one way to find out. As Lord Bledsoe walked away from his wayward son and Stoneworth exited the ballroom, Jane leaned in closer to her employer and her friends. Certainly she would hear more than she ever needed to know from them.

"There now," one of the women, Lady Abebowale, said as she spun back on her friends with a cruel light of pleasure in her eyes. "You see, Stoneworth is determined to ruin the entire family! He shall *never* return to polite Society no matter what he does. He has become a heathen, through and through."

Lady Ridgefield shook her head. Unlike her friend, she was charitable and didn't have an unkind bone in her plump body. "But the new viscount *did* come here tonight, surely that means he will make some attempt to do his duty in the end."

Another of the older women, Lady Campbell-Carlile, sniffed. "And there are some who value a title and the large fortune Stoneworth has over all else. *They* will accept him."

Lady Abebowale's eyes bugged. "Well, we would not accept any of those people again, that is certain. Can you imagine having *him* appear at country parties? He would diddle all the maids and fight with the gentlemen before supper the first night."

Jane bit her lip. When she was in Society, no one ever would have spoken so plainly in front of her because she was unmarried. But now that she was considered a servant, the women never hesitated to be blunt. So Lord Stoneworth had a lusty reputation, as well as a violent one. That seemed to fit.

She would have to be very careful with him once she got the one key piece of information she was lacking.

Leaning forward, she whispered to Lady Ridgefield, "Where is he living?"

Her employer was accustomed to such intrusions on her part. Jane often reminded Her Ladyship about the key pieces of gossip she might have forgotten in her excitement at these parties.

Lady Ridgefield's head bobbed up and down. "Where *is* Stoneworth staying now? Not in the home occupied by his late brother?"

Lady Campbell-Carlile was the one who answered. "Great heavens, no. The viscountess and the children still live there. I heard Stoneworth would not move into the place for the shame he brought his family, though I cannot imagine that blue-eyed devil feeling shame over anything."

Jane shifted in frustration. Damn it all, why did they not say where Stoneworth was living and be finished with it?

Her employer seemed to read her thoughts, for she said, "Where then? Certainly not with his father and mother if tonight is any indication."

Lady Campbell-Carlile shook her head. "No,

gossip has it that he let a home in Abernathe Court, near St. James. And his new neighbors are quite put out by the company he regularly keeps."

Jane no longer heard any more of the women's conversation. Now she knew everything she needed to know. All she had left to do was gather her courage and do something about it.

Chapter 2

Nicholas had opened a bottle of whiskey the moment he returned to his town home. A good, strong alcohol that would do what the watered-down version at the ball could not. But now he stared at the bottle that had been sitting going stale on his desk for some time.

It wasn't that he didn't want to numb away the memories of the night. It was that he wasn't sure he deserved such an escape.

"Was it truly necessary to do all that, Nicholas?"

He turned at the soft voice at his door. There, framed by the light from the hallway behind her, stood his sister-in-law, Lucinda. His brother's widow.

Over the years, Nicholas had wondered at many things about his twin. Like how Anthony could stand the life of a respectable man. Or how he could endure their father's constant interference and suggestions.

But one thing he had never questioned was why his brother had married Lucinda. She had always been stunning, *the* diamond of the first water the year she made her debut. And kind. Even when Nicholas was utterly shunned by Society, Lucinda never asked Anthony to extract his twin from their lives. A fact Nicholas had never mentioned, but always appreciated.

And now she stood in his doorway, unable to look at him because Nicholas's face was the same as that of the man she had loved and lost. Even now, as she accused him with just the quietest of words, the faintest lilt of disappointment, Lucinda kept her eyes trained anywhere else.

"Hello, Luc—" he began.

She held up her hand. "Please," she whispered, and her voice cracked. "Please don't call me by my given name. You sound too much like . . ."

She trailed off, and a heavy silence hung between them. Nicholas didn't need her to finish the sentence.

"I did not know you were in attendance tonight," he said quietly. As far as he knew, Lucinda hadn't even left her London home since his brother was buried.

"It has been six months, and your mother was worried that I had locked myself away entirely. It is against protocol, but she was so upset, I could not deny her. I would not have attended if she had not practically begged me. So I stood in the background, wearing my widow's weeds, and did my best not to speak to anyone, but I was there." Her voice was so bitter that Nicholas wanted to cover his ears.

"I should not have behaved that way," he finally admitted, feeling a more magnified version of the shame he had experienced when he looked at his mother across the ballroom earlier in the evening.

"No," she agreed, lifting her gaze to him finally and flinching away immediately. "You should not have. I realize you take a childish pleasure in twisting your father about, but you must know what damage your surly attitude and poor dress and generally wicked behavior do. Don't you?"

Nicholas ran a hand through his hair. "I embarrassed the family, yet again. But you have been in this family for nearly five years. You know that has always been my role."

Lucinda shook her head with a deep sigh that made Nicholas feel like a spoiled youth, although he was a good half a decade older than his sister-in-law.

"Your role is different now. It must be," she whispered as she half turned.

She still hadn't fully entered the room, merely stood in the doorway as if she couldn't wait to leave. Nicholas supposed that was accurate. Being in the same space as he was, seeing her beloved late husband's face on some other man, it had to kill her a little every time they met.

Yet another shame to add to his many recent shames.

"Yes, I am the viscount," he said, choking on the words. "I must have honor and fidelity and duty and—"

"I don't give a damn about that," Lucinda suddenly snapped, her harsh tone unlike any he had heard from her before. Normally she was gentle, almost to a fault.

Nicholas lifted his gaze to her in surprise. She clenched her fists at her chest, and in the dim light he saw tears glitter on her cheeks.

"What I *do* care about is your brother's memory. Like it or not, you share Anthony's face. When people judge you, they judge him. It has always been that way, but at least when he lived his actions spoke for themselves. Now . . ."

She trailed off, and Nicholas tasted bile in his throat.

Lucinda drew a long breath. "If you will not change for yourself, for your family, and all those things you listed a moment ago, will you not change for Anthony? For his memory?"

Nicholas swallowed hard. "I—"

She wouldn't allow him to continue. "And if not for Anthony, then what about your nieces? I know it is hard to remember when Margaret is only three and Georgina barely six months, she never even met her father, but your actions *will* affect their futures, as well, for good or for ill."

All the anger seemed to deflate out of her when she mentioned her children, leaving her slender shoulders to roll forward in pure exhaustion.

"Oh, Nicholas." She sighed. "I know you. All those times you visited us, I came to adore you as my own brother. You do not want to be responsible for ruining my daughters' futures. For making it so that no amount of dowry can erase the weight of their names. I also know that you may want to shame your father because of some age-old grudge I never fully understood. But you loved Anthony." Her voice broke painfully. "And you do not want to shame him."

Nicholas lifted his hand, wanting to touch her arm, to offer her some comfort. But he didn't.

"I don't want that," he finally admitted softly.

"Then before you return to Society again," she whispered, "please, you must gain some control over yourself. I know it has been many, many years since you were part of polite company. You have probably forgotten many of the niceties that are the rituals of our lives. Relearn them, Nicholas. I beg of you."

Nicholas stared at her a long moment. She had to know what she was asking of him. That her request was the pull against the noose around his neck. More than anything in the world, he wanted to deny her appeal. To sink back into the underground haven he had built, where he was revered almost as a god and whatever he did made no difference.

But that option had been taken from him the same moment his brother drew his final breath. There was no abandoning his duty now, or the life his brother had left behind for Nicholas to step into. Or the truth of Lucinda's words.

"I will not force you to endure the humiliation of tonight again," he finally whispered, his stomach turning with each syllable. "I swear to you that I will not destroy what my brother built."

Lucinda nodded. "Thank you. Now I must go back. Margaret still cries for her father every night. If I am not there when she wakes from her nightmares, she cannot be consoled."

His sister-in-law moved toward the door, but Nicholas stepped forward. "Luc—my lady, if I could trade my place with my brother, I hope you know I would do it in a moment. Without hesitation."

Lucinda shuddered before she turned back. She looked at him squarely, the first time she had done so since her husband's death. "You know I do adore you, as your brother did. So please know that I do not mean to sound harsh when I say, I wish you *could* trade places with Anthony, Nicholas. I wish you could."

And then she was gone, her soft footsteps disappearing down the hall.

Suddenly his office felt small, confined . . . like a cage, and Nicholas could hardly breathe for the walls closing in on him. Wrestling with his poorly tied cravat, he staggered from the chamber and down the hall. He had to get out. Out of this life, away from the burden of respectability and the weight of the consequences that would now follow his every action.

His stomach roiled, twisting as he rushed through the hallways toward the French doors that led to the garden terrace behind the small home he had let. When he burst into the night air, he gasped, lifting his face to the moon and wishing he could bolt like a wolf over the gate and disappear forever.

Only that was impossible.

With a long sigh, Nicholas leaned on the railing with all his weight.

"My lord?" came a voice from the doorway behind him.

Nicholas flinched at the use of the title, but did not move. Perhaps the servant would take the hint and go away.

"Lord Stoneworth?" the insistent butler said, this time a bit louder.

Nicholas scrubbed a hand over his eyes with a frustrated growl. After tonight, the last thing he wanted was an interruption. Right now he wanted a woman to drown his anger and pain in, a drink to make him numb, and a dreamless sleep. Not necessarily in that order.

"Sir?" his servant said a third time.

"Go away, Gladwell," Nicholas growled as he finally turned to face the man. His body hurt as if he had been in a fight. Bruised and battered, but without the excitement to dull the pain.

"I'm sorry, sir, but you have a very strange visitor."

"I'm not expecting anyone," Nicholas said. "Tell him to go away."

"It is not a *he*, sir, but a she. And *she* refuses to leave until she sees you," Gladwell said, giving a sniff that left no amount of guessing to how he felt about his employer or his uninvited "guest."

Nicholas arched a brow. The cool night air was beginning to calm him, and his mind was clearing from the painful haze his encounter with Lucinda had caused.

"A woman?" he asked.

The servant nodded, and for the first time all night Nicholas smiled. Perhaps he would get one of his wishes without even having to search for it. Few people knew he was here, but perhaps one of the actresses or dance hall girls had gotten wind of his new title and home.

"Bring her to me," he murmured as he perched himself on the edge of the veranda.

The man's eyes widened as he looked around the darkened terrace. "Here, sir?"

Nicholas arched a brow. "Yes. Here."

"It is not . . . er . . . you are certain you wish to receive a lady outside in the middle of the night?" Gladwell asked slowly.

He nodded. It wasn't that he wasn't aware of the breach of protocol. It was that he didn't care. And he had a sneaking suspicion that the kind of woman who would come for a meeting this late wouldn't care, either. Hell, a tryst in the moonlight might do him some good. Just one last time, he could feed that beast within him that Lucinda said he had to tame.

"I would like to see my 'strange' guest, after all. And I want to see her right here."

Jane clenched her shaking hands behind her back as she waited near the servants' entrance of the town home Nicholas Stoneworth had been letting for the past six months. She had never been so terrified in her entire life as when she rapped on the kitchen door and demanded to see His Lordship. And when the butler initially refused her request, she had almost, *almost* run back into the night and home in failure.

But one thought of Marcus, lost somewhere and possibly needing her help, had stiffened her resolve. And her "lady of the manor" tone had seemed to work, at least for now, for the servant had stomped off to find the gentleman in question and report her arrival.

The kitchen maid who had been left to make

sure she didn't steal the silver looked at her out of the corner of her eye before she smiled awkwardly and shot her gaze away. All the servants Jane had so far seen in this house looked a little . . . tired. Which made the mysterious Viscount Stoneworth even more terrifying. The man was looking to be an utter beast.

But he was her only hope.

The butler stepped back down the short flight of stairs into the kitchen and glared at her. "His Lordship will see you. How shall I announce you?"

Jane stiffened. "I shall tell the viscount my name myself, thank you."

The slightest twitch around the servant's eye was the only outward indication he gave of his annoyance. "Very well . . . *madam*, please follow me."

Jane stared for a moment as the man turned and began to make his way back up the stairs. She couldn't move. Had her wild scheme truly worked? Somehow she hadn't really expected the viscount to see her, and now she was frozen with uncertainty.

"Don't worry, luv," the maid who had been watching her said from behind her, low enough that the butler wouldn't hear. "No woman His Lordship has had here has ever left with complaints. Fact, most of 'em look happy as can be when they leave his bed. I'm sure you'll be fine."

Jane blanched as she stared in shock over her shoulder at the young woman. She wasn't oblivious to the assumptions people might make if she came here uninvited, but she hadn't exactly expected them to be spelled out so bluntly.

"Are you coming?" the butler asked, his tone sharp from the top of the stairs.

Jane rushed forward, ignoring all her remaining fears. None of that mattered now. All that mattered was that Stoneworth was her last hope. Her only hope. And if she concentrated and focused, appealed to him in the right way, she was certain she could obtain his assistance. *That* would be worth any humiliation.

She scurried behind the butler, struggling to keep up with his long strides as she moved down the hallways. They twisted and turned in a maze. At every doorway she expected the servant to stop, but he never did, passing every lighted room without faltering in his steps.

Until he reached the back French doors that led to the very dark garden behind the town house. They had been thrown open, despite the late hour. But no. They could not be going outside . . .

Could they?

As if in answer to her question, the butler stepped out onto the veranda and said, "Your visitor, my lord. She would not give her name."

Then he stepped aside and motioned Jane outside. She swallowed hard, that urge to run filling her yet again. With all her might, she fought it, straightened her shoulders, and stepped onto the stone terrace that overlooked an untamed garden below.

There was no light save for the sliver coming from the door and the full moon overhead, so it took a moment for her eyes to adjust. When she could finally see beyond shadows, she looked around for the man she had come to see. To her surprise, he sat on the stone edge of the veranda wall, arms folded . . . watching her.

Great God, up close he was a sight to behold. Like no other man she had ever met. Most of the gentlemen in her acquaintance were a bit soft. Even those who were in good physical condition didn't have the air of danger, animal strength, or unpredictability that this man did.

And the moonlight only magnified that air. It was almost as if he didn't belong in the house with the civilized people. There he was caged. But here . . .

He rose to his feet and stepped toward her. Instinctively she turned away, but before she could bolt, the butler returned inside and quietly closed the door behind him, leaving her at the utter mercy of this stranger.

Jane recognized, in that moment, that she was entirely out of her league.

"Well, well, my dear," Stoneworth drawled. "*You* are not what I was expecting at all."

"Yes, sir," she said on a forced breath. "I am sorry that I did not give your butler my name. I feared you would not see me if you knew who I was."

The corner of Stoneworth's lips lifted, but it made more of a snarl than a smile. "And who are you?"

Jane lifted her gaze to his, startled. "Oh, yes. I apologize. My name is Jane Fenton."

"No, not your name. *Who* are you?" He tilted his head. "I don't think we've met before. Although you do look . . . *familiar* somehow."

She nodded, thinking of the brief way he had looked at her earlier in the evening. Trying not to think of the shameful thrill his meaningless perusal had given her. Now he didn't even recall her face.

"Y-you might have seen me tonight at the Glouchester ball," she explained.

"In that gown?" he asked, tilting his head to the side as if he were examining her serviceable woolen frock.

More heat flooded Jane's cheeks, but this time it was angry, as well as embarrassed. "*Your* cravat was crooked and you haven't shaved for two days, at least. You have no room to judge—"

She caught herself, swallowing back the rest of her heated response to his jab. When she was pressed, Jane often had the terrible habit of letting honesty get in the way of tact. Her father had sometimes joked that she got her temper the moment she inherited the ruddy highlights in her otherwise plain brown hair. Now that "red-headed temper" might have cost her dearly.

She held her breath as she awaited Nicholas Stoneworth's reaction.

But when he moved even closer, she found he was smiling at her. Something a bit more genuine than the feral snarls and false smirks she had seen him exhibit tonight.

"It seems I have hit upon a sore spot for you," he said with an exaggerated bow. "I do apologize."

Hating the heat that continued to rise in her cheeks, Jane shrugged. "I am a lady's companion. I do not dress in a fancy fashion, I am meant to fade into the background."

"Ah." Again his gaze swept over her from head to toe. "I doubt you fade well, Miss Jane Fenton."

"That is an entirely inappropriate thing to say to a woman you don't even know," Jane snapped, hating how breathless her voice sounded.

"As inappropriate as coming unescorted to the home of a man *you* don't know?"

He moved on her so swiftly that she didn't have a chance to back away. Suddenly she was staring at the twisted remnants of the cravat he had apparently wrenched free from his neck after the ball. His body heat surrounded her and overpowered the cooler night air. He was so close that she could have sworn she heard his heart beat, but perhaps it was just her own roaring in her ears.

His hand came up and he pushed a loose lock of hair away from her face. Rough hands with pronounced knuckles stroked over her skin and sent a shiver through her that was unwanted.

"I did not come here for this," she said, but her words wavered.

"No?" he whispered, his rough voice seductively dark and smoky in the otherwise quiet night. "Are you certain you didn't come here to test the theories about my prowess? Or perhaps to make your cruel parents sorry that they allowed you to fall into ruin? Or maybe in the hopes that I would make you my mistress and give you enough of a monthly stipend that you could quit the dreary life of a companion in trade for one where you didn't even have to get out of bed?"

Jane stepped away from him, although it took far more effort than she would ever admit, even under torture. She folded her arms as a protective shield over her suddenly tingling breasts.

"No," she snapped. "None of those things. I have no interest in theories about your 'prowess,' my parents were far from cruel, and I don't mind being a companion." She hesitated. For some strange reason, she felt compelled to explain herself further. "My father was a viscount, so I have lived the life of a lady. And although it is not the future I once imagined for myself, serving a lady is not as bad as I once thought it would be."

Stoneworth seemed surprised at her retort, but not angered. He was still smiling at her, that feral expression that said he could own her if he chose.

"Then why *are* you here, little one?" he asked. "Tell me before I lose interest."

Jane clenched her fists. She would have only one chance at this, her plea could be nothing less than perfect.

"I may not know much about your 'prowess,' as you put it—" she began.

He interrupted her with a deep, throaty chuckle before he reached into his breast pocket and withdrew a cigar. She watched in fascination as he bit off the end and pressed it between surprisingly full lips.

"Would you like one?" he asked without looking at her.

She wrinkled her nose. "Of course not." She hastened to continue with her story before he distracted her once more. "But there *are* many tales circulating about you. Some say that while you were away from polite Society, you existed in the underground."

He froze, totally still for a long breath. Finally he said, "I see. Well, let me disabuse you of any incorrect rumors."

Jane's heart sank. So he had no connection,

which meant she was here enduring his mocking for no reason whatsoever.

"I never owned a brothel . . . or is it a gambling hall that I am supposed to be proprietor of?"

He pressed his lips as if considering the rumor, and Jane's nostrils flared. His ridicule was almost too much.

He held up a hand as if he'd given up trying to remember. "Either way, I know enough about both their workings to likely do quite well at it." He took the cigar from his mouth and smiled. "And I have not fathered a hundred children. None that I am aware of, as I am exceedingly careful, you see. When it comes to the underground . . ."

He looked away, turning his face full into the moonlight, and Jane caught her breath. There was something *sad* in his expression. Just for a fleeting moment, but she saw it nonetheless.

"That is true. I did box in the underground matches. And made myself a tidy fortune that has nothing to do with my father's coffers. So you can report that back to whichever lady you work for. I assume she sent you here to find out about me and see if I'm worthy of marrying. Or bedding."

With heat burning her cheeks, Jane shook her head. "You misunderstand me, sir. I was not sent here by my employer. Lady Ridgefield is not looking for a husband. She doesn't know I came at all."

"Lady Ridgefield?" Stoneworth repeated in surprise. "Ah yes, well, Her Ladyship and I are not quite of an age, are we?"

Jane felt her lips twitching with a smile that she suppressed. "My errand is none but my own. You see, four years ago my elder brother disappeared after a series of increasingly bitter rows with my father. Since my father's death, my cousin has had my brother declared dead and taken over the title, but I do not believe that declaration to be true. I have pored over my father's papers, but there is little information. Only that Marcus was last seen two years ago in the underground by a man my father hired to bring him back to us. And then . . . nothing."

Stoneworth stared at her blankly. "If your father was titled, why do you work as a lady's maid? Surely your cousin will provide you with some living."

"He has offered to do so." Jane lifted her chin with as much pride as she had left. "But I would not take a farthing from that charlatan. Acting like he has the authority to do anything with the title or the money that is rightly my brother's."

"Why not marry then?" he asked.

She pursed her lips. "Who would have me? My brother's reputation is out in enough circles, and then there is the tiny fact that I am essentially a servant now." She straightened her shoulders. "But even if those things were not true, I could not put my thoughts into marriage, not with Marcus still missing. My whole attention must be put toward finding him. And helping him back to health once he *is* found and returned to his lawful position."

Nicholas's brow wrinkled as if he had some argument with that, but he didn't press the issue. "And where do I come into this somewhat tragic little tale?"

Jane pursed her lips at his dismissive tone. "If you did, indeed, live in that underground world, then you may have connections with those who knew my brother. I thought that if—"

He held up a hand as he let out a long sigh. "What is your brother's name?"

She stepped forward, her blood quickening with excitement. "Lord Marcus Fenton. He would have been Viscount Fenton after my father's death, but my cousin—"

"Stole the title, yes." Stoneworth stepped away from her, his earlier flirtatious demeanor gone. Now it seemed he did not even want to look at her. "I do not know his name, I am sorry, miss. You will have to find someone else to help you."

Jane shook her head in disbelief. "N-no. There is no one else! Do you not think I have looked? Since my father's death last year, since my cousin instigated his treachery, I have searched far and wide and spent what little money I saved from my pin allowance over the years, but with no results."

"And why do you think my help would bring you more results than you have obtained already?"

She stepped toward him, hands held up in mute entreaty, though she hated to beg. "I never had someone assisting me who actually knew the world Marcus may be trapped in. You are the only one. Please, I—"

Stoneworth reached out and caught her hands. He cupped them between his larger ones, cocooning them in warmth even as he squeezed.

"Jane Fenton, I am not a hero, do you understand?" His voice was low and harsh. "I cannot help you. I *will* not help you. Now go."

He released her and stepped away.

Jane stared at him in utter shock. She had been picturing for the entire evening what she would do when she encountered this man. She had run over all the scenarios in her head again and again.

But now that she was staring at him, dismissed like a common lightskirt he picked up off the street and determined he did not want, she realized she had never truly believed he would refuse her. She had thought that as a gentleman, he would be compelled to at least hear her out.

Tears stung behind her eyes, ones that she had forced away time and again over the past year. She blinked furiously, refusing to shed them before this . . . this . . . *person*.

"You are not only uncouth, sir, but you are cruel," she whispered. "I asked you for help and you dismiss me like I am a bug on your boot. You have no manners, no charm, no niceties in you at all. No wonder the *ton* despises you."

She turned on her heel and headed for the house. But as she grasped the door handle with a shaking hand, Stoneworth's deep voice came from behind her.

"Wait."

Chapter 3

Nicholas stared as Miss Jane Fenton pierced him with a look so cold and dismissive, he might have mistaken her for an icy queen if it weren't for her ugly gown and sensible hairstyle.

Despite those things, he could not ignore what a beautiful young woman she was, especially in the intimacy of moonlight. He could well imagine she had been an incomparable when her family provided her with expensive gowns and she had nothing to do all day but take care of her hair and skin in the hope she would catch a titled man.

As he was now.

Only she wasn't his type. Normally Nicholas was attracted to women with a far different kind of beauty. Something more blatant, a coy turn of the head that said he would find pleasure in his paramour's bed if he asked. Jane didn't possess that kind of appeal. Her beauty was more wholesome. Pure.

Entirely out of his reach, even if he *had* wanted it.

Still, she could be of some use to him. Despite her lowered position as a lady's companion, Jane was cultured. That was evident in her posture, her voice, even the way she moved her slender hands when she spoke. And she had handled him well when he knew that his forward approach shocked and even frightened her.

"I would like to make a bargain with you," he said.

Jane's eyes widened, and then understanding dawned. Followed swiftly by appalled anger. She folded her arms across her chest for the second time that night. Nicholas doubted she realized how the action lifted her breasts ever so slightly and drew his attention to the luscious swell.

"How dare you, sir! I am not that kind of woman. I may be fallen, but I have never in my life considered taking money or help in exchange for—"

Nicholas held up a hand to stop the stream of words.

"Not that kind of offer, sweet," he interrupted with a grin, although her misunderstanding of his intentions conjured a swift, unbidden thought of this woman spread across his bed, her dark hair with its ruddy highlights down around her and her back arched in offering of those perfect breasts she kept trying to hide. "I don't pay for that, not with blunt or assistance. No, I want something else from you."

Her eyes narrowed, and Nicholas found himself looking at her face closely. Even in the dim light, he could see her eyes were very dark, like pure chocolate. And they reflected the depth of her emotions. No pretense here, no pretended offense. Jane Fenton truly did not trust him.

Clever girl.

"What do you want?" she asked, cautious as if she feared he would pounce on her as an answer.

He briefly considered doing just that, but put it out of his mind. Those wayward thoughts were part of what was getting him in trouble.

"If you saw me tonight, then you must have been privy to the, er, *exchange* I had with my father. As well as my behavior in general."

Nicholas shifted, suddenly glad for the light breeze that stirred around them. He was surprised by how uncomfortable this topic made him. He wasn't accustomed to explaining himself to anyone, but especially virginal lady's companions who had come uninvited to his home.

Jane's gaze flitted over him from head to toe, and from the way her lip curled ever so slightly, he could see she thought very little of what she saw. Which was utterly fascinating. Most women fell at his feet with little urging. This one looked at him as if he wasn't fit to shine her shoes.

"I did indeed," she said with a sniff of disapproval. "You drank far too much, terrified half the guests with your glower, and entertained the other half by having a rather loud argument with your father, who is one of the most influential men in the Upper Ten Thousand. All in all it was a devastating night for your reputation."

Nicholas flinched at her blunt assessment. "I would say thank you, as my reputation amongst the circles I moved in tonight means very little to me. However, it was recently brought to my attention that my actions also could adversely affect both the memory of my . . ." He hesitated as a stab of pain unexpectedly hit his gut. ". . . my late brother, as well as his two young daughters. And that is unacceptable. I have begun to realize that I have but two options: to leave Society entirely or to make an effort to fit back into it."

Jane stepped forward, and her expression had softened a fraction. He saw that she understood his concern for his brother. That was one commonality they shared. Although he feared her hopes that her brother was alive were foolish dreams rather than reality.

Still, *she* didn't know that.

"And?" she encouraged, her voice low.

He cleared his throat. Here was the difficult part. He was unaccustomed to asking for help.

"I was raised to be a gentleman, of course, but I was never very good at it. And over the past seven years I have forgotten most of my lessons in good manners and grace. I need a—well, a *tutor* for lack of a better word." He tilted his head. "If you will help me to find my way back into Society, I will do my best to uncover your brother's whereabouts."

Jane stumbled away from him, her eyes wide. "You cannot mean that."

He arched a brow. "I assure you, I do."

"You are asking the impossible!" she said on a humorless laugh. "From what I saw tonight, you would need months of training and study to make any good impression as a gentleman."

Nicholas clenched his fists. This woman did delight in insulting him. Very few people had ever dared to do that, and he didn't think any of them had ever been of the fairer sex.

"Then we shall make an even match, for your request to find a man missing in the underground for two years or more is just as complex and time-consuming." Nicholas shook his head. "But I will still make the attempt, if you promise to remind me of the niceties of Society."

"Why me?" she asked, her hands moving to her hips. "You could hire any number of people to do this for you."

He shrugged. To be honest, until his encounter with Lucinda less than an hour ago, he had never even considered becoming a gentleman again. But he could well imagine what kind of hell it would be to hire a tutor. People would know, people would talk. His father would get a huge amount of pleasure out of the knowledge and probably take credit, if he didn't swoop in and take over the arrangement entirely.

A childish reason to ask this woman to repay her debt this way, but she was here and she was convenient.

"You're a hell of a lot prettier than any ludicrous fop I could hire to do the deed," he said.

He could have sworn that a tantalizing pink blush briefly colored her cheeks, but then Jane turned away into a shadow out of the moonlight, and he could no longer see.

"No!" she said, her voice shaking. "I could never possibly do such a thing. The risk—"

Nicholas's eyes narrowed. "Isn't finding your brother worth a little risk?"

She sucked in a breath and turned back to him suddenly. All the color drained from her face the moment he spoke those words. And almost as swiftly, Nicholas wished he had not said them at all. They were a cruel manipulation, beneath even him. But he *needed* Jane Fenton. And he was willing to do whatever it took to have her help.

Aside from which, if he did, by some off chance, find her wayward brother in his search, she would be thankful for the bargain they had made.

"I-I—" she stammered. Then she slowly shook her head. "I cannot do this. I *cannot.*"

Without looking at him, she yanked the terrace

door open and fled down the long hallway toward his front door.

A strange sense of emptiness remained in her wake. Nicholas hadn't realized how much he hoped she would accept his terms. Now if he hired a tutor, it would have to be the kind of person his father would approve of instead of a lady who smelled faintly of ripe peaches and had eyes so dark he could surely drown in their beauty.

Jane took great heaving breaths as she sat in the hired hack while it wound its way back to Lady Ridgefield's home on Bond Street. Nicholas Stoneworth's words still rang in her head. His offer and his final question taunted her.

Isn't finding your brother worth a little risk?

Jane groaned in pain. Finding Marcus had been the main focus of the last year of her life. The way she had dealt with the pain of her beloved father's passing, the shock when she realized just how many secrets he had been keeping to "protect" her, and the betrayal when her cousin took advantage of the situation and had Marcus declared dead.

And yet she had been unwilling to risk something so pitiable as her reputation to find him.

"What reputation?" she groaned as she rested her hand against her aching head.

No one even *saw* her when they looked at her anymore, except for a handful of women she had once been friendly with. And they seemed to take cruel pleasure in how far she had fallen over such a short time.

Except Nicholas Stoneworth saw her when he looked at her. And like it or not, she saw him. Not the snarling tiger he'd been at the ball or even the seductive scoundrel who had been expecting a whore as his visitor . . . but something deeper.

She had sensed his pain when he spoke of his brother. And she had felt undeniable empathy for it.

But that didn't mean she could turn him into a gentleman. She wasn't even certain that was possible. Seven years of hard living had squeezed gentility out of him, wrung it away like water from a cloth. She could only imagine making him sit at a table with twenty different forks and explain the order. Or forcing him to try to balance a tiny tea sandwich in his big hand while he chatted about the weather. Or spinning around a dance floor, with his hand against her hip, demonstrating the waltz.

She shivered.

No, she was not the right woman for such things. The idea of doing them was terrifying, actually. Being alone with Nicholas for half an hour had been trying enough.

So she would have to find some other way to find her brother. Again.

She was out of money, there was no way to hire

another investigator. But perhaps if she read over her father's papers one last time she would decipher some clue that she had missed in the past. She'd gone over them a hundred times before, but once more couldn't hurt.

But that would mean going back to her old home. Seeing her cousin. Facing the man who had tried to steal her brother's life.

Her stomach turned at the thought, but now that Stoneworth had refused her, she had little choice. So tomorrow she would take a few hours in the afternoon and do what she had to do, no matter how distasteful the idea was.

Because turning Nicholas Stoneworth into a gentleman was not an option.

Chapter 4

J ane blinked back tears as she looked around the front parlor of the city estate she had called home for more than twenty years. It looked exactly the same as it had when her father was alive. Memories of him and her mother and her brother came flooding back to her as she waited for her cousin.

She sighed as she crossed to the broad window seat that overlooked the street. Sinking down onto the cushioned ledge, she looked with unseeing eyes at the bustling scene below.

As a child, she had sat here while her mother read her stories in the afternoon after tea. Later, she had laughed here when her brother told fantastical tales of his days in school. And more recently, she had cried here when her father passed of a sudden apoplexy and she was left utterly alone in the world.

"Good afternoon, Jane."

She stiffened as she got to her feet and

watched her cousin Patrick enter the room. He was a tall man, though not as tall as Nicholas Stoneworth. And certainly not as muscular, but no one could call him fat, either. Actually, he was a rather handsome man, with the strong features that were common to so many of the men in her family. His dark green eyes were just like her father's. The lock of black hair that fell across his forehead put her to mind of her brother.

Which made the fact that he had betrayed that same family all the more distasteful.

"Good afternoon," Jane said with barely concealed disdain. She would not call him "my lord." Not ever.

"I am pleased that you came," her cousin said as he motioned to the two chairs that were situated before the fire. "Especially since you have left my past three missives unanswered."

Jane clenched her fists as she sank into the chair slowly. Her desire was to refuse his polite overtures, but she couldn't do that.

"I had nothing to say to you after our last argument."

Patrick pursed his lips. "If only we did not have to argue at all, Jane. I wish you were not so insistent on making me out to be a villain. I know you don't understand—"

Drawing in a harsh breath, she snapped, "I

understand perfectly. You *want* my brother to be dead so that you can have the life that was meant for him."

Her cousin's cheek twitched. "Jane," he began, his tone a warning.

One that she ignored, although her rational mind screamed at her to be civil. It was impossible to heed that call. Patrick forever brought out the worst in her and made her say things she shouldn't.

"Somehow you managed to convince the justice that my brother is dead. I don't know how you did it, though I assume it involved a great deal of money. But I am not so easily swayed as some greedy barrister. I know Marcus is *not* dead. And I will use every breath in my body to prove it and take back what you stole."

Patrick drew in a deep breath, but he did not get angry. He never got angry, even when they argued. That fact drove Jane mad. She wanted to rile him. To make him as frustrated and annoyed as she was every time she looked at him.

"How could you do this?" she asked, and hated how her voice broke.

He shook his head slowly. "I did what needed to be done to protect the family name, and continue the family line. You may not wish to believe that, but it is the truth. And I offered to help you, to marry you. I still would."

Jane surged to her feet. "Please do not claim that your distasteful offer was made to help me. You did it only to legitimize your claim to the title and to soothe your own guilt over your betrayals. Nothing more. I told you then that I will never marry you, and I meant it. But I *will* find my brother, and then you will be revealed for the charlatan and liar you are."

Patrick got to his feet slowly. He looked at her, and his expression was one of sadness. Pity. Which caused the anger that boiled out of control in Jane's chest to burn even hotter.

"You may continue to try, Jane," he said softly. "But you might do better to accept what has happened. And accept help. You do not have to continue on as a companion to Lady Ridgefield. At the very least, I could sponsor another Season for you, I could—"

Jane turned her back, and the action silenced him midsentence. "I did not come here for your false charity, Patrick. I came to review my father's papers once more. In fact, I would like to take them with me, so that I will have access to them at all times."

Patrick sighed. "I have told you before, those items belong to the estate. You may make as many copies of the information as you like and visit as often as you care to for examination. But I cannot allow my uncle's papers to leave this house."

Jane spun on him, fists shaking at her sides. All the emotion she normally tried to control was alive at that moment. Transformed into the powerful hatred she had developed for the man before her. He was a person she had once thought of as a friend. But now she could see only his detestable qualities.

"Fine," she finally managed through clenched teeth. She wanted to say so much more, but feared Patrick would use his power to keep her from reading over her father's papers at all if she continued to press the issue.

"Then I will have Jenkins show you to the archive. I assume when you are finished with your work, you will not want to see me, but if you do I shall be in my office. Good day." Her cousin turned and quietly exited the room.

As Jane waited for the butler who used to serve *her* to come and collect her, she paced the small parlor restlessly. Her cousin's words echoed in her head. Patrick had told her to accept help. He meant his own, of course, but that was not a scenario she would ever allow herself to become a part of.

However, *another* man had offered his help. With a price, of course, but if Nicholas could find her brother . . . perhaps he was right that the ends would justify the means.

And how hard could it be to "train" a man to be a gentleman?

She shut her eyes as she thought of Nicholas Stoneworth. An image of him came far too quickly, standing in the cool moonlight, his bright blue eyes glittering with sensual promise and debauchery.

It would likely be impossible to transform him into the kind of man who would be welcome in the ballrooms of the best of the *ton*. But *he* didn't have to know that. She only had to help him until Marcus was found. Then she could renege on their bargain. That was not honorable, perhaps, but neither was asking a lady to pay for the help of a gentleman.

She didn't have any choice. With Patrick keeping her from any kind of private investigation and without money for any other search, Jane needed Nicholas Stoneworth.

And as long as he needed her in return, then she would have a little bit of power. She could only hope it would be enough.

Jane stood at the back door of Nicholas's town home, rapping on the hard surface. She shivered, though the spring night's breeze was far from brisk. Nervousness caused the motion.

The door came open and a disapproving female servant stared at her. From the apron she wore, she appeared to be a cook.

"Another one?" she snapped with a cluck of her tongue.

Brow wrinkling with confusion, Jane said, "I am here to see your master. Will you tell him that Jane Fenton has returned?"

The cook turned her back with another harrumph. "Not my job to show his hussies around."

Jane took a step inside, though she hadn't yet been invited. "Madam, I am not a hussy, I am—"

"You again."

She looked up as the butler who had shown her in the night before came down the three steps into the kitchen.

"G-good evening," she stammered, thrown off by the tall, thin man's utter disdain. "I have come to see your master."

"Clearly, but I'm afraid I cannot allow that. Lord Stoneworth has asked not to be disturbed tonight. I shall be sure to tell him that you called."

He started to depart the room, but Jane rushed toward him before he could utterly dismiss her.

"But he is expecting me."

The man turned and speared her with a look full of disbelief. "I somehow doubt that."

"Please, won't you ask him? It couldn't hurt, could it?" she pleaded, hoping her mournful expression could manipulate the situation a little.

She *had* to make Nicholas agree to her scheme as soon as possible, before he changed his mind or found another tutor and she was back where she started.

"It will hurt far more than you imagine, miss," the butler said. "Do you have any intention of leaving?"

Jane shook her head quickly.

He shut his eyes with a long-suffering sigh. "Then follow me."

He led her through the halls a second time, but tonight he took her to a small parlor rather than the terrace where she had met with Nicholas before. She tapped her toe restlessly as she awaited the man's return.

Looking around her, she took in the room, which was in some state of disarray. Not dirty, of course, but as if someone had moved the furniture and it never quite found itself back in the right place. She made a mental note to include lessons on the maintenance of one's home as part of the gentlemanly instruction she would conduct if Nicholas agreed.

He *would* agree. He had to.

She heard masculine voices in the hallway and rushed to the door. She staggered back at what she saw. Nicholas was with his servant, but he was not dressed. He wore a black silken robe, tied negligently around his hips. Tanned skin, rippled with ropes of muscle, seem to be everywhere she looked.

Was he doing that on purpose to stymie her?

She forced her hands to stop shaking and tried to appear bored as he entered the room.

"Miss Jane Fenton," he drawled, not even looking the slightest bit embarrassed at his lack of attire. "I did not expect to see you this evening. Or ever again. Last night you made it clear you wanted nothing to do with me unless it was on your own, rather narrow terms."

Jane forced herself not to stare at his bare, muscular legs, or the expanse of chest that was revealed in the deep vee of his dressing gown, or his broad shoulders. Instead, she stared straight into his pale eyes, but found them almost as distracting as his shamefully uncovered body.

"I-I—" she stammered.

"Stone?" came a female voice from the door.

Jane froze, then slowly peeked around Nicholas to see a disheveled blonde smiling at the viscount. His face briefly tightened with what looked like annoyance before he turned.

"Lydia, I thought we had already said our good-byes," he said as he made his way to the door. The pair of them spoke for a moment quietly before the other woman pulled a childishly pouting face and then left.

Jane opened and shut her mouth in shock. So he had been . . . been *bedding* that woman when she arrived. That was why he was wearing naught but a robe. Strange emotions troubled her at the realization. Embarrassment, of course, but she was also intrigued. The cook had said "another one" when Jane entered the house, so she must have believed Jane was there to join in the viscount's fun.

Did women actually *share* men in bed?

And another emotion made itself known. Faint, but still there in a troubling degree.

Jealousy. She didn't like the idea that Nicholas Stoneworth had been upstairs pleasuring some lightskirt while she was downstairs awaiting him.

Which was ridiculous! She was being foolish to even consider it, just overly emotional after her troubling encounter with Patrick and her terrifying decision to accept Stoneworth's bargain.

She was not, she could *not* be jealous of this man's conquests.

Nicholas gently shut the door, the sound ricocheting off the walls like a gunshot. She stared at the barrier with a frown.

"My apologies," he said, though he didn't sound sorry for anything. "I did not intend for us to be interrupted."

She pursed her lips. "Indeed."

"Now what were you saying?" he asked as he continued to move toward her step by long step. "Something about why you came?"

Suddenly Jane was having a hard time recalling her reason herself. All she could think about was how tall Nicholas Stoneworth was.

"How did you blacken your eye?" she found herself asking. She shook her head the moment the question left her lips.

He stopped stalking toward her and stared at her. Then a little smile quirked his lips. "Is that why you came here? To inquire about my eye?"

She frowned. He was toying with her. "Of course not," she said, though her tone was not as harsh as she had wanted it to be.

"I was punched," he explained without any indication of how he felt about that fact. "In this very room, in fact."

Jane swallowed. That might explain the disarray of the chamber. So this man could not even control himself enough not to brawl in his own home. She had a large job in front of her to make him into a gentleman, but there was nothing to be done about it.

"If I am to train you, you must realize that fighting in the front parlor is not done," she said.

He folded his arms, and in the process his silk robe rose a few more inches, revealing a tanned expanse of very muscular thigh. With a gasp, Jane looked away.

"*Are* you training me, Jane Fenton?"

She nodded, making certain she did not look at him at all. He was far too distracting in his current state. "If you would still agree to help me find my brother, I shall."

"That was my initial offer," Nicholas said on a low chuckle. "I see no reason to change the terms. Unless there is something *else* you would like to barter with."

There was no mistaking his meaning. For a brief moment, Jane considered what he was saying. The idea of bartering her body for his help was not as distasteful as it should have been. She recalled the way her pulse had quickened when he brushed her hair away from her face the night before.

With a shiver, she pushed the thoughts away. Stiffening her spine, she shot him a glare. "You are shameless, sir."

"So I have been told." Nicholas moved to the poor boy across the room and poured two glasses of sherry. He held one out to her.

She took it carefully. "My first lesson to you is that a gentleman does not meet a lady in his robe."

For a moment, Nicholas stared at her. Then he set the fresh drink down on the tabletop and moved for his robe tie. Jane staggered back, splashing alcohol onto the wooden floor in her hasty retreat.

"No!" she yelped as she covered her eyes with her free hand.

"A pity," he said. When she didn't uncover her eyes, he said, "Jane, you may remove your hand, I will not do it."

Slowly, she lowered her fingers, half believing he would actually be standing naked in front of her when she did. A strange mixture of relief and disappointment greeted her when she found him still clothed in the dressing gown. And she also felt a very strange desire to laugh at the boyish grin on his face. That flash of amusement was something she had not felt for a long time.

Instead, she straightened her shoulders and tried to remain distant and businesslike. "Very well, we are agreed on the terms of the bargain. So let us speak about the mechanics, shall we? I cannot come here during the day. Lady Ridgefield is a little—"

"Daft?" Nicholas supplied.

"Flighty," Jane retorted sharply. "But not so much that she wouldn't notice my absence if I left her constantly. I have a job to do and I cannot abandon those duties."

Nicholas nodded. "There is more of a chance of you being caught if you come here during the day at any rate. I do not think either of us wants that, for it can only lead to more damage to both our reputations."

Jane shivered at the thought. "So what are we to do?"

"Why not come at night as you have been doing?" Nicholas asked. "I assume leaving Lady Ridgefield in the evening is easier."

Jane pondered that. "She often entertains guests and gives me the night off. When she does not, she almost always retires early. Nights of balls or parties are different, of course, but after those events I am generally free."

He nodded. "Very well. Then you will come here in the evenings. How have you gotten here before?"

"Hack," she admitted.

He moved on her a step. "Hack?" he repeated. "That is far too dangerous, and I imagine it is very expensive. I shall send an unmarked vehicle for you in the alley behind Lady Ridgefield's."

"But I—" Jane began, though she could admit the idea of not having to take a smelly, drafty hack was a nice one.

"No buts. That is part of the arrangement."

He waved off any further arguments with every bit of the arrogance of a man of his station, and Jane stifled a smile. Perhaps this wouldn't be so difficult after all.

"As for you, I would like to receive a report about your progress in your search for my brother each time we meet," she said.

He wrinkled his brow. "I may not uncover information for some time. You are asking for a very difficult trade from me, you know."

She shook her head. "I don't care. I want to know what you are doing to look for Marcus, and whether or not those searches bear fruit. Otherwise, how am I to know this isn't just some fraud on your part?"

"You cannot trust my word," he said, leaning closer. "As a gentleman?"

She pursed her lips. "You aren't a gentleman yet."

He chuckled. "Very well, I agree to keep you informed of my attempts to determine where your brother has gone."

"Then it seems we are agreed, Viscount Stoneworth."

The smile faded from Nicholas's face, and he turned away a fraction. "Don't call me that."

Jane watched him in surprise. "I-I beg your pardon?"

"I don't wish to be 'my lorded' or called viscount," he snapped, his tone suddenly harsh.

She folded her arms, refusing to be intimidated by his peevish demeanor. "Whether you like it or not, that *is* what people will call you. You should become accustomed to it with me so that you will answer and not pull that angry face each time someone does it in polite company."

He spun on her, and the anger she had seen before was even stronger. Only it was laced with something else. Pain. And she realized in that moment exactly why Nicholas Stoneworth did not want to be called viscount.

Her lips parted. "It is because of your brother, isn't it?"

He stiffened, all his normal rakishness gone. "Don't be foolish."

"It is."

She moved toward him and hesitated before she placed a hand on his arm. She meant the gesture as one of comfort, but she couldn't ignore the snap of attraction touching him caused. His arm was muscular, like the rest of him, and warm beneath her palm.

She shook her head and recalled her purpose, shoving her strange reactions to him aside. "I can imagine this is all very difficult for you. To lose someone so close to you as a twin brother and to have to take his place—"

He yanked his arm from her grasp. "I will *never* take his place."

She tilted her head in acquiescence. "Of course."

He moved away from her. "You may call me Stoneworth or Stone, hell, even Nicholas. But I shall not answer if you 'my lord' me. Or if you call me viscount. *That* is not up for debate."

Jane folded her arms in frustration. Although she understood the emotional reaction Nicholas was experiencing, it did not change the fact that he was, indeed, viscount. But perhaps that was a fight to have with him another day. When he was a bit more . . . tamed.

"As you wish," she said softly.

He cleared his throat uncomfortably. "As for my part, I will require more information if I am to find your brother. Why don't we discuss that instead of this highly unpleasant topic?"

She bit back a bark of humorless laughter. As if talking about her own brother's disappearance was any more pleasant.

"What do you need to know?" she asked through clenched teeth.

"You say he disappeared," Nicholas pressed, tilting his head to examine her as she spoke. "What does that mean? Was he abducted? Did he leave any indication of his whereabouts? What precipitated the break with your family?"

She shut her eyes but couldn't block the pain of memories. "I don't know much. Unfortunately, my father 'protected' me from most of what occurred during that time. I know they fought. My brother's behavior had grown increasingly erratic and my father tried to rein him in."

Nicholas grunted, as if he understood that.

"Our interactions with him grew further and further apart and finally they ceased all together." She gripped her hands into fists. "I pressed my father, but he would not tell me anything. It was only after his death that I realized my brother had apparently developed some kind of dependence on opium. My father had reason to believe he went into the underground to feed his demons."

She shook her head, willing tears not to fall. "That was where he conducted his investigation."

"I see."

Nicholas gave no indication of his feelings or thoughts on her story, which she had all but torn from her heart. He simply stared at her, unreadable. Unfeeling. She shifted.

"I have brought some materials my father collected during his own search for Marcus," she said as she reached into her reticule and pulled out the items.

Nicholas took them and scanned over the neat lines of her handwriting. "These are not the original notes."

She shook her head. "My cousin refuses to allow me to take the originals from the house. These copies are the best I can do. I assure you, I was careful to leave nothing out."

"Nothing you could see." Nicholas's lips thinned. "There may be things in the originals that I could use in my search. Nuances. You are certain your cousin will not allow them to be removed, even temporarily?"

More angry tears stung Jane's eyes as she thought of Patrick's stubbornness earlier in the day, but she blinked them away. "He refuses to relinquish control of anything that could prove his claims false. I would not put it past him to destroy my father's papers entirely just to keep me from the truth."

Nicholas's gaze slowly moved to her face, and he examined her closely. Jane shifted under the scrutiny, trying not to look away and show him weakness, but uncomfortable under his stare.

"Could your cousin have been involved in your brother's disappearance?"

His tone was utterly cool for such a devastating question. Jane sucked in a breath of shock as she realized what Nicholas was implying. That Patrick would—would—

"No," she whispered. "I cannot believe he would do such a thing. He was out of the country when my brother first went missing. It was only after my father's death that he came forward and began his foolishness about Marcus being dead as well."

She shivered. Strangely, as much as she despised Patrick at present, she couldn't believe him capable of any kind of murderous intent to obtain the title. His crime was the fraud he had committed, it could not be anything deeper.

Or at least she hoped that was true.

No, according to her father's notes, it was Marcus's own sad desire for opium that had driven him further and further into the madness of the underground. Something Jane found equally difficult to believe.

She shook away her troubling thoughts and dipped back into her reticule. When her fingers touched the smooth round disk of metal within, she shivered. Slowly, she withdrew the item and held it out.

"I also brought this, in the hope it will aid you in your search."

She clicked the release on the side of the silver and the disk opened, revealing it as a framed miniature. On one side was a portrait of her beloved mother, but on the other was an image of Marcus, as he had been a few months before he disappeared. Young and handsome, his face filled with hopes for the future.

"This is your brother?" Nicholas asked, his voice suddenly more gentle as he took the frame from her shaking palm.

On reflex, Jane lifted her hand to cover her heart, hoping the ache of losing this last vestige of her lost family would fade quickly.

"Yes," she whispered.

"You share his eyes," he murmured, though he did not look up to verify the statement. "Is this woman your mother?"

She nodded, blinking back more tears. "She was. She died when I was just a girl. My lor—" She cut herself off when Nicholas's stare came up to hers. His brow arched in warning. She sighed. "In the four years since my brother's disappearance, I have never let these miniatures leave my possession. Please . . ." She hesitated. ". . . take care of them. I would like them back when you have no further need for them."

He snagged her gaze with eyes so bright and blue that they almost hurt to look at. Then he nodded, as solemn and serious as she had ever seen him.

"I swear to you, I will be careful. And I will return these to you as soon as I am able." He closed the frame and placed it on the table beside his drink.

"Very good," she said softly, forcing herself not to stare at the silver circle that held so much of her heart. "Now I should return to Lady Ridgefield's home. I do not want to rouse any suspicion. Shall I return tomorrow night for our first lesson?"

Nicholas nodded. "Yes, I am agreeable to that. If you give me a moment, I will have a carriage brought around to the servants' entrance for you."

She nodded wordlessly and watched as he departed the room. Once he was gone, she let out her breath in a whoosh. Finally she had someone on her side in her search for Marcus! Now she was certain she would find the answers she had sought for so long.

And if those answers came at a price, then that was the way of the world. She was willing to pay it, no matter how high, no matter how tempting.

Chapter 5

"**I** heard your little mouse returned. Your charm is commendable. It seems it stretches beyond opera singers and courtesans, after all."

Nicholas started. He had been staring out the window to the street down below where Jane had disappeared more than an hour before. He'd been so focused on his musings, he hadn't even heard the entrance of his best friend, Ronan "Rage" Riley.

He turned with a smile. "She did, indeed, Rage. Walked back into my lair like she wasn't even afraid of me. Fascinating creature, that one."

Rage tilted his head. "Fascinating. Who ever would have thought that a virginal fallen debutante would inspire you to look her way, let alone call her fascinating. She must be a pretty little mouse, indeed."

Nicholas shrugged, dismissing the comment as if he hadn't noticed Jane's appearance. But the truth was that he couldn't get her beauty out of his mind. It was so strange. Innocence didn't normally attract him, but there was something about this girl. Something about her full, red lips, her dark, haunted eyes that he found himself wanting.

"I can only assume she returned tonight because she changed her mind about helping you," Rage continued, interrupting Nicholas's thoughts.

He nodded. Since he had returned to London, Rage had been staying in the town home, acting as Nicholas's confidant, affairs manager, even sometimes-valet. In short, his best friend was the only person Nicholas could fully trust.

Rage poured himself a drink. "How dreary, to have to take gentleman's lessons."

Again, Nicholas shrugged wordlessly. Actually, the thought of Jane being the one to teach him made the idea of lessons far less unpleasant. She would be here, alone with him, close to him. It could actually be quite entertaining, especially since she was so bent on pretending she didn't notice he was a man.

But he had caught her looking at his bare legs, his chest, watching his mouth move. On some secret level, Jane Fenton wanted him.

He was accustomed to that, of course. Women had desired him since he was out of short pants. And even more of them since he became a boxer. Pugilists, especially successful ones who managed to keep their teeth, were in great demand from women of all stations. Christ, after the party, where he was decried as a heathen, he had still gotten several clandestine notes from women of the *ton,* making all kinds of offers for sin and passion.

And that was the problem. He didn't need rich women throwing themselves at him for secret affairs. What he needed was the attention of the right kind of woman. The fastest way to get back into the good graces of the *ton* and repair whatever damage he had already done to Anthony's reputation was to marry someone of good name and fortune.

Not sleep with every widow in heat. And not, sadly, pursue the charms of a woman fallen in station like Jane. If he could manage to clean himself up, he would be on the lookout for a wife, not a mistress.

"Stone?"

Nicholas shook his head. Again, he had been utterly distracted by thoughts of Jane. "Yes?"

"So what about Miss Fenton's brother? A man who disappeared into the underground so many years ago is likely going to be impossible to find, even if he is alive, which we both know is highly doubtful." Rage leaned back on the edge of the desk. "How do you intend to get what you want without Miss Fenton discovering *that* nasty little truth?"

Nicholas flinched. When he'd first offered to find Jane's brother, he hadn't cared if he misled her. He still intended to do so, since it would garner him what he desired, but now it left a rather unpleasant taste in his mouth. Especially when he thought of her crumpled face when she turned over the miniature of her mother and brother.

He knew something of her grief. He certainly felt some version of it whenever he thought of Anthony. If only *he* could pretend his brother wasn't dead, but lost somewhere.

"I will make some effort to find the man," Nicholas said as he fingered the silver frame he had put into his pocket when he got dressed after Jane's departure. "But if she has more faith in my ability than I deserve, who I am to disavow her of that notion? Especially if her continued confidence affords me her assistance?"

Rage smiled. "Ah, well, her inexperience will come in handy then. From a distance, she certainly looked innocent. Like a—"

"Fresh lily," Nicholas finished quietly.

Rage arched a brow. "I beg your pardon?"

"Nothing." He paced the room and returned to his spot looking out the window.

After years living a profligate life, Nicholas had to focus. To become a "better" man, at least on the surface. And Jane Fenton was going to be there to ensure that happened.

Nothing more.

* * *

Jane twirled a loose lock of hair around and around her finger as she stared into her rapidly cooling cup of tea with unseeing eyes. In the background, Lady Ridgefield chattered happily, completely unaware that Jane was lost in her own world.

Actually, that was the problem. She *wasn't* in her own world. She was in the dark and dangerous world of Nicholas Stoneworth. And she had been for more than twenty-four hours. Every time her mind was not occupied, it seemed to drift to the man. And more often than not, in her mind he was in the same state of undress as the last time she was with him.

Very distracting when she should have been focusing on what steps she would have to take in order to turn him back into a gentleman.

She shivered as the memory of the dark timber of his voice echoed in her ears. One could not deny that the man had an animal magnetism. That fact had probably done him wonders with loose women over the years. But could it truly translate into the kind of charisma impressive enough with the *ton* that it would erase years of bad behavior and innuendo?

More information was what she needed.

Lifting her head, she looked at her employer. As Lady Ridgefield slathered butter onto a piece of lightly toasted bread, she continued a long listing of the personal business of every member of the *ton*, without drawing breath. When she did finally pause to take a bite of her breakfast, Jane took the opportunity.

"The gossip must be buzzing about the new Viscount Stoneworth after his appearance at the Glouchester ball."

Lady Ridgefield's brown eyes lit up with excitement. Not the wicked pleasure of some of her friends, who took great joy in reveling in the pain of others. Jane had learned over the past six months that her employer more enjoyed knowing something that others didn't. In fact, when the gossip she imparted was bad news, she often became forlorn and Jane had to tease her out of her melancholy.

"Indeed," Lady Ridgefield answered on a deep sigh. "Nicholas Stoneworth is all the talk, unfortunately little of it is good."

Jane shifted. She would have to be careful in her approach. Even with Lady Ridgefield, too much interest would bring attention to her, which was the last thing she desired. If she was to work with Nicholas for their mutual benefit, it had to be in complete secrecy.

"I was too young to remember him, although I believe I did meet his brother once or twice before I left Society," Jane said with an affectation of bored interest. "What exactly has the viscount done to deserve such ire? Certainly many men leave Society to see the world, only to return to open arms. Why is Stoneworth so different?"

"The underground, my dear." Her employer sighed between bites of toast. "*That* has made all the difference. You know as well as I do that our Society is separated into very different worlds. Once you desert one for another, it is almost impossible to make the worst of our class forget it."

Jane flinched. How well she knew that, indeed. Friends she had been close to since childhood now ignored her, or worse, treated her like she was beneath them because she had been forced to take a position as a lady's companion. Any illusion Jane had that she could ever return to the place she once held had faded months ago.

Strangely, she found she didn't miss the idea of marrying some pompous lord her father chose for her and being paraded around until she birthed a few sons and became less useful. No man who had courted her in the brief years she had been considered a lady had ever come close to capturing her interest, let alone her heart.

Besides, she could hardly think of her own happiness when Marcus needed her full attention. After she found him, after she helped him return to his rightful place . . . *then* she would think about her own future.

Shaking her head, she cleared her thoughts away. This conversation was not about her, it was about Nicholas Stoneworth.

"Was he *truly* in the underground, though?" she pressed, though she knew the answer. One only had to spend five minutes with Nicholas to feel the darkness and danger of his person. "How in the world did the son of a well-respected marquis ever turn to such a place?"

Lady Ridgefield dabbed her lips with her napkin as she pondered that question. "No one really knows the cause of the marquis and his son's ultimate breach, at least no one in my circles."

Jane stifled a smile. If Lady Ridgefield's circles knew nothing, then no one did. Those women were like hungry lionesses. Nothing escaped them once they went on the hunt.

Her employer frowned. "But it seemed to me that the young man and his father always had trouble. While Anthony Stoneworth was everything a father could want in an heir, Nicholas seemed to revel in causing trouble. He was never quite as accepted as his brother to begin with, so when the rumors began that he was going down to dangerous parts of London, participating in questionable activities . . . I suppose people were almost relieved to have a reason to shun him."

Jane's brow wrinkled. She could well imagine Nicholas, as a twin, must have been somewhat hurt to see his father embrace his brother and dismiss him. And yet, instead of trying to fit into some kind of mold, he had rebelled.

So he had never *really* been a gentleman to begin with, at least not in action. Which would likely make her training all the harder.

"But his family must have tried to keep him from those types of places, to keep him away from danger?" Jane asked.

She flinched as she thought of her father's paperwork, which had detailed so much about his desperate attempts to save her brother after Marcus disappeared into his own underground hell.

Lady Ridgefield laughed. "That boy was never one to heed warnings. In fact, just the opposite. At some point I believe his father found out he was earning a *living* fighting at some of those underground clubs. They had a row and Nicholas left. They say Stoneworth kept in touch with his brother and perhaps occasionally met with his mother, but he and his father only spoke again because of Anthony's death."

"How tragic," Jane said softly just as the door opened and a footman entered to discuss something about Lady Ridgefield's schedule for the day.

As her employer spoke quietly to the man, Jane shivered. She had been so close to her family, she couldn't imagine parting ways with them purposefully. Breaking so completely that she didn't even speak to them. No, she had been *torn* from her family by death and circumstance.

How could Nicholas Stoneworth be so cavalier in throwing away his connections in this world? Could a man like that truly be redeemed?

She shook her head.

None of those things mattered in this instance. She wasn't out to make the man a saint, only give him a few reminders about gentlemanly behavior. And until he found her brother, which she was convinced he could do, she had no choice but to do her best with him.

And hope that her best would somehow be enough.

THE NOTORIOUS LADY ANNE

Chapter 6

Nicholas checked the clock, then immediately cursed himself for doing so. It wasn't the first time that he'd done it. In fact, in the last hour alone he had found his eyes slipping to the timepiece five times. Each time it seemed the minute hand had moved only a few slots.

Why he was obsessed with the clock, he refused to ponder. Jane had not given him a specific hour that she would come to him tonight. It would all depend upon Lady Ridgefield.

And yet still he watched, his body coiled and tight. It was not a very different feeling from what he got before a fight, when anxiety made him restless and ready. Only there would be no fighting tonight. At least not the kind he was accustomed to. The kind he thrived on and lived for. The kind he might never be able to participate in again.

His heart ached dully at the thought. He hadn't started out fighting to earn a living, rather to survive. When he first began frequenting the underground bars and gambling establishments, he had been a target. Soft, he had reeked of money and privilege, despite his attempts to be rough. But after one particularly bad night, when he managed to fend off three men attempting to rob him in an alley, he had been approached to fight for a purse.

And everything about him had changed. The more he learned about the game, the more fighting had transformed beyond necessity to art. And he'd become very good at it.

"My lord?"

Nicholas shook off his thoughts and turned to glare at his butler. "We have discussed this, Gladwell. I do not wish to be referred to in that manner."

His butler's lips pursed. "*Sir*, Miss Fenton is here. Shall I show her in?"

Nicholas straightened up. "Yes. Bring her to me."

The servant stifled a sigh and stepped aside. In a breath Jane was standing before him.

Nicholas couldn't help but move toward her a step, nor was he unaware of the way she caught her breath when he did so. It was unfortunate that her gown was so plain. A drab muslin that was too big for her slender frame. But he had always had a fine imagination when it came to women, and Nicholas was still aware of the smooth curve of her breasts, the narrow expanse of her hips. He could easily imagine just how lovely she had looked when she wore fine silks and satins.

"Is there anything you will require?" Gladwell asked, startling Nicholas into reality. He had actually forgotten that his servant was still standing there.

"No, thank you. I will ring if we do," Nicholas said with a nod of dismissal. The butler left, but did not shut the door behind him.

With a roll of his eyes, Nicholas moved forward and did it himself before he turned to Jane with a smile. "He does not approve of our being alone. I assume he believes I'll be ravishing you tonight."

Jane swallowed hard before she moved into the center of the room. "As long as he doesn't share that belief with anyone who might tell those outside of this household, his misguided thoughts matter very little. There will be no ravishing."

Nicholas smiled. "Pity."

He expected her to turn or blush or acknowledge his quiet comment, but instead, she continued to look around the room, a finger pressed to her full bottom lip.

"Hmm. We have much work to be done and I believe we can start much of it here. Later, of course, we shall need use of the dining room.

And your ballroom. Do you think that can be arranged?"

She turned to look at him, and Nicholas stared for a moment before he said, "Of course. If you tell me what you require, my staff will ensure it is done. I am at your beck and call, my lady."

He gave her a gallant bow and an audacious wink, but she did not react to either. Instead, she withdrew a small notebook and a small charcoal pencil from the pocket of her ugly gown.

"Proper address," she murmured as she scribbled something.

Nicholas couldn't help but notice that several of the square sheets were covered with her broad scrawl. He wrinkled his brow.

"And just what is that?"

She looked up at him as if she had forgotten his presence entirely. "It is a list of some of the items we will need to cover in your education."

She flipped the notebook to its first page and then turned the sheets until she reached her latest entry. Nicholas's heart sank when he realized there were at least twenty-five entries on her list.

"Is that all?" he said, sarcasm dripping from every syllable.

She shrugged as she pocketed the notebook and pencil. "Probably not. I tend to think of a few additions every day. I'm certain I will find more as I come to know you better."

Nicholas suddenly wanted a drink, but he forced himself to remain where he was. He watched as Jane took a slow turn around him, examining him from head to toe. Normally such bold scrutiny by a lovely young woman would have been shocking. And this was. Only for a different reason than one might have expected.

Jane seemed to be sizing him up as she would a pony or a fillet of beef at market. There was nothing blatant in her stare. In fact, she appeared to be unmoved by him in the slightest. No amount of flirtation seemed to make her even aware of him as a man at all, beyond her first unguarded moments when she stepped into the room.

Despite himself, Nicholas was fascinated by this. This woman was a challenge. An utter riddle, and he found himself wanting to solve it. Find some way to break the protective shell she had put around herself.

"Well, you are certainly going to look very well once you have some proper clothing," she said, but it seemed she required no answer. "However, it is often not the clothing that makes a man, but how he wears it. If you stagger or lumber about like a giant, your fine accoutrements will do you no good."

"Do you require my participation in this conversation at all?" Nicholas asked, folding his arms across his chest.

She frowned. "Of course. I require your participation in every aspect of our time together, otherwise we won't get far at all. Now then, I would like to see how you move."

Nicholas felt his eyebrows knit together in surprise. "I beg your pardon?"

She looked at him as if he was quite daft. "Please walk about the room, like you would do normally. Try not to think about what you are doing or that you are being watched. Be as unpracticed as possible."

Nicholas stared. Well, this was the very end. He had never experienced a woman like this. When he made his offer to her, he hadn't thought that she would take her charge so seriously that she forced herself to tamp down and forget all the attraction between them.

It seemed his duty to remind her. If only to see her cheeks flush.

"But my dear," he drawled. "How should I walk?"

"As I said, just move as you would normally," she repeated, again looking at him as if he were not intelligent in the least.

"But you see, a man walks differently in various situations. If I am in an unfamiliar surrounding, where I'm not certain if I'm in danger, I might be cautious."

He turned away and demonstrated what he

meant, his shoulders back so he looked as big as possible, his fists at the ready, his eyes flitting to every corner in a subtle analysis of his surroundings.

"Or if I were relaxed, comfortable, amongst friends, I might move quite differently." He changed his gait, relaxing his shoulders, slowing his steps.

Then he turned back to her. She was staring at him, her expression unreadable. "Or would you prefer I walk like I would while pursuing a woman?"

He stepped toward her in a few long strides, possessive. Feral. Slowly, he inched around her as she had done earlier, but while her examination of his form had been clinical, this was something entirely different. He moved in close, almost touching her, but not quite. He circled her frame like a cat, stalking and inviting. Making it clear with every step that he could claim her any time he desired to do so.

When he moved to stand before her again, she looked up at him. Her bottom lip trembled ever so slightly and her eyes had become a fraction glazed. Her throat worked as she swallowed.

There it was. Nicholas could have crowed. He *could* move her. Remind her that he was a man, after all.

"You have grace," she said softly, when a long

moment of silence had passed between them. "Perhaps you are not a lost cause after all, my lord."

Nicholas froze. He had been "my lorded" twice that night. Both times, the address had cut him. His eyes shut, and he worked to block out thoughts of Anthony. Thoughts of the gravity of his situation.

When he opened them again, he found that Jane's expression had changed as well. The desire he had inspired still lingered in the background, but something far more potent had come to the forefront.

Pity.

And he had to wipe that away.

"Oh my dear, I *am* a lost cause. Trust in that," he said, his voice rough.

He reached for her without realizing he intended to do so. She stumbled forward in surprise at his sudden movement, falling against his chest, and his arms came around her, almost of their own volition. She was warm, fragile, and he felt her heart fluttering with a wild beat against his own. Her face tilted up and he couldn't help himself. Couldn't stop himself.

He leaned down and pressed his lips to hers.

She tasted like tea with honey, sweet and rich. And while her lips pursed together in surprise, they were still soft as satin and smooth against his own. He increased the pressure of his mouth, coaxing and demanding a response even though his rational mind told him to stop. That by doing this, he was threatening their bargain and his own promises to change.

But he couldn't listen to that voice. Kissing her had been as much a surprise to him as it was to her, but now that he was doing it, he wanted more.

Her lips relaxed beneath his, and her hands, which had been balled into fists at her sides, slowly lifted to his forearms. He realized that was all the invitation he would likely get. He parted his lips and gently traced the crease of her mouth with the tip of his tongue. She gasped, and he took that moment of weakness, tasting her, savoring her flavor like a man starved.

Her fingers bunched against the linen fabric of his shirt, and her heart rate increased. He felt her fighting, not him, but her own desires. Yet she didn't pull away. Couldn't pull away. That was a triumph, but it was nothing compared to when she hesitantly let her tongue touch his.

An explosion of lust so powerful that it took him off guard made him pull her closer. He crushed her to his chest, desire driving him to arch against her, to lose finesse in trade for pure, unadulterated need.

This was not a feeling he'd had with many women. This excitement so wild and passionate that it threatened to rage out of control in a moment. It was heady and powerful.

But suddenly Jane stiffened and shoved against his chest, rending herself from his arms with a fierce cry. She backed away, wiping her mouth with the back of her hand as she stared at him as if he were a beast free of his cage.

"If this is how you intend to behave, your grace will be of little help to you," she snapped, her voice trembling like her limbs and her skin hot pink, but not with arousal.

Nicholas recognized, as he stared at her, that she was *angry*. Offended. Even though she had reacted to him, allowed him the liberty of her kiss for a moment, now she wanted nothing to do with it or him.

She pulled at her gown to straighten it, although he had done nothing to mar it. Likely that would have changed within the span of five minutes if she hadn't broken away. She glared at him with all the censure and haughtiness of the highest duchess in the Empire.

"I am leaving now," she said. "I think I've learned quite enough for one day, and I don't know that you will be able to absorb any further education in your current"—she glanced down pointedly at the erection that now made itself known—"state."

Nicholas stared at her. "You are leaving?" he repeated stupidly.

She nodded once. "I will return tomorrow, though. And I expect you will have some information for me regarding your own search for my brother by then. Good evening, *my lord*."

Nicholas flinched as she left the room and slammed the door behind her. He stared at the place she had stood. In his thirty years on this earth, he had been with many women. His reaction to them and theirs to him had varied, of course, but none of them had ever kissed him and pulled away first. None of them had ever looked at him like his touch was akin to acid.

None of them had ever been so unmoved by his prowess as Jane Fenton. And he had never been so driven to prove to a woman that he could make her tremble.

In the carriage winding its way through the London streets, Jane leaned back against the leather seats. Her entire body was trembling. Not from fear, not even from the anger that she had turned to for protection once she regained her senses.

No, her body now shook from something else. Something she did not want any more than she could control it. She trembled from the force of her desire. The desire she had felt when she walked into the room and saw Nicholas waiting for her, a tiger still pacing his cage.

The desire she had been unable to ignore when

he circled her, whispering words she should have censured him for, but instead had made her stomach flutter wildly.

And the desire that had washed over her in an overwhelming wave when he kissed her. Tasted her. Made her realize, for the first time, just how powerful a man could be. How much control he could wield with one heated touch.

It was a solemn reminder that Nicholas might be the student, but that didn't mean he was naïve. If she intended to continue with this "training," she would have to be very careful of him. Careful of his body . . . and careful of his dark and dangerous soul, as well.

The underground was not one specific place, though those of the *ton* often spoke of it as if it was. Of course most of them had never left the safety of Bond Street to investigate their ideas on the place they decried. Those who did were generally like Jane's brother, lost in their own pains and obsessions. The underground was an end for them.

But to Nicholas, it had been a beginning. And now, as he walked with Rage down Jermyn Cross at a broad, wide clip, it was like coming home. The dirty street was dangerous, yes, but it had a frantic energy about it, as well. This was a place where a fortune could be made or lost; where the next person one met could become a lifelong friend or turn out to be a murderer; a place where spirits and women ran free in equal measure, and neither were weak or watered down.

Clubs lined each side of the narrow, dirty expanse, but they were not the fancy ones like White's or Boodle's that catered to men of his class. There were no cigar rooms in *these* places, no liveried footmen to bring fresh port. Nicholas almost chuckled when he thought of what would happen if such a person entered these pits.

No, one had to be sharp here. And a man like Nicholas, who had enough of a reputation that the lightskirts hawking their wares in front of an open pub door called out to him by name and offered him free tumbles as they walked by, had to be especially alert. There were dozens of men who would love the prestige of taking down the most celebrated underground fighter. And most of them would not fight fair.

Which meant it was the perfect place to go to forget his troubling encounter with Jane Fenton earlier in the night. Kissing her had been a huge mistake. A great pleasure, but a mistake nonetheless.

But then Nicholas had never been one to learn from his mistakes, and he wanted to repeat this one again and again.

"Hey, stay alert." Rage's whisper was harsh at his side.

Nicholas shook off his thoughts and looked around. A group of four men had just stepped from one of the gambling hells. Although they were all staggering, they also had guns strapped to their hips, and they were watching Rage and Nicholas closely as they passed by.

"What's wrong with you?" Rage snapped once the men had weaved their way into another hell instead of pursuing them. "You didn't even glance their way until I mentioned it. You know you can't daydream here, friend. Wait until we get to Ruby's where you've got folks watching your back."

"Sorry," he mumbled. "It was a slip."

"One I've never seen you make," his friend pressed. "So do you want to tell me why? And why are we here? I thought you were in for the night once Miss Fenton left."

Nicholas sighed. There was no use lying to Rage. His friend had the uncanny ability to see right through him every time. "The answer to both your questions *is* Miss Fenton."

"Let's go inside and you can tell me all about it." Rage motioned to the gaming hell where he had stopped.

Nicholas smiled as he looked up at the battered wooden sign swinging in the early summer's night breeze. Ruby's.

They entered the hall and were immediately greeted by the smell of nervous sweat, cheap cigar smoke, and spilled whiskey. For a long time those scents had been repugnant to Nicholas, but over the years they had come to symbolize a kind of comfort. Here, he belonged.

Except now he didn't.

Rage wove his way through the teeming crowd of desperate men and sly women until they reached a bar in the back. As people cast glances at them, a reverent hush moved through the bar. Nicholas shrugged it off. He had become accustomed to such attention after years of fighting. Both he and Rage were popular pugilists, and the men in this bar had won and lost small fortunes by betting on their battles.

Many of the women had been part of the celebrations or consolations after them.

A weathered barkeep stepped up and gave what was as close to a smile as one was going to get on such a scarred face. "Rage, Stone, haven't seen you two for a bit. What's your poison?"

"Whiskey for both. And is Ruby here tonight?" Rage asked as he motioned his head toward the back where most of the higher stakes gaming went on.

"Ruby's here," the barkeep said as he set two grimy glasses on the tabletop. "Be up soon enough when word gets around that you two are here."

Then he turned away, making no further effort

to make conversation. In the hells, it was best not to hear or see anything when you weren't invited, and everyone knew it.

"So, Jane Fenton," Rage said as he took a sip of his drink. "How did she chase you into the hells? Were her lessons so dastardly?"

Nicholas groaned. "The lessons were hardly anything to speak of. She asked me to move for her—"

Rage interrupted with a devilish grin. "And I'm sure you were most happy to oblige her."

He shrugged. "She seemed immune to my subtle attempts at charm. And then to my blatant ones. I've never seen anything like it, actually. And then I, er, kissed her."

Rage set his drink down with raised eyebrows. "And this set you on your heels . . . how? You've certainly kissed women before her, and I'll wager you'll kiss plenty more after. No kiss has ever sent you running from your own home."

"But Jane isn't like the other women I've kissed," he explained, trying to clarify the problem for himself as much as his friend. "She isn't some whore or an opera singer or a married woman slumming in the hells with a fighter. She is a lady, whether she is still treated like one or not. And if I'm to become a gentleman again, I cannot just go around kissing ladies like her without consequences."

Rage shivered. They both knew the consequence Nicholas referred to. Marriage. It wasn't something often forced upon those who lived in the world around them. But in the *ton*, one could be shackled to a woman faster than one could say devil's daughter.

And while Nicholas knew that his new life would eventually lead to marriage, he wasn't about to be run into it by a careless kiss. He would choose the woman he took for a bride carefully. A woman of influence would be best, one who could continue to improve his reputation.

"The last thing I need is for it to be said that I seduced some poor fallen lady," he groaned. "My reputation is wretched enough as it is."

Rage shrugged. "Is she the type to spread such stories, perhaps in order to better her situation?"

Nicholas paused. He hadn't even considered that idea. But as he thought of Jane, he couldn't imagine her doing such a thing. After all, she had been offered an escape from her current position by her cousin's offer of marriage. If she had refused that, it didn't seem likely that she would use their strange situation against him to force a union.

"I couldn't see her doing that. She is the one who insists on secrecy and propriety," he said, though he couldn't help but think of her brief responsiveness before she turned the fiery spark of her anger on him.

And what a spark it had been. He smiled just thinking of it. It might be worth kissing her again, just to make her rail and flush like that.

"My boys!"

Both men looked up as a woman entered the main room from the back gaming hall. With a grin, Nicholas pushed to his feet to greet her.

Ruby Hathaway had long passed the bloom of her youth, but there was still something about her. A middle-aged queen who ruled her gaming hall with an iron fist. She had been married to the man who first put Nicholas in the ring, and though he was gone, Ruby still looked at the fighters her husband had trained as her own children.

"Didn't think we'd see you back, Stone, after your poor brother cocked up his toes," Ruby said as she pressed a kiss to first his cheek, then Rage's. "I am so sorry."

Nicholas accepted her sympathy with a tight smile, knowing she meant only the best, despite her crude, blunt terms. "Thank you, Ruby."

She squeezed his arm gently, then released it, and her pity was gone. "So, how *is* life in the grand halls? Are those goosecaps giving you hell?"

"As much as they can manage without lowering their noses," Nicholas admitted.

For a few moments, they talked, reminiscing and catching up on the goings-on in the gaming hell that they had missed. Then Rage shot him a look from the corner of his eye, and Nicholas nodded.

"Ruby, I wondered if you can put out a word for me amongst the rabble and the opium men. I'm looking for someone who they might know."

She tilted her head to the side and examined Nicholas carefully. "You never ran with their lot, Stone. Never touched the stuff, if I recall, and better for ya."

He nodded slowly. A few glimpses of the men who had become obsessed with the drug, and Nicholas had never felt any desire to test his luck. Even when he was injured, he refused the medicine for fear of developing a craving for it.

"True, but a . . . friend is missing her brother and I promised to investigate." He withdrew the little silver frame from his pocket and showed Ruby the miniature of Jane's brother. "The man's name would have been Marcus Fenton, though he might have gone by something else amongst this society."

Ruby took the little frame carefully and looked at both Marcus's portrait and the one of Jane's mother. "Don't seem familiar, though if he took to the opiate, he might not have looked much like that by the time he was through. Pretty lady, though. She don't look like no whore to me. You've made friends with a rich lot already, then."

Nicholas took the frame back and carefully closed it as he shrugged. "You know me, Ruby. I'm the kind of man that women befriend."

She laughed, her voice husky from years of smoke and drink. "That you are, boy. Well, might as well tup the rich ones as well as the poor, eh? I'll put out a word about your foppish opium hound. Come back in a few days and we'll see if I've come up with any answers. Now I best be back to my business."

She waved to them both before she returned to the back room where the deepest cards were played. Rage looked at Nicholas when she was gone.

"She might have something for us in time, but I think we both know she won't. What will you tell Jane next time you see her, to keep her from realizing there is no hope?"

Nicholas took the last sip of his drink, unable to think of a good answer. Again, his rarely demonstrated conscience tweaked him. Jane had such high hopes in his miraculous ability to find her lost brother.

"Stone!"

He looked to the left at the voice that had mercifully kept him from answering his friend. Through the crowd, two young men, probably too young to be in such a place, were approaching, their eyes bright with excitement.

"You're Stone, the boxer, ain't you?" one boy asked, while the other boy kept nudging him for encouragement.

Nicholas sighed. "That I am, boys. And this here is Rage Riley."

The two exchanged awed glances before the braver boy said, "Will ya be fightin' tonight, Stone?"

Nicholas looked at the door behind the bar wistfully. Behind this room was another larger room where bare-fisted brawling went on late into the night. How satisfying it would be to go a few rounds with one of these drunks. To pound out his frustration and dissatisfaction with something physical, rather than *thinking* incessantly.

"I don't think so, boys," he finally said, turning away from the room. "Not tonight at any rate."

They both made a sound of distress as they faded back into the crowd. Nicholas stared at his empty glass, feeling Rage's stare on him, but unwilling to answer his friend's unspoken questions and comments.

The fact was that this place used to feel like home to him. But he no longer belonged here. Just as he didn't belong in Jane's world. He was a man with no country, in a way.

And he had yet to figure out what to do about it.

Chapter 7

~~~⁓⁓~~~

Jane stood staring at the back servants' entrance to Nicholas's home. She had been standing there almost a full five minutes and yet felt no closer to knocking and facing him again.

She was a coward. Never before had she felt that. She had faced the deaths of two parents, the disappearance of a beloved brother, and the betrayal of a favorite cousin without allowing fear to mob her. She had gone into the house of a woman she did not know beyond mere passing and become a servant without trembling. She had faced the loathing and mockery of her former peers without a flinch.

Yet one uncouth man . . .

No, it wasn't the man she feared. It was the kiss. The feelings inspired by the kiss. The deep longing in her soul that she hadn't even known existed.

The most ridiculous part of it all was that last night had not been the first time she was kissed.

To be precise about it, it had been the third. The first was when she was ten, and it had been with her hated cousin Patrick. Of course, he hadn't been hated then and had also been all of thirteen. It was a child's peck, not something she'd thought of until she began pondering her history of kisses in the wee hours of the morning when sleep would not come.

Her second kiss had been more proper. It had occurred the year before her father died, on the balcony at a ball. This time her partner had been the youngest son of Lord Harrington, what was his name . . . Rupert or something close to that?

They had been dancing, and he had taken her out onto the balcony for a little air. She had felt like something was coming, and sure enough, he had kissed her. She recalled it as a nice experience. A brief brush of strong, firm lips on hers before they both pulled away with a blush.

But Rupert Harrington had nothing like the crushing, consuming power of Nicholas Stoneworth. The kiss on the balcony hadn't tested her resolve or made her stomach flutter or her legs shake. It hadn't kept her awake all night or distracted her the next day. And it hadn't had such consequences as she faced now, either.

What if Nicholas believed he could kiss her any time he liked? Or take even further liberties with her? She shivered and tried to convince herself that it was out of fear and disgust. But it wasn't.

Excitement would have been more accurate. The idea that he would kiss her again, perhaps do more than just that, gave her a thrill.

And the thrill was troubling, too. How could she be consumed with thoughts of kisses when she was so close to finding Marcus? It was *wrong* to let her mind wander from her task. Wrong to think of Nicholas Stoneworth as a man and not a means to her brother.

She leaned forward and rested her head against the cool door. Perhaps she should leave. She could run away into the night and never see Nicholas Stoneworth again. She could pretend she'd never made this bargain or even met the man at all.

Slowly, she turned and faced the street. In a moment, she could hail a hack and be gone.

Before she could make that final decision, the door behind her opened. Spinning, she turned, expecting to find the heavyset cook or stern Gladwell judging her.

Instead, Nicholas Stoneworth framed the door. The light from the warm kitchen outlined him like a dark, fallen angel. He was wearing trousers that hung casually around his hips and his shirt was stripped open, so there was a shocking expanse of bare, tempting skin for her eyes to feast upon.

She had never seen a man's fully bare chest before, just hints of Nicholas's in the past. Muscle. There was muscle everywhere. Curved and toned from work, from fighting, from God only knew what activities. Light chest hair curled against his skin and a line of it trailed down his stomach, making a path that disappeared into his waistband.

He made a deep, throaty sound before he said, "Leaving?"

Jane started. She had been staring quite blatantly at his half-naked body and now snapped her gaze to his. He was staring at her evenly, his impossibly bright blue eyes reflecting amusement and something else. Something hot and heady that she fought to ignore as she scrambled for some kind of decorum.

"I-I—" she stammered, then paused for a deep breath. "No. I wasn't going to leave."

She couldn't. After all, this man was her last hope.

"Then step inside, my lady. Join me." He moved back to allow her to come in.

The kitchen was empty except for the two of them. A fact that startled Jane almost as much as Nicholas's appearance.

"Were you waiting for me here?" she asked, her mouth dry.

He nodded as he motioned her toward a seat at the plain, serviceable table and took his own place to stand before the stove with his back to her. Jane sank into the chair and watched in wonder as he gently stirred a pot of something that smelled like chocolate.

"I saw no need in making my servants stay up waiting to let you in and show you out. You are later than I expected."

"Yes. Lady Ridgefield had a letter from her eldest daughter. She was so excited that she asked me to read it to her tonight and write one in return immediately." Jane smiled as she thought of her employer's excitement. "Unfortunately, Lady Ridgefield dictates just as she speaks, in one uninterrupted sentence. She also tends to want to include everything that comes to mind in her letters without filter. Her correspondence can take hours to compose."

"Ah," Nicholas said as he added a bit of spice to whatever he was concocting. "And yet you still like her."

Jane straightened up, protectiveness making her heart pound a little stronger. She knew what some people said about Lady Ridgefield behind her back, and it angered Jane to no end.

"I *do* like her," she said with no hesitation. "She is as kind and decent a woman as I have ever known."

He looked at her over his shoulder. "I recall her from my childhood."

Jane laughed despite herself. "She recalls you, as well. And always speaks of you with much affection."

"Of course she is talking about me," he groaned.

"*Everyone* is talking about you," she replied.

Slowly, he turned and looked at her full-on. "Everyone?"

Jane cleared her throat. "You know that full well, for it is why you have asked for my assistance."

"Indeed, it is," he replied, his voice faraway as he turned his attention back to the stovetop. "Perhaps I should visit Lady Ridgefield, then. Give her something to talk about with those biddies she calls friends."

Jane shoved to her feet in surprise. The idea that Nicholas would bring himself to the home where she lived, insert himself into the society of her employer, was terrifying. What if someone guessed about their clandestine meetings? What if all was revealed and ruined?

Then she noticed him toss a wink over his shoulder at her.

"You are teasing me," she said with relief as she sank back down.

"You make far too easy a target. So serious."

He turned and brought a steaming cup of chocolate to set before her on the table. He took a seat across from her with his own mug. She couldn't help but notice that neither cup matched. Hers actually appeared to be fine china, and she could well imagine the cook's horror when she noticed *that* the next day.

She stared at the mug before her, breathing in

the delicious smells of thick, rich chocolate. She hadn't indulged in this pleasure since before her father died. Carefully, she lifted the mug to her lips, blew on it, and took the first sip.

Whatever he had added to the concoction gave it a heady, spicy flavor that melded with the rich chocolate. She shut her eyes and let out a low moan of pure pleasure as the brew slid down her throat.

When she opened them again, she found Nicholas staring at her, his cup lifted halfway to his lips, eyes wide and focused on her mouth.

"Good?" he asked, but his voice was suddenly strained.

She nodded. "Delightful," she admitted. "I cannot believe you made this yourself."

He shrugged, lowering his cup. "The world of the *ton* is very sheltered. Those of our class never learn to do anything for themselves. Leaving this world showed me how little I was actually capable of. So I learned to take care of myself in every way. Including the occasional cup of chocolate." He winked at her again, and the tension that had hung between them faded a fraction. "I can also sew a button and make a broth that will help speed away a winter cough."

Jane smiled. "You are a man of many talents."

"You have no idea."

Her smile faded as another blush heated her

cheeks. Nicholas was incapable of not flirting. He had to make everything an innuendo. Which only taunted her with two facts.

One, that she was just another in a long series of women with whom he had played this game. And two, that she couldn't stop herself from reacting to the way he looked at her, the warmth of his skin, which was so close that she could have touched him if she dared.

She cleared her throat, hoping it would help clear her mind. "H-have you made any headway with your investigation into my brother's disappearance?"

Yes, that was right. She needed to refocus on the matters at hand. Keep her mind on Marcus and on her promise to help Nicholas. Everything else had to be forgotten. Ignored. Crushed down where she would no longer think or want it.

Nicholas frowned as he downed his chocolate in a few great gulps. He wiped his lip with the back of his hand and said, "Indeed, Rage and I went into the hells last night after you departed and spoke to an old friend. She will be getting in contact with those who might have known your brother."

Jane nodded, waiting for happiness and relief to wash over her. It didn't. All she could concentrate on was the fact that Nicholas had turned to a *woman* for help. Probably a beautiful one, too. And in trade for her assistance, he had . . .

"It will likely take a few days for any real information to reach us." Nicholas took her empty cup and set them both away. He remained standing, leaning against the lower cabinetry with one ankle crossed over the other.

Reluctantly, Jane pushed to her feet. "And this woman, you think she has connections enough?"

He hesitated for a moment, but then nodded slowly. "She is not the only person I will make inquiries with, but she's the best start. She didn't recognize your brother when I allowed her to view the miniature, but that doesn't mean someone else won't."

Jane's heart lodged in her throat. Some stranger had pawed over her precious miniature. Looked at Marcus's face and dismissed him. For the first time, the full weight of that washed over her. And the weaknesses she always fought so hard to control took hold of her.

With a gasp, she grasped the back of the chair she had vacated and clung. Tears stung her eyes, threatening to humiliate her in the kitchen of this man who inspired such a strange mixture of feelings in her.

He stared at her, his expression a combination of understanding and discomfort. Then, without a word, he stepped forward and placed a remarkably gentle hand on her shoulder. His long fingers curled around her, soothing and lightly stroking before he drew her against his bare chest and held her there.

Propriety dictated that she pull away, but Jane found she couldn't do that. It had been so long since someone offered her tenderness or reassurance that she ached for it. A few tears slipped from her eyes, touching Nicholas's hot skin. Yet he didn't pull back, and still he did not speak.

She allowed his embrace a few moments before she gathered her composure, remembered her place, and stepped back. He made no move to force her to stay close to him, and for that she was equally relieved and disappointed.

"I'm sorry," she said, grasping for a handkerchief in the pocket of her plain pelisse. "I don't know why I did that."

He frowned, but then said, "I understand."

Jane looked up at him and saw the wealth of true empathy in his expression. He, too, had lost a brother. He might be better at hiding it, but her sorrow and pain mirrored his own. Only she still had hope for Marcus. Nicholas could have none, for his brother was already cold in the ground. Lost to him forever.

"Yes, you do." She dabbed her eyes. "This is enough nonsense. Thank you for the update on your search. I can accept that it may be a few days before you have more information for me. In the meantime, we have our training to attend to."

He seemed as relieved as she was to get away from the tender subject of their lost siblings. "Where would you like to begin, Jane?"

"Your wardrobe."

She looked him up and down, concealing a shiver at the utter beauty of his masculine frame. Certainly he could not go out half naked, as pleasant an image as that idea created. And so far she had not seen him in anything approaching appropriate attire. Even when he attended the Glouchester ball, he had not looked totally correct.

The spark of mischief returned to Nicholas's stare, and Jane almost wanted to smile at it. Until he said, "That is absolutely agreeable to me. All you must do is accompany me to my chamber."

Nicholas couldn't help but grin at Jane's outraged expression. He much preferred that to the crumpled nature of her earlier anguish. Especially since he had no illusions that his "investigation" would bring her relief. She was pinning her hopes on a fool's notion. And it wasn't one he could disabuse her of.

"I will not go to your chamber, Lord Stoneworth!" she snapped.

He flinched at the use of his brother's title, but ignored it this time. "Then how do you propose you examine my wardrobe, my dear?"

She sputtered and blinked as she pondered that

question. A few times she parted her lips, but then snapped them shut as if she had come up with an idea, but reconsidered it. Finally, she pursed her mouth in frustration.

"I suppose it is the only way. But I cannot teach you to be gentlemanly and then allow you to do something so *ungentlemanly* as taking me to your room alone."

Nicholas smothered a smile. He didn't think any other woman had ever argued so strenuously against joining him in his chamber. Which made Jane utterly tempting.

But after his loss of control the last time he kissed her, he supposed she was correct in her assessment of their situation. If he was alone with her, with no chance of being caught, and passion struck him . . . well, it might not end with a mere kiss.

"My valet of sorts is upstairs and not yet asleep like the remaining servants. I could have him stand by in the room with us to ensure that I do not ravish you."

She stiffened at his choice of words, but then nodded once. "Yes. That would suffice. For future reference, though, an ideal chaperone would be another woman. Normally she would be older and married. But under these strange circumstances, I would accept a servant of any kind. As long as you feel you can trust him."

Nicholas motioned to the door and led her

down the hallway and up the stairs toward the bedchambers. "Oh yes," he murmured as he paused at Rage's door. "I trust him."

Jane blinked as he knocked. "You have your valet sleep in a family chamber?" she whispered. "Honestly, Nicholas, we must talk about—"

But before she could finish her admonishment, the door to Rage's chamber opened.

Jane broke off as she looked up and up at him. Nicholas had never uncovered many facts about Rage's upbringing, but had always assumed his friend was raised on the streets. Despite the fact that he was well-spoken and highly intelligent, Rage had a rough, wary quality that most street folk had. A wan, sad knowledge of the world and all its evils.

But unlike some, who became beggars or were crushed by the experience entirely, Rage had become strong. He and Nicholas had only fought in matches a few times, but even when they sparred, Rage was a handful for Nicholas. Powerful, skilled in his knowledge of where a punch could do the most devastation.

Rage's nose was a bit crooked from one too many fights, his skin was dark with sun, and his hair was close cropped to his head. Jane shot Nicholas a glare, and he realized she recognized his friend for what he was.

And that was no servant.

"Miss Jane Fenton, may I present to you Ronan

'Rage' Riley. He is my best friend, my sparring partner, and yes, occasionally my valet. And Rage, this is Jane."

"Miss Fenton," Rage said coolly. Nicholas saw his brief, blunt appraisal and then the quick, roguish grin of approval.

"Good evening," she said, hardly looking at Rage. Instead, she folded her arms and glared at Nicholas. "You know this still isn't proper! This man is no ordinary servant. In fact, he's not really a servant at all, is he?"

Rage remained silent, even when Jane sent him a quick side glance, as if her question were for him, not Nicholas. But she didn't quite understand how loyal the men were. Rage wouldn't reveal anything until he was certain of Nicholas's motives.

"Perhaps not," Nicholas answered instead. "But since most of the other servants are off doing personal business or sleeping in their warm beds, you have few choices. We either use Rage as chaperone or we wake everyone else and line them up so you can choose the correct one, and thus expose yourself to their remarks and questions later."

Jane let out a sigh so loud and low that it seemed to vibrate from her chest. Then she threw up her hands in surrender.

"Very well. I suppose you would not try to 'ravish me,' as you put it earlier, with your friend standing by."

Rage flashed a quick smile since that had never stopped either of them before, but Nicholas sent him a look to keep him quiet.

Luckily Jane hadn't noticed and continued, "Have I mentioned to you before that you are utterly impossible?"

Nicholas grinned as he motioned for Rage to accompany them down the hallway to his own chamber. "At least once, my dear. But it never hurts to hear a compliment over and over."

Chapter 8

Nicholas flexed his fingers at his sides, clenching fists and releasing them as he breathed. He never should have asked Rage to "chaperone" him and Jane. He'd done it to annoy her in one way, and in another it had been a chance for his friend to meet Jane and garner his own impressions.

But now all that was flying back in Nicholas's face because after her initial shock at encountering yet another uncouth boxer, Jane seemed to have fallen under Rage's sway. Every time the other man spoke, she smiled. His ridiculous jokes about the "sad state" of Nicholas's wardrobe made her laugh. And she seemed endlessly interested in his fighting career and past.

In short, everything that irritated her about Nicholas seemed to delight her in Rage.

Jane turned to him for the first time in what felt like an hour.

"It is clear to me after examining your attire

that you need an entirely new set of clothing." She motioned to his open wardrobe with one hand. "Most of your things are befitting your activities in the underground, but will not suit in the life you will now embark upon. And those things that you have that are more sophisticated seem to be from the time before you left Society. They no longer fit you well, and fashions change, even for men."

Nicholas set his jaw. The last thing he wanted was to waste some ungodly amount of time standing for a tailor. But there was nothing to be done about it. Even before they had come upstairs, he'd known what Jane would say.

He just hadn't realized it would amuse Rage so damned much. His friend was grinning like a fool.

"Fine," Nicholas said through clenched teeth.

Jane acted as if he hadn't spoken and turned to his friend. "Mr. Riley, can I depend upon you to ensure that Lord Stoneworth arranges for a tailor to come here tomorrow? And if I leave a list of items he will require, will you see to it that those things will be measured for and ordered?"

Nicholas moved between them with a growl of displeasure. "I said yes. I do not require supervision in such a simple task."

Jane shrugged as she snapped his wardrobe shut. "If you want to convince anyone that Mr.

Riley is your valet, then these are the sorts of things he will be required to arrange. You are no longer living in the underground, gentlemen. A man of Nicholas's stature does very little for himself."

Nicholas felt all the fire bleeding out of him at that comment. That was what he hated most about this entire situation. If he fully accepted the burden of his brother's life, he would be subject to all manner of rules, regulations, and expectations. His independence would be torn away, leaving him nothing more than a dressed-up tiger in a circus. Caged, toothless, unable to change his fate.

"Are we finished here?" he asked.

His feelings must have been reflected in his voice, for both Jane and Rage looked at him with twin expressions of surprise. Then Jane's look softened.

"Yes," she said. "It is very late and I should be going. Lady Ridgefield is planning a party in three days. Until it is over, she will likely keep much closer watch on me." She sighed softly. "In these situations, she sometimes even comes to me in the night with new ideas."

Nicholas shot his friend a look and Rage held out a hand to Jane. "Miss Fenton, it has been a pleasure."

She extended her own hand without hesitation and even blushed when Rage lifted it to his lips instead of shaking it. Nicholas's humor dropped even further as his friend left them alone.

"Well," she said softly, moving toward the door. "Good night."

"Wait," he said, suddenly loath to have her go since they would not see each other for a few days. "Let me accompany you."

She hesitated. "But—"

He cut her off. "It is late. I would feel better if I saw you to Lady Ridgefield's. I won't exit the vehicle, simply wait until I see you go inside."

Jane worried her lower lip a moment. "Very well."

Jane wasn't exactly certain what she had expected when Nicholas offered to take her home, but it wasn't this. He was slouched down like a petulant child on the opulent leather carriage seat across from her. He wouldn't even look at her, and an undefined tension coursed between them.

Was he angry that she couldn't come back to him for a few days? Did he think she was trying to renege on their agreement? And if he was, would he go back on his end of the bargain?

Well, there was only one way to find out.

She straightened up and looked him in the eye. "Are you angry with me because I cannot return tomorrow?"

He started, almost as if he had forgotten she

was there at all. Slowly, he maneuvered to sit up straight. "I knew that your employment might prevent you from coming to my home at will. I assume you are not lying to me about Lady Ridgefield's gathering."

Jane cocked her head. If it wasn't her absence that upset him, then what was it? For she felt his mood was directed toward her, not just some general aggravation.

"Then have I offended you by my assertion that you need new clothing?" She leaned forward. "If I was too blunt—"

He actually smiled a little, which gave her great relief. "You could never be too blunt for me, my dear."

"Then allow me to be blunt now," she said, her frustration with his attitude mounting, though she wasn't certain why she cared. "You seem to harbor some ill feelings toward me at present. I would like to know what I have done to offend you. If it is not my absence, nor the clothing—"

He moved so swiftly that she hardly had time to react before he was right on top of her. He shifted to her side of the carriage, caught her arm in one hand, and with the other softly covered her lips to stop her talking.

"Look at me, Jane. Do you think I give a damn about clothing?" His thumb moved against her lip, stroking over the skin there.

Jane caught her breath beneath his touch. Her entire body tingled, making her overly aware of her reactions to this man. Her heart pounded so loudly it drowned out nearly all other sounds. Her legs shook, despite the fact that she was seated. And she felt her nipples tighten beneath her gown, although it wasn't cold in the carriage.

And she was also suddenly hyper aware of the man next to her. How big he was. How he smelled deliciously of sandalwood and foreign spices and something she couldn't place, but spoke to her on an almost elemental level. She found her gaze drifting from his bright eyes down to his lips.

"If I am in an ill humor," he continued, his voice low and rough, "it is because I did not like watching you with my friend. I hated that you laughed at his pathetic jokes. That you looked at him at all."

Jane snatched her gaze from his mouth and back to his eyes. In a hundred years, she never would have guessed that was what troubled him. That . . . that . . . well, it was jealousy, wasn't it?

And it made so sense.

"But—" she began.

He shook his head. "I realize it is utterly foolish. I don't care about you, so I have no reason to give a damn about who makes you smile. And yet tonight, I did."

Then his fingers traced up the curve of her jaw and found their way into her hair. He tilted her face gently, and she recognized what he was about to do. And to her shock, relief washed through her as his lips came to press against hers for the second time in as many days.

This time his kiss didn't surprise her, as it had the first time. What did shock her was the strength of her own reaction. Just as before, a weak, needy feeling spread through her body, starting at the point of contact of their lips and cascading downward until her entire body was on fire.

She didn't fight the flames, although her fading rational mind screamed at her to do so. To stop him.

Instead, she found herself lifting her hands to the rough material of his sleeves, clinging to his arms and feeling them contract beneath her fingers. Then she was sliding across the carriage seat as he tugged her even closer.

His mouth moved, slow and seductive. Infinitely gentle and powerfully erotic.

It was strange, before he touched her, she would have thought such a large, powerful man would demand with his kiss. Steal. But Nicholas didn't. He coaxed.

Perhaps because he knew he could take any time he liked, he had trained himself not to do so. He didn't have to prove his superior strength when it was such an obvious fact.

Whatever the reason, the slow, seductive kiss tore down her defenses, stole her breath, and made her utter a low moan against his lips.

The sound seemed to incite his passions. His fingers stroked along her spine, and she arched against his chest with every wild sensation.

But as quickly as the kiss had begun, he thrust her aside, pushing himself into the farthest corner of the carriage seat and staring at her from the half dark.

"You should go, Jane."

She shook her head, hoping she could somehow shake away the troubling effect of this man, and found that the carriage had stopped. Out the window, she could see the dark shape of Lady Ridgefield's house.

She glanced back at him. His eyes practically glowed in the low light, giving him that feral, animal look that she didn't think she'd ever manage to "train" out of him.

"I—" she began, her lips hot, her hands trembling.

He growled as interruption. "Run, Jane. Before you cannot."

Without replying, she wrenched the carriage

door open, ignoring the footman who had come to offer her assistance, and scurried away across the manicured grass toward the servants' entrance she had left unlocked earlier in the evening.

And though she never dared look back, she was all too aware that Nicholas didn't leave until she was safely inside . . . nor did he tear his hot gaze away from her retreating form.

Chapter 9

Nicholas shifted uncomfortably on the settee that was far too small for his frame, but his mother did not seem to notice. She was preoccupied by watching him, an utterly happy beam on her normally somber face.

"I am so very glad you accepted my invitation today, Nicholas," she said breathlessly, and not for the first time. Every time she repeated it, it drove a stake into his heart.

He smiled stiffly, unsure of how to behave with his mother. She felt so small, so delicate, so ladylike, that it made his own failings all the clearer. All the more distasteful. But it was more than those things that made him squirm like a schoolboy in her presence. Although he had not cut himself off from her entirely over the years, as he had from his father, there remained a distance that was hard to bridge.

"I assume Father does not know of my presence here," he said, and instantly wished he could take back the blunt words when his mother's smile dropped.

She shrugged one slender shoulder delicately. "He is aware, but he . . . he . . ."

"He did not wish to see me," Nicholas finished in a bland tone that did not reveal the tiny hurt he felt at that fact. "I don't find that surprising."

His mother sighed before taking a sip of tea. "The ball last week did upset him, Nicholas. He was furious that you would behave in such a manner. That you would—"

Nicholas held up a hand. He had heard this enough times by now that he could recite it by heart. There was no need to continue repeating it.

"I realize my actions put a blight on Anthony's memory," he said quietly. "Lucinda spoke to me after the event."

His mother straightened up in surprise. "Did she? That is a shock to me. Since your brother's death, Lucinda has been locked away in Winchester Court. She will hardly see anyone, and it takes enormous effort on my part to force her to go on any outings. She is taking her mourning period quite seriously. Enough so that it troubles me. And I know that seeing you—"

"Hurts her," Nicholas finished, clenching his fists beneath the table. "Anyone can see that."

His mother sighed, her expression faraway and sad. "Time is all that will heal her. It is what will heal us all."

He nodded to placate her, but he didn't think what she said was true. What did the passing of twelve months or twelve years matter? His brother would still be dead. That other half of himself that he had always taken comfort in would never return.

"Have you thought about taking over Winchester Court?" his mother asked.

Nicholas started. "Great God, Mother! No!"

His mother didn't seem surprised by his outburst. "I only ask because it is the home that goes along with your title."

"I don't want it," he snapped, more sharply than he intended. "It is Lucinda's home and her children's. I would no sooner take it than stab out my own eye."

His mother smiled, but it was a sad expression. "You always did use vivid language. Yet the fact remains that it *is* your home now. And at some point you will need to move into it. You will need to take over the title in a way that is complete, not simply surface."

Nicholas shut his eyes. If only his mother knew just how surface this entire experience was to him. This was not his life. No matter how he pretended, no matter how he "learned" to behave as if it was, it never would be.

"This has been thrust upon me," he said quietly. "And I realize that I have not accepted it with much . . . *grace* as of yet."

He opened his eyes to find his mother's gentle stare focused on him.

"But I am . . ."

He hesitated. His mother and father were close. If he told Her Ladyship of his plans to better himself, she would likely share it with her husband. And Nicholas did not desire that.

"I'm working on it," he finally said.

She nodded, but now tears had sprung up in her eyes. "This is a difficult time for us all. Losing your brother has been—" She stopped and sucked in a broken breath. "I imagine it is even more difficult for you. You've given up a great deal and I appreciate it, even if your father cannot yet."

Nicholas dipped his chin down in a combination of awe and shame. Here was his mother, who had lost her son, who had lost so much more over the years, and she was offering him her gratitude, although Nicholas had never done anything to earn it. Nothing but humiliate her, even if that wasn't his intent.

The self-reflection stung and he decided to change the subject. "I hear Lady Ridgefield is having a party."

"Is she?" his mother said, and she seemed as relieved as he to move away from the painful, emotional topic of their strained relationship. "I have always liked her. A silly woman, but well meaning."

Nicholas nodded. That was how Jane saw her, as well. He looked at his mother. Was it possible she knew more about Jane?

"She has a companion who seemed familiar to me when I saw her at the ball last week," he lied.

His mother tilted her head. "Her companion? I suppose it is possible you might have met her as a younger woman. She is Jane Fenton, the daughter of Viscount Fenton, who passed away a year or more ago. I believe his nephew inherited the title. For some reason Jane took a position as Lady Ridgefield's companion."

"Strange that she would do so, considering she was from a family of rank," he mused, hoping his mother would take his interest as mere small talk.

But it was not to be. The marchioness was instantly on the prowl, taking in his every reaction with careful intent. "I believe she had a falling out of some kind with her cousin. I recall her to be a headstrong girl."

"Perhaps the cousin did her a wrong," Nicholas offered, still curious about the man Jane believed had betrayed her.

She had claimed he could not in any way be involved in her brother's disappearance, but if she was wrong, Nicholas might need to offer more than assistance. Protection hadn't been in their original bargain, but he would not leave Jane to the mercy of someone who might have killed for title.

His mother shrugged. "I don't know. I've never heard of such a thing, but it is possible, of course."

She tilted her head to examine him more closely, the way she had when he was a boy and she was trying to determine if he'd done something naughty. Which he almost always had.

"Why all the interest, Nicholas? I don't think I've ever known you to notice any young lady over another, even before you left home."

He stifled a curse. Damn, he'd gone too far. His mother, longing for some stability in his life, would not let this be unless he quelled her curiosity now.

"I have no interest in Jane Fenton," he said with a sniff, although he couldn't help but think of the passionate kiss they had shared in his carriage just the night before.

It had been a long, very hard night recalling it over and over, actually.

"Then why the questions?"

"Her cousin owes me money," he lied easily.

His mother's nose wrinkled delicately, as if the idea offended her. Damn, he couldn't win. If he put her off one notion, then he offended her with another. No wonder he had left this society. And no wonder it was so damned hard to get back in!

"Well, if you *were* interested in her for some other purpose," his mother pressed, "then I can tell you that Jane's mother was a beauty of much renown and a lovely woman. And though Jane did not have an unsuccessful first few seasons herself, I don't recall her garnering excessive interest from suitors."

Nicholas drew back despite himself. How was that possible? Every time Jane was near him, he was utterly aware of her. Could the men of the upper class be so blind to her charms?

Idiots.

"Hmmm," he said, noncommittal when in fact he was far too interested.

"You *will* have to marry one day, you know, dear," his mother pressed. "To carry on the line, at the very least."

"Yes. I'm not unaware of the fact that a marriage is also one of the quickest ways back into Society's good graces," he said, stifling a groan.

"I suppose that is true," his mother said slowly.

"Choosing a woman of high rank with power in her family is my only option."

The marchioness's brow wrinkled. "Is that truly what you think? That you must marry for position?"

He nodded once. "Anthony's children should not be harmed due to their uncle's choices, should they?"

Her face softened. "But my darling, what about love? What about joy? What—"

Nicholas rose to his feet swiftly. "My, is that the time? I'm afraid I have another appointment."

His mother's eyebrows knitted together in annoyance, but she got to her feet and turned her cheek so he could kiss her farewell. "Yes, yes. I understand, you do not wish your life to be meddled with."

He smiled as she escorted him to the foyer.

"I only want you to be happy." His mother shook her head. "God knows, after all this family has suffered, I would *love* to see you happy."

"I will be," Nicholas said as he squeezed her hand and then slipped from his childhood home. But as he stepped into his waiting carriage, he thought about the promise he had just made. It wasn't one he could keep. Because the life he was leading now was nothing more than a prison.

And he would never escape.

Jane smoothed her plain dress and smiled at one of Lady Ridgefield's guests as she walked past. The woman did not even acknowledge her existence, and Jane fought to keep her expression pleasant. At some point the blatantly rude, dismissive behavior would stop stinging. It had to.

Didn't it?

She silently admonished herself for the thought. It mattered very little what anyone else thought of her. Lady Ridgefield was pleased with how her garden party was progressing, Jane could tell by the bright expression on her employer's face.

And that was all that mattered after the past few days' frantic work to ready for the gathering. Jane was ragged from the planning of the details and last-minute changes, but in truth she had come to welcome the busyness. It had been helpful in forgetting Nicholas and the confusing thoughts and feelings he put into her mind.

She frowned as some small part of her whispered that she was lying to herself. And her frown deepened as her mind turned, once again, to the soft sweep of his tongue against hers when he dragged her to him in the carriage. Of her own heated response to his touch when she should have pushed him away and demanded he put a stop to such shockingly ungentlemanly behavior.

It wasn't right. And yet she had allowed him that liberty not once, but twice! In fact, if he hadn't stopped in the carriage, she might have allowed much more. It was almost like he was training her in wicked ways, even as she trained him in the proper ones.

She shook off her thoughts as another lady

approached. Her heart lodged firmly in her throat as Jane realized it was Marchioness Bledsoe, Nicholas's mother.

Despite her son's poor reputation, the marchioness was one of the most influential and sought-after ladies in Society. What she wore, the *ton* copied. What she did, they emulated. And perhaps that fact was one of the only ones that could save Nicholas if Jane managed to tame him even a little.

The woman had been a late addition to Lady Ridgefield's gathering, and one that had so delighted the countess that Jane had hardly felt any anxiety at the time.

But there it was, rising in her chest now, making her palms sweat as she shoved them behind her back and gave the woman a smile she assumed would be ignored. But instead of dismissing her like so many others, Lady Bledsoe stopped before her.

"You are Jane Fenton, are you not?" her Ladyship asked in a light, almost musical voice that was soothing.

Jane nodded mutely, caught up in the same spell Lady Bledsoe had woven around Society more than thirty years prior. No one could deny that the other woman was still beautiful, despite her advancing years. Nicholas did not resemble his mother in many ways, for Her Ladyship's hair was far more fair and her eyes a dark brown rather than that shocking blue.

But there was something in her expression that put Jane to mind of Nicholas nonetheless. It was that faint essence of sadness and loss that called to Jane's own lingering grief.

Lady Bledsoe tilted her head slightly, and Jane shook away her thoughts and recalled her manners.

"Yes, my lady. I am Jane Fenton."

"And your mother was Elizabeth Fenton, yes?"

Her nervousness nearly forgotten, Jane smiled. "Indeed, she was. You have a good memory."

Lady Bledsoe stepped beside her, her posture clearly indicating that she was chatting with Jane, not demanding she do the duties of little more than a servant. Jane couldn't help but look around to see if anyone else noticed that fact.

"She was a beautiful woman, a diamond of the first water in every sense of the word. I was already married by the time she came out, but I enjoyed any exchange we shared. And she remained just as lovely up until—"

She broke off with a sad frown. Jane drew in a long breath. "Yes. She *was* lovely. I miss her still. But you know of that pain. I am sorry for your own recent loss, my lady."

The other woman tilted her head in acknowledgment of Jane's sympathy, but then she seemed to push those more painful subjects away.

"But now you are here," Lady Bledsoe said with a quick motion around Lady Ridgefield's sitting room. "And Lady Ridgefield speaks very highly of you."

Jane crinkled her brow, confused. Lady Bledsoe seemed to have some kind of purpose in this unexpected exchange, but Jane could not yet determine it.

"My employer is very kind, but I am surprised that the subject would come up. I am . . . I'm very happy working for her," she added, on the chance that Lady Bledsoe was somehow trying to steal her away from Lady Ridgefield.

Wouldn't that be the perfect addition to her strange situation? If Lady Bledsoe knew Jane had been kissing her only son, she might not be so friendly and accommodating.

But Her Ladyship only chuckled. "I am not looking for a companion, dear Jane. I asked for a different purpose entirely."

"My lady?"

"My son, Nicholas," she said with a smile.

The entire room around her faded away as Jane stared at the woman before her. Lady Bledsoe was looking at her with a bland expression, entirely unreadable. But she was also waiting, expecting Jane to respond in some way to her shocking statement.

"Lord Stoneworth, you mean," she said, her voice little more than a harsh, shaky whisper.

Lady Bledsoe's expression pinched a moment, just as Nicholas's always did when he was called by that title.

"It is hard for me to think of him as that, but yes. He is Lord Stoneworth now. And he tells me that he knows you."

Now Jane's eyes were wide, almost painfully so. Lady Bledsoe was talking to her with such knowing certainty, with such a conspiratorial gleam in her eye that Jane could not believe it. This woman *knew* about Jane's arrangement with Nicholas. There was no other explanation for her sudden interest, her hints that the two of them had a deeper relationship, her implications that her son had revealed something to her.

"I-I—" she stammered.

"Something about your cousin or your brother," she murmured, almost more to herself. Jane flinched, her hunch now further confirmed.

"My lady, I do not know what you must think of me," Jane blurted out, unable to contain herself any longer. "I'm sure you cannot approve, but Nicho—" She gasped in horror at her slip and quickly corrected herself. "But Lord Stoneworth and I came to an agreement. I am training him in exchange for his help. I swear to you it is not a bargain of the flesh or—"

Lady Bledsoe now stared at her like she had

sprouted a second head. Her lips parted as Jane continued to ramble, until finally she lifted a hand to silence her.

"Wait. Am I to understand that you are training my son"—her voice dropped as she cast a quick glance around the room—"to become a gentleman?"

Jane stopped midsentence as horror washed over her. She had assumed Her Ladyship knew the truth from her demeanor and the way she had phrased her initial mention of Jane and Nicolas's relationship. But now . . .

"Lady Bledsoe . . ."

The other woman shook her head. "Come with me, Jane. We must find a private room where we can talk."

Chapter 10

⁓⟡⁓

J ane wrung her hands as she followed Lady
   Bledsoe into one of Lady Ridgefield's unoccu-
pied parlors. As the door clicked shut behind her,
it was as if she were being led to an execution.

And perhaps it was in a way. If Her Ladyship was angry about the strange arrangement
between Jane and her son, she had the power
to utterly destroy Jane if she chose to. Lady
Ridgefield might even be forced to terminate her
employment. Without a reference, she could easily
be out on the street.

And Jane could hardly bear to think about
Nicholas. He had made it clear more than once
that his parents were the last people in the world
he wanted to be aware of his attempt at transfor-
mation. He would be livid when he heard what
she had done.

With all those thoughts plaguing her, Jane
turned, expecting to find a furious, cold marchioness staring back. Instead, Lady Bledsoe

was . . . *beaming*. Her dark eyes were lit up with joy and her cheeks were pink with pleasure. Instead of looking like the powerful, distinguished woman she was, she seemed more like an excited schoolgirl.

"Oh, my dear, you do not know how happy this news makes me," she gushed as she reached out and caught both of Jane's hands.

Jane stared in wonder, too dumbstruck to formulate any kind of reasonable reply.

Not that the marchioness seemed to expect or desire one. She continued to speak, almost in one interrupted sentence. More like Lady Ridgefield than her normally calm and refined self.

"No one must know, of course, for this arrangement is most unorthodox. If you were found out, it could damage you both. Trust Nicholas to pick a beautiful woman to be his guide." She rolled her eyes. "But it matters little. He is making things right. He is coming back to us."

Jane bit her lip. There was no way she could deny what she had already revealed. And when she looked at Lady Bledsoe's face, which had been so sad and somber since her son's death, Jane couldn't bear to snatch away the other woman's happiness, even to protect herself. It wasn't right to change Lady Bledsoe's good humor with any facts about what a difficult charge Nicholas was.

Or what an excellent kisser.

"Do say something, dear, you are so pale, you're beginning to frighten me," Lady Bledsoe said, leaning in closer.

Jane shook her head. "My lady, in my nervousness in speaking to you, I made a poor assumption that somehow you knew the truth about my arrangement with your son. But I should not have revealed it."

"Why not?" Lady Bledsoe said with a smile. "It is the best news I have had in an age."

"Because it was not my secret to tell," Jane insisted, pacing away from the bubbling marchioness.

That seemed to affect Nicholas's mother, for she stopped chattering and sighed. "Yes. I suppose that is true."

"He will be so angry at me for revealing this. And to you." She gave Lady Bledsoe an apologetic glance. "You of all people. He made it clear he didn't want anyone to know of his attempt."

"Nicholas and his father have long been . . . *strained*." Lady Bledsoe was serious now. "But you didn't tell me this to harm him, did you?"

"No!"

"So you did not reveal his secret with malicious intent?"

"Of course not!"

"Then you have nothing to be sorry about." She smiled as if that were the last word on the subject.

"But I broke his confidence nonetheless," Jane insisted, distress taking over her with increasing urgency. She covered her eyes as she sank into the nearest chair.

Lady Bledsoe rushed to her side and took her hands. "There is a simple solution to this, Jane."

She lifted her gaze, willing to hear anything that would soften the blow when she revealed what she'd done to Nicholas. "Yes?"

"Don't tell him."

Jane's mouth dropped open in shock. That was the one suggestion she hadn't been expecting. And she found it tempting, indeed.

But still . . .

"Lie to him, you mean?" Jane whispered.

It would certainly make her life easier. But she had spent the last few years being lied to. "Protected," so many people had said. And every time she uncovered the truth, she felt like a fool. It was the worst feeling in the world to know someone she believed she could trust was playing her for false.

And with what she already knew of Nicholas, she was certain his feelings on the matter would be the same.

"It is a small lie," his mother reasoned. "One that will not hurt him, for I will not tell his father. And his father is the real issue for Nicholas."

Her mouth turned down with regret.

"It doesn't seem right." Jane stared past Lady Bledsoe to the low fire across the room.

The marchioness's gaze snagged hers. Jane felt the full force of her scrutiny, as if the lady had a sudden notion she was now trying to prove by a thorough examination of Jane's expression. Then the other woman smiled, this time reassuringly.

"I understand why you hesitate and I commend you for your honesty when it comes to my son. Under any other circumstances, I would agree with you that he should know the truth. But I—"

Now she hesitated, and Jane found herself leaning forward.

"I'm sure you do not know this, but I lost several children at birth. The twins were our miracle after years of heartbreak and pain."

Jane gasped. These private losses were rarely spoken of outside a family, and a swell of pity rose in her chest. "I am so very sorry, my lady."

Lady Bledsoe swallowed, fighting back tears. "When Nicholas left us, it tore me apart. Since then, he has been little more than a ghost in my life. Passing through from time to time, but always distant. After his brother died, he was all I had left. I long to renew our relationship."

Jane nodded. She understood the other woman's feelings. Being alone in the world, watching those she loved fade away, was the greatest pain imaginable.

"All I ask is that you keep this secret, at least for a little while. Let me share in what you are doing, perhaps I can even help my son, without interfering, of course. It would mean a great deal to me." Lady Bledsoe squeezed her hands again, gently. "Please?"

Jane found herself nodding. She couldn't help it. The other woman's plea was just too close to her own heart to deny. And perhaps having a silent ally in her dealings with Nicholas would make it easier. If not that, it could serve as a sharp reminder of propriety whenever she was tempted to give in to his kisses.

"Thank you," Lady Bledsoe said with a wide smile. "And perhaps I can be of assistance to you, too. Use my influence on your behalf."

Jane pushed to her feet. "My lady, I have not done any of this to gain influence, I assure you."

Lady Bledsoe straightened up and looked at her evenly. Then she nodded. "Very well. Now we must hurry back to the party before Lady Ridgefield and the others notice my absence and begin asking questions. But before we go back, there are a few things I think you must know about Nicholas."

"Yes?" Jane found herself leaning closer, desperate for insight into the man who affected her so keenly.

"First, my son may look gruff and behave with little manners, but he is kind. He would sacrifice his own life to save another or give away all he had if it would help someone else."

Jane blinked. That certainly did not describe the feral, prowling man she had been meeting with. A man who refused to help her unless she paid a high price in exchange. So perhaps this statement was a mother's wishful thinking.

Or perhaps there was more to Nicholas Stoneworth than what she had seen so far.

"Secondly, I realize he resists becoming all his brother was." Lady Bledsoe frowned, deep sadness darkening her eyes. "I assume he is not an easy pupil in that regard. But it is not out of spite. It is out of grief. Those boys were best friends, brothers in the deepest sense of the word. Even after Nicholas parted ways with good society and his father, he and Anthony remained close. His brother's death weighs heavily upon him."

That Jane *could* agree to. She nodded as she thought of the pain she had seen Nicholas display. Sometimes he attempted to mask it with anger, but the pain lingered. Harsh and raw and deep.

"Finally, you must know that he is a frustrating, willful man, but I ask you not to give up on him." Lady Bledsoe held her stare. "I'm afraid his father did. But I ask you not to do so, no matter how difficult he makes this for you."

Jane's eyes widened. As she and Lady Bledsoe

stood, hands clutched, staring at each other, it seemed the other woman was speaking of things far deeper than her training of Nicholas.

"Jane? Jane?"

The two women broke apart as Lady Ridgefield burst into the room with a smile. "There you are, my dear. And Lady Bledsoe, I have been missing you, as well."

Her Ladyship smiled kindly at Lady Ridgefield. "Your lovely companion was good enough to give me a tour of your home, my lady. It is a beautiful estate. Did you pick out these stunning moldings yourself?"

As Lady Ridgefield launched into an explanation of her taste in art and decor, she moved into the hallway. Lady Bledsoe trailed behind her, but not before she sent a quick, meaningful glance to Jane. And then the two women were gone, mere echoing voices in the hallway.

With a weary sigh, Jane sank back into the chair she had been occupying. Suddenly her training of Nicholas had taken on a much deeper meaning, with far higher stakes. A twinge of shame made Jane flinch. She had entered her agreement with Nicholas as a means to find her brother. She hadn't even really cared if she helped him, giving him up for a lost cause almost before they started.

But now it was time to renew her focus. Perhaps she could *truly* help this man. Even if she never recovered the remains of her own fractured family, perhaps by helping him she could repair his.

The idea of that brought some peace to her tangled, out-of-sorts mind. She had to have imagined the deeper meaning when Lady Bledsoe told her not to give up on Nicholas. All Her Ladyship could have meant was his training. There could be nothing more to it than that, for she was no longer a part of the world he would one day conquer.

A fact she needed to remember.

"Can you trust your servants?"

Nicholas looked up from his mind-numbing study of the latest copy of *Debrett's*. Jane had brought the book of influential families with her tonight as part of his lesson on proper address. The names and titles were beginning to swim together, as were her short, curt descriptions of who the families were.

"Why?" he asked as he rubbed his eyes.

When the fog cleared, he examined Jane more closely, but she wasn't looking at him. She sat across the room, as far away as was humanly possible. As she stared out the window to the darkened gardens behind the house, it was almost as if he wasn't there at all.

That was how she had been all night. Polite, yes. Helpful, yes. But this was the first time he truly felt like she was nothing more than his teacher and he, her student.

He shouldn't have cared about that, but he did. Her resistance only made her all the more fascinating and made his desire to press her all the greater.

"It might help if we could involve at least some of your staff in your training," Jane explained with a quick glance his way. She turned her face just as quickly when she saw he was staring at her. "You will require lessons on dining and dancing, and those would be far easier with someone to set the table and accompany us on a pianoforte."

Nicholas pushed to his feet, stretching his back and neck as he considered her question. Beyond not stealing the silver, he hadn't really considered the trustworthiness of his servants before. He didn't care if tales were spread about him . . . or at least he hadn't until Lucinda shamed him. And as long as their duties were done, he didn't really care what the men and women in his employ did in their free time.

But now he thought of each person, picturing their faces, imagining the actions he'd seen them take in the past six months. It was easy enough to make judgments based upon those brief interactions. He had learned to be a good assessor of character early on in his days in the underground. If he hadn't been, he would have been dead.

"Well, Gladwell, despite his piss-poor attitude in general, is trustworthy to a fault. And he is the leader in how the others behave." He shrugged. "As for the cook, Mrs. Fieldframe, she is gruff, but I've heard rumors that she can be kindly when no one is looking. I cannot imagine her breaking a confidence or doing something to purposefully ruin either one of us."

Jane stood up now and moved to the window. Her back was to him, so he could not read her face, but her body was rigid as she stared outside into the dark.

"They both think I am a whore."

Her statement surprised him. After only mild resistance, Jane had agreed to his proposal, although their clandestine meetings put her at great risk for ruination. Never had he heard her complain about it, or ponder aloud the consequences of their bargain. Somehow he had always imagined Jane to be above those worries. She was no longer out in Society, after all.

He moved a step closer. "Do you care?"

She hesitated, and there was a long moment of silence while she pondered that question. She turned her face and provided him a glimpse of her profile. Her mouth was drawn down and her eyebrows knitted together.

"I wouldn't have in the past, but now I am a part of their society. I suppose it does bother me that they look down upon me with such contempt."

"Do you really consider yourself a part of the servant class?" Nicholas asked in further surprise. When he looked at Jane, even with her serviceable gowns and plain hairstyles, he always saw a graceful and refined lady.

"I *am*," Jane insisted. "There is no denying that. I accept money in exchange for my services. I do what Lady Ridgefield desires. Despite my true affection for her, and I believe hers for me, we are not friends. I am her employee." She paused with a frown. "And yet despite all that, I do not fully fit. Not in the servant world. And not in what was once my own."

"Like me." Nicholas was an arm's length away from her now. He had the strangest urge to reach out and touch her, comfort her. But that seemed too intimate, too close. Even kissing her seemed less personal.

She turned at his statement, and when she saw how near he was, her eyes widened. "Yes, I suppose that is true."

She fidgeted her hands behind her back and refused to look at him. Nicholas frowned.

"You are nervous," he said softly. "Why?"

Jane's lips parted. "You read me so easily."

"It is old habit," he explained. "In the underground, it was a way to protect myself."

"Do you feel you need to protect yourself from me, then?" She laughed, but the sound was strained.

"Perhaps." His reply was stone serious, and her smile fell.

"You are twice my size, I could not hurt you," she murmured, yet she couldn't meet his eyes. Nicholas wondered at the reason.

And wondered why her withdrawal didn't keep him from finally closing the distance between them to touch her face. He tilted her chin so she could no longer avoid his gaze.

"Not physically, no." His fingers moved across her skin almost against his will, and he thrilled as her eyelids fluttered shut on a soft sigh. "But there are other wounds you could easily inflict, Jane."

She blinked as if waking from a dream and lifted her hands to his chest. For a moment, they rested there, and she continued to stare up at him. Like she was trying to decide if she should draw him close or push him away.

The second choice won out. She shoved back, extracting herself and moving away in a few stumbling steps. Nicholas frowned at the loss of her body heat, the lingering soft, floral scent of her skin.

"We should not—" She cut herself off with a vibrant blush that seemed to color all her skin a most fetching pink. He couldn't help but wonder if it flushed places where he could not see. "You and I have crossed a line more than once, Lord Stoneworth."

Nicholas's nostrils flared as she reverted, yet again, to that hated title, but he did not correct her. "Indeed we have, to my great pleasure."

She let her gaze fall on his face again, and there was unmistakable regret reflected there. "Yes. But unfortunately one of the lessons of good Society is a bitter one. Sometimes we must trade pleasure for propriety."

"Must we?" Nicholas asked, a suddenly acrid taste in his mouth. That was the main problem with this new life. It seemed there would be no pleasure ever again.

She nodded. "You know it is. No matter what I do, there are some things that will never change. You and I are not in the same . . . *realm*. And I have allowed myself to forget that too many times. But I cannot any longer. From now on we must be professional in our dealings. I can be nothing more than a teacher to you."

Nicholas stepped away. There it was in plain terms. No matter what Jane did, some things would never change. His barbarian heart, for one. His inability to be gentleman enough for his family. For Society. For her.

An unfamiliar feeling spread like poison through his body. An ache similar to that when he lost a fight. Physical pain laced with self-directed anger.

"Yes," he growled, turning that anger outward. "You are correct, of course. How foolish of me to believe otherwise. Your lessons are beginning to stick, Miss Fenton. We wouldn't want to be slumming, would we? That is a valuable lesson I will carry with me always."

Jane blinked, and her confusion and hurt over his suddenly harsh tone was clear in her expression.

"Yes," she whispered.

"I will speak to a few servants about our true purpose for these nightly meetings and request whatever assistance they can provide. I will also return to my source in the underground tonight, so you can expect another report on your brother when we next meet." He turned away as a method of dismissing her. "Off with you, then. I believe we've made great progress today."

"Oh. Well, good night then, my lord."

He hesitated, longing to turn back and say something else. Instead, he snapped out, "Good evening, Miss Fenton."

And then she was gone, the door to his study closing softly behind her. With a growl of displeasure, Nicholas moved to the poor boy and made himself a stiff drink. As he tossed it back in one long gulp, he looked up at the mirror above him.

In his finer clothing, with his hair tamed, he did look like a gentleman. He looked like his brother.

And that was the last thing he desired, especially tonight.

He slammed the empty glass down and strode from the room. He would speak to his servants, as he had promised Jane, but then he was going to find Rage. Before they headed into the underground, he needed a sparring match to purge these ugly feelings and make everything else fade but physical pain.

Chapter 11

Jane stared at her plate, but hardly saw the heaping pile of breakfast treats that had been placed before her. She was too distracted, and to her dismay it wasn't for the right reasons. Thoughts of her brother and anxiety about what Nicholas might report to her tonight about his whereabouts should have been in the forefront of her mind.

But to her dismay, she had hardly thought about Marcus since she'd left Nicholas's home the night before. And she hadn't thought about Nicholas's training, either.

No, it had been something else entirely that had been plaguing her. A weakness she hated to admit, but could no longer deny or ignore.

Her feelings were hurt.

When she had spoken to Nicholas about the difference in their status, she hadn't expected him to agree so readily and then dismiss her like so many others of his stature. She supposed she should have been happy, even proud. His new attitude meant that he *was* recalling his place in the world.

One day he might very well be a celebrated member of the *ton*. One day she could watch him spin around the dance floor while mamas schemed for their daughters to be the next in his arms. One day he might treat her like everyone else did. Like she didn't exist.

And that was what hurt most.

"I'm sorry you had to wake so early today, my dear," Lady Ridgefield said, dabbing her lips with a napkin. "Especially since Ursula said you were tossing and turning late in the night."

Jane straightened up, brought back to reality in an instant. "Ursula heard me?"

Lady Ridgefield nodded without looking at Jane as she motioned for a footman to pour more tea. "Yes, she was passing by your door around two and said she heard you moving about."

Jane sucked in a breath. She had come in right around that time. How close she had come to being caught sneaking into the house! She would have to be more careful in the future.

"Just a touch of restlessness," she explained. "I do not mind being up early, but I wonder why the break in your regular routine."

Normally Lady Ridgefield awoke at nine, but did not rise until ten. Her breakfast was always laid out around eleven. Today, though, it was nine and they were already eating.

"Lady Bledsoe and I had such a lovely time at the tea yesterday that she invited me to spend the day with her." Lady Ridgefield was practically bouncing with excitement. "I did not mention it to you earlier because she wasn't certain of her plans until this morning. But I will be meeting her at Hyde Park in an hour."

"Ah."

Jane swallowed. Another day with Nicholas's mother. As much as she'd found herself liking the woman the previous afternoon, it was such an awkward thing to know Lady Bledsoe was aware of the truth.

"Then I shall ready myself for an outing at once and prepare the rest of your things," she said as she rose.

Lady Ridgefield waved her back to her seat. "No, no. She made the suggestion that you might like a day off, my dear. And I agreed. You worked so hard to make my tea a success. The least I owe you is a day to yourself. So you run along and take care of any private matters. I shall see you after supper."

Jane blinked in disbelief. Although Lady Ridgefield was nothing but kind to her, she enjoyed having company almost constantly. Jane loathed taking a day off, for she knew her employer would grow forlorn at the thought. Now Lady Ridgefield was beaming at her.

And Lady Bledsoe had arranged it all. Of course, she meant for it to be helpful in Jane's charge to help her son. Instead of a few stolen hours in the dark when she was exhausted, this meant she could meet with Nicholas now and have an entire day to work on his training.

An entire day with Nicholas.

A temptation and a fearful prospect. Especially after last night. But this was what she had agreed to do, for Marcus's sake. And the sooner she got there, the sooner she would know what Nicholas had uncovered on that score.

"Thank you," she said when she realized her employer was awaiting her reply. "I appreciate your thinking of me."

Without hesitation, Lady Ridgefield reached across the table and covered Jane's hand with her own. The gesture was so quick and genuine that Jane found her eyes filling with tears.

Ones that pricked even more sharply when her employer said, "You have seemed tired of late, my dear. I would like for you to have a lovely day for yourself."

The lump in Jane's throat was hard to swallow around, so she nodded instead of speaking.

Lady Ridgefield squeezed her hand, then leaned back to finish the last few bites of her breakfast. "Lady Bledsoe was very impressed by you. She asked about you quite often as we took our tour."

"Did she?"

Of course, Jane knew the only reason for Lady Bledsoe's interest was Jane's involvement in her son's success. But it was still pleasing to hear that such a fine lady paid her any mind at all.

Lady Ridgefield nodded. "If a woman like that took you under her wing . . . well, you might not have to be my servant for long. She could help you arrange a fine marriage for yourself if she decided to do so."

"Certainly that was not the line of her questioning!" Jane gasped, nearly choking on her tea.

Lady Ridgefield shrugged one shoulder delicately, but there was a knowing smile on her face. The idea that Nicholas's mother would arrange a match for her troubled Jane. Since her father's death, she'd had no thought of marriage. Marcus was lost somewhere, and she was the only person left in the world who cared enough to find him. She couldn't think of something so frivolous as courting when her brother was going through God only knew what. It would be selfish and wrong.

No, she would not even begin to think of such a thing until her brother was back where he belonged. Luckily, she doubted Lady Bledsoe would actually have such a plan.

Honestly, Jane doubted many men of Lady

Bledsoe's acquaintance would have her, even if she *were* interested in such a match. Her own comments on the differences in class and Nicholas's reactions to them were proof of that. Even if they stung terribly.

What she had to do was to forget all that nonsense. Put away her unwanted desire for Nicholas and think of her brother. Nothing else mattered.

Nothing and no one else could.

Jane pulled her hooded cloak farther down over her face as she knocked on the servants' entrance of Nicholas's house. Although she doubted anyone would be watching or recognize her if they did, the idea of being exposed in broad daylight, the danger of being caught, had her on edge.

After what seemed like an age, the door swung open, and Jane tensed. The cook who thought she was little better than a lightskirt was standing there, a bloody cleaver in one hand and a scowl on her face.

"What do you want?" she snapped.

Jane pushed her hood back far enough to reveal her face. "Good morning Mrs.—"

"Why Jane!" the cook said, suddenly all smiles. She stepped aside and motioned her to come in. "What are you doing here so early? The master said you wouldn't be coming but at night."

Jane was almost speechless as she stared at the woman. The cook had transformed from the harsh, judgmental harridan who had always greeted her before into a kindly, almost motherly figure.

And then realization dawned. Nicholas had made good on his promise to speak to some of the servants so they could help in his training. She smiled with relief. It was nice not to be treated as a loose woman anymore. She hadn't realized how much that troubled her.

"I was able to get a day away," she explained. "And I thought since I have more time, it could be an opportunity to work on some of the more intricate lessons on manners."

The cook nodded and motioned to the kitchen table. Jane flashed briefly to the night she and Nicholas had shared their chocolate there. His comforting embrace had moved her more than she cared to admit.

"Would you like to sit? Have you had your breakfast?"

"I have, thank you." Jane was still in a marvel at Mrs. Fieldframe's sudden kindness. "But I *will* require your help, if it isn't too much trouble. I'd like to start the complicated business of training Lord Stoneworth about dining etiquette. Do you think you could prepare us a luncheon with at least three courses? And have the table set as though we were having a formal meal at a party? I would be happy to serve if none of the other servants are to know of our true purpose."

Mrs. Fieldframe nodded immediately. "Of course. And I must say, Miss Fenton, I am so pleased you will be helping the master. As generous an employer as I've ever had pleasure of serving, but he's a hopeless one in many things. Why, just last night he was up with that friend of his, banging away at each other in one of the parlors. I thought poor Gladwell would have a dead faint when they broke one of the vases."

Jane stared at the other woman. "Nicholas and Rage were *fighting* in the parlor last night?"

The cook nodded. "Put the house right back into an uproar. Another maid gave notice this morning!"

Jane sighed. This was bad news, indeed. It seemed every time she made some progress with Nicholas, he slipped back into old habits.

"I would like to speak to Lord Stoneworth. Can you tell me where he is?"

The cook stared at her. "Still abed, Miss Fenton."

Now Jane was truly shocked. "Still abed? Why, it is near noon!"

"His Lordship never rises before two or three. And he insists no one dare wake him, either. The few that have tried have been very sorry they did it. Now they heed his warning, and none will go close to that room until he has been up for at least an hour."

Shaking her head, Jane started for the staircase that led into the main house. "Thank you, Mrs. Fieldframe. I appreciate your help."

"But miss—"

Jane ignored her calls as she made her way to the main staircase and up to the family chambers. It was time Nicholas had another lesson. That a gentleman did not lollygag around in bed all day. In her mind, only a libertine did that. And she was determined Nicholas would not become a useless rake. There were more than enough of those in the world.

She knocked smartly on his chamber door and waited, impatience making her foot tap beneath her gown hem. There was no reply, so she rapped harder. Still, no sound came from within.

Her shoulders tensed as she stared at the barrier. It was bold to consider bursting uninvited into the man's chamber. Just a few short days before, she had berated Nicholas for suggesting the very same thing. And yet she wanted him out of that bed. She wanted him to see that he could not behave in such a manner if he wished to succeed.

She briefly considered calling for a footman to do the deed of waking him, but the cook had said no servant dared to do so. Which left it on her shoulders. She thrust them back and swung the door open to make her way into the darkened chamber.

It took a few moments for her eyes to adjust, but finally the shadowy forms of furniture that were scattered around Nicholas's dressing room began to grow clearer. Carefully, she made her way forward through the adjoining door that led to his actual bedroom.

She had caught a glimpse of his bedchamber the day she examined his wardrobe what seemed like ages ago, although it was less than a week. But actually going inside the room was far different. Dim sunshine edged around the drawn curtains, and it was joined by the dull remains of embers in the fireplace across the room. Combined, they it gave her enough light to see better in this room than the last.

The bed was large, pressed back against the wall between window and fireplace. It took up a good portion of the room. But that seemed to be the only fine piece of furniture Nicholas had kept. A small, rather rickety-looking table that was woefully out of place was beside the bed, and Jane could see a book perched precariously on it. No other furniture filled the room. It was as if he had stripped the chamber of anything a gentleman would desire. As if it was some small bit of defiance of the position he didn't want and hadn't asked for.

A motion on the bed forced Jane to look there. Despite herself, she caught her breath. Nicholas had thrown some of the covers from his upper body with a low groan, and now the scarce light in the room gave her a perfect view of his broad back, his defined, muscular shoulders as he lay sprawled across the massive bed at an angle.

With a fervent glance at his face, Jane ensured that he remained asleep. From all appearances, he was, so she allowed herself what she had tried to deny in the past. She stared.

She had seen his chest before, but his back had always been covered. Now she noticed a tattoo on one shoulder, though it was too dark to make out the shape clearly. And a scar marked the other shoulder, standing out stark against his darker skin.

His body was strong from work and fighting and life in general. And it was real, just as he was real. There was nothing about this man that was false, as so many men of the *ton* were. And that, she could finally admit to herself, was exciting.

His body was breathtaking, too. She had felt his strength drawing her in, been enveloped by his warmth, tasted his desire. But there was more to his draw than just that. *He* was exciting. Unpredictable, honest to a fault, truly unconcerned with what those around him thought.

And yet all those were the things she was

charged to change, to tame because he couldn't be accepted by the stuffy matrons and old men of the upper class if he wasn't . . . flat. Dull.

She shook her head. That wasn't her concern. This training was something Nicholas had asked for. He *wanted* to change, to be accepted, in order to ensure his late brother's legacy. That was a noble charge, she had no right to question it.

And now she had to stop staring at him and do what he asked. Reluctantly, she moved away from him to the window, where she threw open the curtain and bathed the room in early afternoon sunlight.

Nicholas let out a groan, his eyebrows knitting together as he rolled to his back, covers tangling around his legs, and threw one arm over his eyes. Jane frowned. Now there was even more of this man to see, and it was clear from the bare hip that peeked out from a gap in the sheets that he wasn't wearing anything under those tangled bedclothes.

She had two options. To run away and let him wake on his own time. Or to do her duty and forget that he made her lose her breath whenever she was near him.

She straightened her spine and came closer to the bed. Drawing in a breath to steady herself and readying for his grumpy response, she leaned down to give his shoulder a shake.

The instant her hand touched his skin, Nicholas was moving. Jane didn't have a moment to respond before he caught her wrist in a viselike grip and tugged. She found herself falling over him as he rolled and yanked at the same time.

She hit the mattress hard, but before she had time to say or do anything, Nicholas's heavy, hard body moved over her, pinning her arms at her sides and keeping her from moving any more than a slight squirm. She gasped as she felt the heavy length of his erection pressing against her belly.

He stared down at her, face a frightening mask of anger and power, but then recognition seemed to dawn. Jane realized, with a start, that he hadn't even been awake when he moved so forcefully. His thrusting her into her current position was all done on instinct. A protection.

"Jane?" he said, his face softening a little, though there was still enough anger there to make her shiver. "What the hell are you doing here?"

She stared up at him. God, he was so close and so beautiful. She wanted nothing more than to lean up and kiss him. The press of his body didn't hurt her or frighten her, it only continued that excitement she had felt when she looked at him as he lay sleeping.

"Jane!" he snapped.

She shook away her reactions and began to struggle. "Let me up," she whispered, but the sound of her plea wasn't believable even to her own ears.

"Do you know I could have killed you before I even recognized who you were?" he asked, his anger still bubbling at the surface. "What were you thinking, coming into a man's chamber?"

Jane's body was completely out of her control now. With their chests molded so tightly together, Jane could feel her nipples swelling, and between her legs a shocking, heated wetness had begun. It was madness.

"My lord," she panted, squirming harder against him, but still unable to free even an arm from beneath his hard and heavy weight. "Please let me up."

"You must know how foolhardy it was—" he continued, seemingly unaware of her distress and arousal.

"Nicholas!" she finally cried, her voice cracking.

That stopped him. He stared down at her for a long moment, finally truly taking in their positions. He adjusted himself against her, allowing her arms to be free, but he didn't move off her. She dragged her hands to his chest and pushed, but he was as unmovable as granite.

Through now heavy lids and eyes dilated with what she recognized was desire, he watched her.

"But you *did* know better, didn't you?" he asked, his voice silky and seductive. "My servants must have told you I was abed. I might not be an expert in the actions of a gentleman, but I am willing to wager most would not see it as ladylike for you to come up here alone"—he cast a glance over his shoulder—"and with the door shut behind you so we would have no interruptions."

"Please," she whispered, hating that he was exposing her every desire.

She had tried to convince herself of a dozen "good" reasons to come into this room, but he was right. She had ached for this moment without fully recognizing it.

But he would not be stopped. "What did you want when you came here? Do you even know?"

She turned her face away from his, but he was so close to her now that there was no escaping him, or his pointed questions. He was stripping her bare, her raw emotions and uncharted needs out for him to see. And for her to finally admit.

Despite what she had said about their differing classes yesterday . . . or maybe *because* of what she had said . . . there was still a part of her that longed for the emotions he had roused when he kissed her. When they touched, she forgot every other painful thing in her life and only focused on him. It was selfish, but she craved it nonetheless.

She blushed. "I'm sorry."

"I don't want your apologies," he said softly, his breath stirring her skin and lighting her on fire even as she fought to break free of his spell. "I want you to tell me why you came up to my room."

She squeezed her eyes shut, fighting to regain control. To remember herself.

"To talk to you," she choked out. "I'm only here to make you a gentleman. That's the only reason."

The lie didn't sound believable in any way. And when Nicholas responded by arching his body into hers, letting the harsh ridge of his erection press into the soft flesh of her belly even further, she moaned.

"This is not gentlemanly," he whispered.

She opened her eyes, shaking her head with effort. "No."

He smiled. "So how should a gentleman touch a lady if not like this? This could be a very important lesson for me."

Jane gasped for air. She had to get away from this situation immediately because in a few moments she wasn't going to be in control of her body anymore. She was going to beg for things she didn't fully understand.

"A gentleman would . . . he would remember he was with a lady," she gasped, trying to press him away, but not quite able. "He would think of her and—"

He cut her off by leaning down to nuzzle his lips against her neck, and any thoughts and words Jane had left faded as she moaned again.

"Quite right." His tongue darted out to flick along her suddenly sensitive skin. "He *would* think of her, wouldn't he? This is an easy lesson, then."

Jane arched, helpless, all her protests gone. She didn't care anymore if she broke that code that a lady should not allow a gentleman to take liberties. She wasn't a lady anymore. And she wanted this man, she craved his touch with a desperation that terrified and thrilled her at once.

And she knew, in that wicked moment, that she was going to let him do anything.

Chapter 12

❦

J ane's hips lifted, rubbing against Nicholas's as his mouth dipped lower to the rounded neck of her plain gown. Shivers and sighs escaped her, ones she couldn't control and no longer tried to do so.

"You are sweet, Jane Fenton," he whispered as his hand drifted down and cupped one breast.

Her eyes fluttered shut at that intimate, shocking touch. It was abundantly clear that she had been asleep before this moment, before this man. And now, just as she had tried to awaken him moments before, *she* was being awakened, but from a very different kind of slumber.

He massaged her breast, infinitely gentle despite his big, rough hands. His thumb strummed across her now distended nipple, rasping the thin fabric of her gown across the sensitive peak with a rhythm she feared would drive her mad.

And all the time he watched her, looking down

at her through hooded lids as she arched and moaned with pleasure at each new sensation. Under any other circumstance, she would have been embarrassed to have such intimate reactions observed, but she was too far gone with desire to consider that now.

All she could think about was the stunning, tingling pleasure that eased its way through her aching body as he touched her. No wonder women threw away everything, wrecked themselves, for this. It was too powerful to deny.

His hand drifted lower now, skimming over her belly and then resting on her hip as his mouth followed the path. Through her gown, she felt the humid heat of his breath against her nipple, and she cried out, wishing her skin was bare like his. Knowing instinctively that the pleasure would be magnified if nothing stood between them.

But he didn't seem to be interested in removing her gown. Instead, he caught the hem with one roving hand and pushed it up, lifting it higher and higher until it was bunched around her hips. He found the slit in her drawers and then his hand was inside, and this time there *was* the touch of bare skin on skin.

Jane bit back a cry when his palm rested against her thigh. Rough fingers smoothed up the hot skin there, questing, reaching until they found the juncture where her legs met. She found them parting in some ancient give-and-take.

And then he touched her. Intimately. His large palm cupped her sex. She turned her head away, blushing at the wetness he found there, burning with desire for more and hating that she didn't know what *more* meant.

Until he gave it to her. His fingers spread her folds, opening her hot flesh so he could stroke across the entrance to her body. When he touched her, his eyes shut and he seemed to be as lost in this moment as she was. As caught up in the pleasure, though certainly he had done this before. Many times.

She put that thought out of her head as she arched helplessly, her body begging for what her mind did not yet fully comprehend. And then one of his thick fingers slipped inside her.

She gasped at the fullness, the unexpected and pleasurable invasion of his body in hers. He held still, staring down at her. Waiting, it seemed, though Jane felt she would burst if one more second passed without *something* happening.

Without breaking the intensity of their stare, Nicholas began to move his fingers within her, curling the digits, thrusting in and out of her questing body. To her shock, Jane found herself arching with each thrust, her reactions as natural to her as breathing.

As heavy and full and magnificent as Nicholas's touch had been before, now the pleasure he brought was wildly out of control. She rode out every wave and tensed with delicious anxiety as she reached for the next one.

Just when she thought the pleasure could get no more intense, no more powerful, Nicholas stroked his thumb across a bundle of nerves hidden within her folds and Jane found herself falling. Falling over an edge she hadn't seen coming, falling into the warmth and power of a pleasure more intense than any in her life.

She cried out despite her attempts to bite back the sound, and her hips thrust wildly. But Nicholas did not slow in his ministrations, continuing to urge her, drive her through wave after wave until she collapsed back against his pillows, utterly weak and spent with pleasure.

Gently, he withdrew his fingers from her still clenching body and carefully smoothed her gown back over her legs. He still half covered her, and Jane felt a powerful urge to wrap her arms around him and hold him against her. To cling to this moment between them, even though what had just transpired was exactly the opposite of every lesson she had been teaching.

And yet it didn't matter. Jane had spent the last year regretting any moment of pleasure she experienced. But she refused to regret *this*. It could very well be the only taste of passion she ever had. And there was no better teacher for *her* than her own wayward student.

Nicholas reached down and brushed a few

stray locks of hair away from her face. He stared at her intently, and for the first time Jane felt the true ramifications of what they had done. She hadn't exactly been ruined, but this *was* the kind of thing that led to forced marriages and duels at dawn.

Nicholas leaned in close, yet didn't kiss her, as she ached for him to do. His breath brushed sweet against her skin, and Jane was shocked that the desire he had awakened and then quenched rushed back in full force.

"Oh, sweetling," he all but purred. "I fear you and I are going to be involved in a battle of temptation for as long as we are near each other. The only question is if you will succeed in corrupting me . . . or if I will corrupt you."

Jane shut her eyes at his statement. It was not said cruelly, of that she was certain, but there was a harsh truth to it. Every time she surrendered to Nicholas, each time they shared a stolen moment like this one, it was a risk to her. Corruption to a woman of her station meant shunning, loss of reputation and employment, perhaps even a life on the street.

And Nicholas would suffer, too. The more conservative mamas would steer their innocent daughters away from him for fear of his seduction. His choices on the marriage mart would be severely limited by such an action.

Reluctantly, she pressed her hands to his chest and shoved gently. "Please let me up."

This time he did as she asked, rolling over on his back. She got to her feet and smoothed her wrinkled skirt as she turned to him. With a start, Jane realized the blankets had fallen away from his body when he moved, and now he was utterly naked. She blushed, but couldn't keep herself from staring.

His hips and legs were as muscular and well-formed as the rest of his fine body. But they were of less interest to her than the harsh thrust of the erection she had felt pressed to her belly a short time ago.

Jane had never seen a naked man before, and it was a shocking sight. He seemed so big, so hard and so . . . so . . . *male.*

When he didn't make any movement to cover himself, she turned her head. But that didn't change her shameful urge to move closer, to stare, even to touch him as intimately as he had touched her.

Trying to ignore all those confusing desires, she said, "I came here today, so much earlier than normal, because Lady Ridgefield was—"

She broke off, recalling that it was Nicholas's own mother who had helped arranged for this day together. What that lady would think if she knew how Jane had started it . . . well, it was too much to consider.

"Lady Ridgefield gave me a day off while she went to visit a friend," she finally finished, avoiding the direct lie. "I hoped that you and I could share a luncheon to discuss table etiquette and perhaps review some of our earlier lessons. I would also like to see any clothing you ordered from the tailor."

"Is that all?" Nicholas asked, his lazy posture and drawl taunting her. He was shameless, never once moving to cover himself.

She nodded and kept her stare away from him. "If you would ready yourself and join me downstairs, I would . . . I would appreciate it."

He sat up a little, and she couldn't help but look at him from the corner of her eye. Lord above, he was temptation and sin embodied, just as she'd thought the first night she saw him.

"Your wish is my command," he said.

Her hands shaking, Jane turned away and staggered downstairs to wait. And try to forget what his touch had awoken in her. And how much she wished she could have more.

As soon as Jane closed the door behind her, Nicholas flopped back on the bed and covered his eyes with his forearm.

"Fuck," he muttered, though the salty curse didn't manage to sum up his feelings on what had just happened.

He hadn't meant to take the encounter so far. That was the root of the problem. He had been angry with her after what he felt was her dismissal the day before. And that anger had grown when he woke to find her pinned and struggling beneath him.

Great God, he could have killed her out of pure instinct before he was fully awake! That had shaken him. To be honest, it *still* shook him.

His touch was meant to be punishment. A way to prove to her that when it came to desire, she couldn't deny that he held sway over her. That *he* was the master and she the student.

And then she had moaned. She had been so wet. She had been so sweet. And he hadn't been able to stop himself until he felt her sheath flutter with an orgasm.

Worse, he had been less than a minute away from burying himself to the hilt in her wet, willing body and ruining her entirely. Only a tiny part of him that was beginning to remember what it meant to be a gentleman had stopped him.

And now he was lying in his rapidly cooling bed, his cock as hard as granite, and Jane was downstairs waiting to torment him. In more ways than one, for he knew every time he looked at her, for as long as they continued this arrangement, he would always see the look of pure rapture on her face when pleasure washed over her.

That was a moment he would never forget.

He slipped his hand down, squeezing his eyes shut as he recalled, in perfect detail, every moment with Jane. He caught his cock in one hand and began to stroke as he pictured her trembling body. Heard her cries.

And imagined what it would have been like to finish what he started. Her body had been so tight around his fingers, around his cock it would be like a wet, hot vise. He bucked against his palm as he thought of spreading her wide, slowly breaching her inch by inch, her nails digging into his back, her moans and gasps encouraging him.

He wanted to take her. Claim her. Own her in a way no other man ever had or ever would. To take her so slowly that she begged for more. To claim her so fast that she whimpered with weak pleasure when it was over.

Suddenly his cock erupted, and Nicholas let out a low, harsh groan of relief. Wiping his hand on the bedclothes, he settled back against the pillows.

Pleasuring himself was only a temporary relief. He had to get dressed, go downstairs, and face the woman who had begun to take center stage in every fantasy he wove. Now that he knew the feel of her body, it was only going to get worse.

Chapter 13

When Nicholas opened the door to the parlor across from the dining room, he was almost surprised to see Jane pacing the floor. Although she had said she would wait while he readied himself, and Gladwell had informed him she was, indeed, inside, he had still had doubts. There were very few women of her rank who would be able to face a man they had just surrendered to so fully.

But Jane stopped her restless movements as he entered and smiled at him as if nothing had transpired at all. Except, as he closed the door behind him and moved a step closer, he saw a flicker of desire and wariness still in her eyes.

Which gave him a bit more pleasure than it should have.

He cleared his throat. For his own sanity, he needed to regain a little distance. A little control.

"Last night I went to the underground," he said with no preamble.

Jane's expression changed instantly. The desire faded away, and wariness became a fear of a deeper sort. Her spine straightened with anxiety and anticipation.

"And?"

The word sounded torn from her throat with effort, and Nicholas fisted his hands at his sides. So much hope was a dangerous thing.

He motioned her toward the nearest comfortable chair, but she remained standing. With reluctance, so did he. A gentleman did not sit in a lady's presence. Ridiculous rules.

"Although most of my sources did not come up with any new information on your brother's whereabouts, there was one woman who told me she thought she saw someone who resembled him. But it was over a year ago and she couldn't be certain."

Jane's hand came up to cover her lips as she gasped out a sound of joy and pain at once. Her eyes glittered with unshed tears, and she stared at him without speaking for a long moment.

"Oh, Nicholas!" she finally breathed as she moved toward him. "This is wonderful news!"

He frowned. She was so lit up with joy, and it was a pleasure to see her happy. But he knew very well that what he had uncovered was barely anything. It was likely a dead end. And though he had started out with the intention to mislead Jane, seeing her like this now, he couldn't do it. He had to let her know that her hopes should not be so high.

"Jane, it is hardly news at all. The woman said she knew a man who looked *like* your brother. Marcus was not so uncommon-looking. And this woman is no stranger to drink. She could have meant a hundred other men, a thousand."

Her joy didn't fade at all. "Or she could have meant Marcus. Nicholas, I have been searching for over a year, desperate to find any scrap of news about him. This is magnificent, for at least it is something. Some hope!"

There was that wretched word again.

She moved even closer, pressing her palms against his forearms and smiling up at him. He stared at her, nearly in his arms, but somehow it wasn't memories of what had transpired a short time ago in his bed that moved him. It was something else entirely. When he looked at her, he thought of summer. Warmth and light, lazy laughter.

"Thank you," she said softly. Then she rose up on her tiptoes and pressed a brief kiss to his lips. "Thank you."

She pressed her mouth to his a second time, and that was just about all his tense body could take. Before she could pull away, he slipped his fingers around her shoulders and held her firm, deepening the kiss. She gasped against him, but then her arms came around his shoulders, her body molded firmly to his, and she clung to him as if he were a lifeline.

Nicholas had never been a clumsy boxer. He prided himself on finesse, both in and out of the ring. And yet today, with Jane, his fingers felt thick and awkward, his body not quite in control. And his mouth was bruising, demanding against hers.

Despite her inexperience, she didn't seem to care. Her breath came in pants between desperate, heated kisses, and her fingers clenched in fists against the fine wool of his new jacket over and over again.

This was a bad thing. His resolve and wavering gentlemanly instincts had been tested once today. He did not think he would succeed at this second test of his willpower. Especially when Jane was as lost in the strange pull between them as he.

He was ready to lay her down on the settee when there was a light rap on the door behind them.

Instantly they broke apart. Jane rushed to the other side of the room, pausing before the picture window that looked out over the grounds behind the town house. Her shoulders lifted and fell with the labor of her breathing.

With a groan, Nicholas wiped his mouth and called out, "Enter."

The door opened, and to his surprise it was his cook who stood there. A smile softened Mrs.

Fieldframe's normally harsh face as she said, "My lord, your luncheon is ready."

"Luncheon?" he repeated in confusion. Then he recalled Jane's mention that she wished to review supper manners. "Yes, thank you."

Jane turned from the window, and now her face was utterly composed. Only the slight redness of her swollen lips revealed her true state.

"Thank you, Mrs. Fieldframe. I will serve Lord Stoneworth today for this first practice."

Mrs. Fieldframe gave Jane a nod, as if she were lady of the house and had some power over the servants. "Yes, miss."

Then the cook was gone, leaving the door open behind her. Nicholas let out his breath in a sigh, partly out of frustration that he was not going to be alone with Jane. And partly out of relief for the same.

"Shall we dine, my lord?" Jane asked, approaching him cautiously, as if he were a beast who could strike.

"Indeed, my dear," he drawled, holding out an arm for her to take. "I suddenly find myself famished."

Jane fidgeted with her place setting, totally ignoring the soup that was steaming in the bowl before her. Although it smelled divine, she couldn't even think of eating it. All thoughts in her mind had been replaced by heated memories of Nicholas's touch. She had allowed it not once, but *twice* in less than an hour.

It should have been shameful, and yet it was thrilling to recall his hands on her, in her, teasing and coaxing out a release so powerful that every other pleasure faded.

"Jane?"

She started, brought back to reality by Nicholas's deep voice. He was staring at her, his expression cloaked.

"Shouldn't you be eating?" he asked, one dark brow arching slowly.

She nodded. "What I *should* be doing is teaching. My apologies for my distraction."

"It is quite all right, I share the source, do I not?" he asked in that low, seductive drawl that seemed to crawl under her skin.

She shivered, but chose to ignore the statement. He was only saying it to get a rise out of her.

"First, I must say that your new clothing is lovely. You look very nice in it, Nicholas."

Of course, he had looked far finer out of the well-made clothing that now accentuated every strong movement of his body. She squeezed her eyes shut as the thought flitted through her mind. She should not keep thinking of that!

When she opened her eyes, Nicholas was staring at her.

"Thank you," he finally said softly. "I am glad you approve. At least the wretched hours being poked and prodded by that horrid tailor are worth something now."

She forced herself to remain focused. It was her only hope. "They are and they will be worth so much more. When you enter a room wearing fine things, the *ton* much more readily accepts you as one of them."

Nicholas snorted out a sound of disgust. "If it is only the clothing that makes a man, then it seems I can do whatever else I please, as long as I do it fashionably."

She shook her head. "It is only a first step. The first impression you make will be favorable when you enter a room dressed as you are, but you must still live up to that impression. Everywhere you go, people will be watching. Especially you, Nicholas."

He smiled. "Because I am so dashing and handsome."

She couldn't help but smile back, even though he wasn't taking her seriously. "No, you oaf. Because you are infamous."

"Mmmm." He sprawled back in his chair and sipped his wine slowly. "The infamous Nicholas Stoneworth. I rather like it."

"But your family does not," she said softly, thinking of Lady Bledsoe's joy that her wayward son was going to return to the fold.

He straightened up. "No."

After a moment of awkward silence, he swept

up his spoon and took a gulping swallow of his soup. Jane's eyes went wide as he bent over, eating with steady, purposeful slurps. He wasn't an animal, to be sure, but he was a man who was bent on eating, not making an impression.

"Slower," she urged, ignoring his glare. "Dinner parties are the perfect place to make polite conversation. You will be seated next to others based upon your importance and theirs. And you may also be seated next to eligible young ladies. I assume that is what you want."

Her voice caught, and she cleared her throat as she erased the idea of Nicholas making love to one of those other young ladies. Of him doing to someone else what he had done with her.

"It is what I need." He scowled. "Very well."

He slowed his eating, and she smiled. Reluctant as he was, he did listen. And when he straightened up and didn't glower, he actually looked like a gentleman. A dangerous one, but one nonetheless.

"Today I am serving," she continued before she took a spoonful of her own soup. "Normally a footman would do that duty. He would come in and serve from your left, then remove the dish and not return until the next course."

Nicholas swallowed and said, "What if I want more?"

She shrugged. "It might be possible to signal

a passing servant, but unlikely. Once you have a serving, that is what you get."

Nicholas frowned. "Great God, these people. No wonder they are so starched and dull. Is there *no* pleasure in their ranks?"

Jane pushed feebly at the memory of the pleasure that had washed over her less than an hour before.

"No wonder the men turn to whores and the underground," he continued. "At least there they can be human. What do the women do? Diddle the footmen?"

Jane's eyes went wide. "This is not dinner conversation!"

He shrugged one shoulder, but did not continue with his rant against the lack of pleasure in Society. "It simply seems like a waste of good food. If one doesn't enjoy life, what is the point?"

Hesitating, Jane pondered that question.

"Or is that not good dinner conversation, either?" he asked, sarcasm dripping from each word.

Jane shook her head. "I think, actually, that might be very good dinner conversation. It might shock some, but if you could avoid making references to whores, there are many men and even women of rank who would love to debate the concept of pleasure versus propriety with you."

"Really?" he sounded less than convinced.

Jane set her spoon down and rose to her feet. As she gathered the bowls in preparation for fetching the next course, she said, "You know, you are a snob, just as you believe those of your rank are. Perhaps you're even worse!"

Nicholas stared at her in shock. "What are you talking about?"

"You make the assumption that everyone you meet in Society will be stuffy, dull, and stupid. In actuality there are many men and women who are bright, amusing, and open-minded."

"Name one," he challenged her, arms folded.

She didn't hesitate. "Your brother."

Nicholas stared at Jane as she finished the last bite of the deliciously poached apple Mrs. Field-frame had presented for dessert. She sighed with delight, and his gut tightened. There was no point denying how much he wanted this woman. Still.

But there was something else. He was beginning to respect her, too. She was a quiet, firm teacher, not allowing him to stray off the course too far, but still willing to smile when he amused her. Whatever had happened in her personal life, no matter how far in position she had fallen, no one could say she was not a lady.

Plus, she had insight. When she reminded him that his brother wasn't the kind of man he now ruthlessly pictured when he imagined those of his rank, it had shamed him. With two words, *your brother*, she had knocked him from the perch he had insisted upon taking since his return to Society, looking down at those who cared about straight cravats and the advantages of a claret versus a port.

If he wanted this to work, for his brother's sake, for his nieces' sakes, he had to try harder.

"We will review all of this further," Jane said, waving to the empty dishes. "I realize it is a lot of information to take in during such a short period of time."

"You are a good teacher," he said softly, leaning back in his chair.

She blushed, the same bright color she had reached when at the heights of physical pleasure, and once again Nicholas was pleased he had a tabletop to cover his lap. Somehow he doubted a raging erection would be considered a compliment by the lady.

"Tell me more about your cousin," he said, wishing both to remain seated and to uncover a bit more about the man she hated so deeply.

Nicholas remained unconvinced that Patrick Fenton might not be somehow involved in Marcus's disappearance. If he was truly the villain Jane believed him to be, there might be something more sinister lurking beneath the surface.

Jane stiffened visibly, and the pleasure on her

face that had lingered after his compliment vanished in an instant.

"What more do you want to know?" she asked, her voice brittle. "He is a usurper and a liar."

He tilted his head. "There must be more to it than that. It might help me find your brother."

Realization dawned on her face. "Do you *really* believe Patrick might have been involved in Marcus's disappearance?"

He shrugged one shoulder. "I don't *believe* anything yet, one way or another. But I am curious."

She sighed, as if the subject was a painful one, and when she began to speak, her voice was low and even, as if the words were difficult.

"There isn't much to tell. Patrick is the son of my father's favorite brother and his Irish wife. His mother was . . ." She hesitated. "She was not a kind woman. Beautiful, but not kind. She ran away from the family when Patrick was still a boy. His father died a few years later. He spent the rest of his growing up shuttling between school and the homes of various relatives. He played with Marcus and me as a boy, and we were actually close."

"How close was he to your father?" Nicholas asked, pleased that his desire was finally back in his control. At least he would be able to stand without shocking Jane yet again.

She pondered the question. "Closer as we grew

older. And once Marcus vanished, Patrick did come to the house more often."

Nicholas steepled his fingers. The hated cousin could have been simply comforting a favorite uncle, or he might have been sowing the seeds of something more sinister.

"And your brother. Were he and Patrick friendly?"

She nodded. "They were of an age. I recall them getting into some trouble together as boys. At some point, though, they had a break of their friendship. The last year before my brother disappeared, he and Patrick did not speak."

Nicholas thought about all the new information for a long moment. "When will your employer expect you back today?"

Jane blinked. "Lady Ridgefield will likely be home in the late afternoon. A few hours more, at least. Why?"

"I think you should pay a visit to your cousin."

She drew back, and he could tell the idea was repellent to her. "*Why?*"

"Because while you talk to him and keep him busy, I want to sneak into the room where he keeps the original letters from your father."

Jane's eyes went wide. "You cannot be serious. You want to break into my cousin's home?"

He shook his head with a grin. "You will let me in secretly, there will be no breaking involved."

"But why?" she asked, ignoring his attempt at humor.

He grew serious. "I want to read those letters myself and see if I can uncover any nuance that may have been missed."

"But it is daylight. Do you not fear being caught?"

With a smile, Nicholas got to his feet. "Oh, sweetling, you haven't seen me sneak yet."

Chapter 14

⌒⌒◯◯⌒⌒

Jane had never been so terrified in her entire life as she was as she stood in the small office where her cousin kept her father's papers. After a brief encounter with one of Patrick's servants, she had gone into the room to "view" the documents.

Now she stood, hands trembling at her sides as she readied herself for the second part of Nicholas's shocking plan. When she felt some semblance of calm, she went into action. Swiftly she withdrew all her father's documents from the cabinet where they were stored and laid them on the desk so Nicholas wouldn't have to search for them.

Quietly she double-checked that the door to the hallway was securely shut before she slipped to the French doors that led to the garden and opened them, allowing Nicholas entry to the room.

He slid inside on silent feet and smiled at her. "Very good. And no one was suspicious of your motives?"

She shook her head. "I have come here many times before to examine my father's things. The servants are accustomed to me arriving uninvited."

"Very good."

"Would you like me to stay here with you?" she asked, dreading the moment when she would be forced to contend with Patrick.

He smiled at her, but she could see it was an attempt at reassurance. Was her worry so clear? To Nicholas, she supposed it was. He had an uncanny ability to read her emotions.

"No, it would be best if you go to him."

"But why?" she asked, clenching her fists at her sides.

He arched a brow at her reluctance. "Because, my dear, he might come in here to speak to you."

"Then can I not leave the house?" she all but pleaded. Now that she felt the strength of Nicholas's suspicions, it would be hard for her to look Patrick in the eye without revealing her hatred of him even more. She was forever blurting out things she shouldn't when he riled her.

"Not if we want to ensure he will not catch me."

Reaching forward, Nicholas caught her shoulders and drew her closer. Jane shivered as his arms came around her and he held her to his chest. She could feel the even rhythm of his heart thumping against hers, and it made her nervousness fade.

"I have no choice but to assume your cousin comes to check these papers to make certain you haven't taken anything each time you depart. If he did so while I remained, it could be disastrous."

Jane looked up at him as the full ramifications of such a thing sank in. If her cousin truly was a villain of the kind Nicholas implied, Patrick could attempt to harm him. And even if he wasn't, if Nicholas was caught stealing in another man's house . . . he would be utterly ruined, with no remaining chance of repairing his reputation.

She drew back, feeling cold as his arms dropped away from her. But she straightened her shoulders nonetheless and tried to match his strength.

"Yes, I see. You are right. I will go to Patrick and keep him occupied. How long do you need?"

Nicholas glanced at the pile of papers on the desk. "At least thirty minutes. Can you do that?"

Jane swallowed hard. "Do you *really* think he checks?"

"For hating the man so much, you are certainly reluctant to make him a villain," he said with a tilt of his head.

Jane dipped her chin. It was one thing to think the man had manipulated the system in order to obtain the title. It was another to think he might be as evil and twisted as Nicholas's theory implied.

"I suppose it is because I know that if there was

some kind of outside assistance in my brother's disappearance then Marcus must be . . ."

She couldn't finish the sentence and blinked hard to control the sudden tears that stung her eyes. Nicholas reached forward, and his big hand cupped her cheek. The warmth and comfort she had experienced when he embraced her returned instantly.

"I am probably wrong," he said softly, but Jane could tell he remained apprehensive. "But I want to be sure. Now go and speak to your cousin. Half an hour and I shall meet you back in the carriage. My driver has instructions on where to pick me up."

She nodded and began to turn away, but then moved back. She caught one of his hands, rough and hard from years of fighting. She held to it tightly as she stared up at him.

"Please be careful."

His face softened, and the bright blue eyes that normally sparkled with mischief were suddenly serious. "I will be, Jane. Don't worry about me."

She nodded slowly, then scurried into the hallway to find her cousin.

Jane was wound as tightly as a ball of twine as she watched the butler knock at her father's office door. Inside, Patrick's voice called out the order to enter.

She clenched her fists as she stepped into the room around the servant. Her cousin was situated behind her father's large oak desk, going over a line of figures in a ledger in front of him. He had a pair of spectacles balanced on his nose. She was struck, once again, by how much he looked like family. He had the Fenton air, the Fenton look.

And she despised him all the more for it.

"Jane," he said, waving off the servant as he got to his feet. "Gregory said you were here looking at your father's paperwork another time. I hope you found everything in order."

She folded her arms, but resisted her urge to lash out. Nicholas needed time, and if she caused a row she might not create enough of it before her cousin asked her to leave in that infuriatingly quiet manner of his.

"Yes. Thank you for allowing me to look at the papers at my convenience," she managed through clenched teeth.

He drew back with an expression of surprise. Then he nodded. "Of course, Jane. I hope you know you are welcome here at any time. Someday I even dare to hope we will be friends again, as we were when we were children."

Her jaw set, and she remained silent. For the first time in a long time, she truly observed her cousin, beyond the family resemblance that troubled her so greatly. Nothing about his appearance said that he could be so twisted as to arrange her brother's disappearance. But did that mean it wasn't so?

"Jane, is something wrong?" he asked, stepping forward. "You seem very *odd* today. Is there anything I can help you with?"

She frowned. "You, help me? I think not."

His mouth thinned and his eyes shut briefly, as if having this conversation with her was a trial. "Great God, Jane, are we going to do this again? It is childish and foolish."

"Perhaps," she said, moving a step away from him, her anger notching up. "Or perhaps it is very wise of me to keep away from you. After all, if you would have my brother declared dead so easily, perhaps you would do something equally vile to me."

"What have I done that is vile to you?" he asked, and his voice actually elevated a fraction before he controlled it. "Offered you assistance? Offered you a respectable marriage? Offered you free access to *my* home to continue a fruitless search for something that doesn't exist?"

Jane bit back a gasp of pain and fury, and promptly abandoned her vows to remain calm. "If it doesn't exist, then why not give me my father's property?"

He opened his mouth to answer, but she cut him off by lifting her hand.

"No, don't. You will only feed me more lies. It doesn't matter anymore, Patrick. You see, you did not think that I would ever get help, but I have."

She shut her eyes the moment the words were out of her mouth. Damn her temper! Once again it had made her say something she should have kept secret.

Now he stared at her, eyes wide. "Help? Who are you mixed up with, Jane?"

She shook her head. "No, you will get nothing more from me."

"Please," he said, and his eyes were almost wild with emotion. "Do not do something foolish. There are men who would prey on you, pretend to help you when they were really stalking your virtue . . . or even worse. They are dangerous men, and you should not put yourself in their path."

Jane snorted her derision. "Do not pretend concern, I do not believe it. Especially now."

"What do you mean?" Patrick said as he moved forward.

This was the first time in any of their encounters that she had managed to break past his calm, restrained demeanor. Now his raw emotion, which she couldn't fully decipher as anger or fear or something else entirely, frightened her.

She stepped away, but he closed the distance, and suddenly she found herself against the wall with little room to maneuver.

"What do you mean 'especially now,' Jane?" he repeated.

She swallowed hard. Nicholas was in the house. If she screamed loud enough, he would come. She knew that as surely as she knew her own name. This was her only opportunity to confront her cousin. And she had to know, to see his face when she questioned him. That would tell her more than any evidence Nicholas uncovered.

"Did you have anything to do with Marcus's disappearance, Patrick?" she asked, her voice low but in no way masking her disgust. "Is that why you're so positive he is gone, because you made certain of it yourself?"

Her cousin's face crumpled, the calm wall he kept up falling as if it had been blown apart with explosive power. He grabbed her upper arms in a grip as powerful as a vise and gave her one shake.

"How dare you?" he growled. "How the hell dare you speak of such a despicable, disgusting thing? What do you know, little girl, of anything I have done in regard to Marcus?"

Jane's heart pounded so hard she feared it would burst from her chest, and her blood roared like a waterfall in her ears. She struggled, but Patrick's grip did not lessen, nor could she escape it. His face was close to hers, angry and wild with emotion. She realized, in that moment, that even if she did scream, Nicholas might not make it in time to save her if her cousin did mean her a harm.

"Patrick, release me," she said, low and firm. "You are hurting me."

Instantly he loosened his grip and stepped back, hands up in surrender. In his eyes, she saw a flicker of horror, as if even he could not believe he had lost control in such a manner.

"I apologize, Jane," he said quietly. "I allowed my frustration with this situation to overwhelm me. I never should have done such a—"

Jane sidestepped away from him, freeing herself from being trapped between her cousin and the wall. She backed up, keeping her eyes on him as she willed her pulse and shaking hands to steady so he wouldn't see how terrifying his sudden attack had been.

What time was it? She glanced at the clock on the mantel beside him. Exactly one half hour had passed, which meant she was free to escape him entirely.

"I must go," she said, hating how her voice shook.

"Jane—" he began, but didn't stop her.

She raced from the room and down the hall. Ignoring the servants who offered to assist her, she rushed outside into the cool spring afternoon. A light rain had begun to fall, and she reveled in the damp splash against her skin. After what had just transpired, she had a powerful urge to be washed clean.

Down the street, Nicholas's carriage awaited her, safe. She stopped running so as not to draw attention to herself and walked as briskly as she could. A servant opened the door, and she threw herself inside. When the door closed behind her, she covered her face with her hands and allowed one sob to escape her lips.

Patrick had always handled her with almost frustrating calm. Never had he been so angry, never had he dared to put a hand on her, not since they were squabbling children! But today she had seen a wildness to his expression. A frightening anger that made her believe, for the first time, that Nicholas might be right. Her cousin could very well be hiding a secret. Perhaps even a deadly one.

But now she had to calm herself. She didn't want Nicholas to see how shaken she was. Although the idea of his comfort was pure temptation.

When Nicholas slipped from the dark shadows in the alley behind Patrick Fenton's home and stepped into the carriage that had just pulled up to the curb, he felt a high. There was nothing better than the freedom of being unknown and uninvited in someone's home. A thief's life had actually appealed to him once, before he found his true calling as a pugilist.

Today had been the first time since his return to Society that he hadn't felt utterly confined.

He settled back into the seat across from Jane and looked at her with a smile. One that almost instantly fell when he saw her expression. She was sickly pale, and although she shoved her hands beneath her knees, there was no denying how they shook. He had never seen her like this, even when she first came to ask him for his help.

Instantly he moved to her side of the carriage. "What is it?" he asked, absently pushing a shiny lock of damp hair away from her face. When it was wet, the red highlights were even clearer. "Did something happen? Are you injured?"

She shook her head, but her gaze darted from his. "Nothing. I was simply worried about you. How did your search go? Did you discover any new information?"

Nicholas frowned. "You are lying to me."

Jane jerked her face up toward his with a gasp. "No!"

"You are." He caught her shoulders and felt her flinch so he gentled the touch, lightly stroking his fingers along her arms. "I don't like to being lied to, Jane. Tell me what happened."

She shook her head, and still she would not meet his eyes. "No."

"Did your cousin do something?" Nicholas asked, alarm rising in his chest. "Did he *touch* you?"

The way her chin jerked down gave him all

the answer he needed. Alarm turned to pure rage in an instant. Rage so deep and dark that he could hardly see as it fell in a veil over his eyes.

With great effort, he reined the anger in. Jane was trembling in the seat beside him, and her fears, her upset, were far more important than revenge and wrath. At least for now. As much as he wished to have the carriage turn around, this was not the time to beat her cousin to a bloody pulp.

Gently he wrapped his arms around her and held her to his chest. Her fingers came up to clutch at his jacket, and she fisted the fabric there, holding tight to him as she shivered in his arms.

"Did he hit you?" he asked, low and even, although the idea made him so angry he could scarce control himself.

"No," she whispered.

"Grope you?" he continued, and that idea infuriated him even more.

She jerked her head in the negative. "No, nothing like that. He just . . . grabbed me, trapped me against the wall. He was angry at something I said. Normally he is so calm. Nothing I do or say can make that mask fall away." She swallowed. "Today it fell, and it made me wonder if what you believe is true. Perhaps he did do my brother a harm."

Nicholas tilted her chin up. "I want you to hear me, Jane. Are you listening?"

She nodded, slow and timid, nothing like the normal strength she had in her gaze. He hated the fear in her eyes and hated her cousin for putting it there. But he also loathed himself. He never should have put the idea in her head of her brother being murdered by her cousin, without solid proof. He should have known that strong, honest Jane would not be able to keep herself from a confrontation. Her cousin could have harmed her, and it would have been Nicholas's fault.

"I found no evidence in your father's papers to suggest your brother was harmed in any way by your cousin. It is still only speculation."

She hesitated, but then nodded again. "One I hope is not true with all my heart. But I have never seen Patrick like he was today."

"But you are safe now," Nicholas soothed.

She smiled shakily. "Yes. I'm with you."

That statement hit him in the gut like a sucker punch. Moved him beyond reason. Without hesitating, he tilted her face up and then kissed her. She leaned into him, hungry and innocent passion pouring from her like the sweetest wine he had ever tasted. But behind that he tasted her fright. And he wanted to make it go away. To never let it return.

Breaking the kiss, he brushed more stray locks

away from her face before he pulled back and withdrew his pocket watch from his waistcoat.

"Damn," he said as he snapped it shut. "No time. You must go back."

She nodded. "Yes. Lady Ridgefield will be home soon."

He thought for a moment. "Will you be able to return to me tonight? Perhaps after Lady Ridgefield has retired?"

Jane dipped her chin. "Today has been very long and trying and confusing. I'm not certain I'm going to be much of a teacher if I return to you tonight."

"If you come back, there will be a lesson," he said softly. "But you will not be forced to teach it. I want to instruct you. I want to teach you how to defend yourself. Will you come back tonight and let me do that?"

Her lips parted in surprise. "Defend myself? Do you mean physically?"

He nodded. It was something he should have done from the beginning.

She shook her head. "I don't know, Nicholas, I—"

He caught both her hands, and the motion silenced her. "Please, Jane. Please let me do this for you."

The ardor in his words and touch seem to astonish her, but she nodded slowly. "Very well. I will come back tonight if it means that much to you."

And as she settled her head against his shoulder and they rode back to Lady Ridgefield's home, Nicholas sighed. For some reason it *did* mean a great deal to offer Jane protection. Whether or not he would remain in her life when their lessons were over.

Chapter 15

Jane stepped into the foyer of Lady Ridgefield's home with a grimace. She was late, despite her attempts to arrive before her employer returned home. There were three fine carriages lined up outside in the turnabout. Even if there hadn't been, the laughter and gossipy voices raised from the nearby parlor were proof enough.

Jane straightened her shoulders before she moved toward the room. It wasn't that she feared Lady Ridgefield would care that she hadn't been there when the ladies arrived, but some of the others might make remarks. After today, which had started out with Nicholas nearly making love to her and ended with her cousin's shocking behavior, she was too shaky to deal with their scorn and distain.

But there was little choice. This was her life now.

With one final sigh, she pushed the door open and stepped into the room. Lady Ridgefield was seated on her favorite chair before a roaring fire, laughing. Beside her in another chair was Lady Bledsoe, her own smile wide and genuine and sweet. Three more ladies perched on the settee across from them, and Jane groaned. Her employer's old friends Lady Campbell-Carlile and Lady Abebowale were two of them and the third was Lady Kirkwood, one of the most influential duchesses in Society.

"Ah, Jane," Lady Ridgefield acknowledged her with a wave into the room. "We were just talking about you."

Jane's heart sank as she trudged forward. That was exactly as she feared, but she forced a smile.

"My apologies for not being here when you arrived, my lady. I lost track of the time."

To her surprise, it was Lady Kirkwood who rose to greet her. She dismissed Jane's apology with an elegant wave of her hand. "Posh, my dear. You are allowed to have your day off as your own, aren't you?"

Jane wrinkled her brow in confusion, but managed to maintain her expected servant's politeness. "Thank you and good afternoon, Your Grace. Is there anything I can do or fetch for you ladies before I withdraw and leave you to your conversation?"

"Leave us?" Lady Abebowale gasped as she leapt to her feet, shooting a quick side glance at both Lady Kirkwood and Lady Bledsoe. "Dear Jane, no. You *must* join us. We have something very important to discuss with you."

Jane couldn't help her stare now, despite how inappropriate it was. She expected kindness from Lady Ridgefield and even Lady Bledsoe. And she didn't know Lady Kirkwood, so she could be no judge of her behavior. But Jane had sat in many a room and ball with Lady Abebowale and Lady Campbell-Carlile, and neither of them had sent her so much as a side glance, despite the fact that the widow Lady Campbell-Carlile had once had designs on her own father!

But now they were being completely cordial to her, as if they had suddenly recalled she once had rank and position. What could she do? Her head was spinning and she desperately wanted to hide, but a servant was expected to serve, no matter how ridiculous or odd the request.

"I-I will certainly join you, if you would like," she said, stepping away to move one of the more uncomfortable wooden chairs from beside the table across the room.

"No, my dear, take my place on the settee," Lady Kirkwood said, motioning to the empty place between the other two women.

"I couldn't—"

"I insist." The duchess arched a brow, and Jane shut her mouth and took the space on the settee.

Lady Bledsoe smiled at her as the others shuffled to move another chair into the circle and re-situated themselves. Jane smiled back shakily and prayed Nicholas's mother would not guess just how eventful her day with him had been. She doubted all this kindness would continue if she realized how far things had gone between her beloved son and a servant.

"Jane," Lady Bledsoe said softly, once the room had settled and Jane had poured herself some tea at Lady Ridgefield's insistence. "All day, I have been talking to these ladies about you."

Jane swallowed as she cast a glance around the room at the others. They were all leaning forward, smiles on their faces, as if in anticipation.

"Have you?" she said weakly. "I don't know what in the world would interest you about me."

"I was once friendly with your mother, as you and I have spoken about," Lady Bledsoe said. "And Lady Campbell-Carlile knew your father before his death. Your parents moved in our circles, and once you did, too. We have determined that it is a shame for you to serve Lady Ridgefield as little more than a common servant when your roots are far grander than that."

Jane's lips parted in surprise. That fact had never seemed to occur to any of the ladies before.

Lady Ridgefield leaned forward now, practically bouncing with glee. "Not that I do not adore your company, Jane. But I have often thought it was not right for you to be lowered to such a position. And now Lady Bledsoe has come up with the best plan in the world."

"Plan?" Jane repeated weakly. Her world felt as though it had begun to spin ever faster and more out of control. This day . . . it was really quite mad. Perhaps it was all a dream.

Except when she surreptitiously pinched herself, she was most definitely awake.

Lady Bledsoe nodded. "The ladies and I all have influence in Society. We have connections, and together we are quite a force to be reckoned with. We would like to . . . *adopt* you, Jane . . . I suppose is the best way to put it. To sponsor you for a Season. You are a beautiful girl, my dear. I am sure you could make an excellent match, despite this last year of service."

Jane opened her mouth and shut it as she tried to formulate some kind of response to this utterly unexpected offer.

To no longer serve, but return to Society, was appealing in a great many ways, but it was out of the question. She felt closer to finding Marcus than she ever had before. She couldn't abandon that! Not to become the charity case of a group of bored Society women.

"I appreciate the sentiment," she said carefully, not wishing to offend. "But I made many of the choices that put me in my current position.

I would not feel right about accepting help from you. You owe me nothing."

"Owe you nothing?" Lady Ridgefield gasped and leaned forward to grasp her hand tightly. "That is not correct at all, my dear! You have been nothing but kind to me, when I know I can be a bit . . . silly. No companion has ever been so thoughtful, nor indulged my eccentricities as sweetly as you have."

Jane blinked, tears stinging her eyes. "But that has been a pleasure, not anything I ever expected this kind of reward for."

Lady Ridgefield dabbed at her own sudden tears. "But whether you expected it or not, I wish to thank you for your wonderful treatment and friendship to me, Jane."

Lady Bledsoe nodded slowly. "Yes. We want to thank you."

Jane swallowed as her gaze slipped to Lady Bledsoe, and she found the woman smiling at her. Now she understood. Lady Ridgefield was the sweetest woman in the world, but in a year she had never considered doing this. It was all Lady Bledsoe's doing. And it was an attempt to make some kind of . . . *payment* for her training of Nicholas. As if Lady Bledsoe felt that if she managed to marry Jane well to some person with a bit of money and position, it would balance out a debt.

A sting of disappointment worked through Jane, though she kept a smile on her face so none of the women would see. They meant well.

"I still don't think I could—"

"Hush!" Lady Abebowale rapped her fan across Jane's knuckles to silence her. As Jane lifted her stinging hand to her mouth, the other woman continued. "There will be no refusals. We will not accept it. You *will* be sponsored by us for a new Season and that is the end of it."

Then she got to her feet. "Now I must go. I will leave the details to the others. Lady Campbell-Carlile, will you go with me in my carriage?"

"And I must return home, as well," Duchess Kirkwood said.

Lady Ridgefield rose to escort them to their vehicles, leaving Lady Bledsoe and Jane alone. As soon as the door closed behind them, the other woman moved to sit beside Jane.

She smiled. "I hope this pleases you, my dear."

Jane hesitated. It seemed she was in a tricky position. If she utterly refused, all she would do was damage her relationship to these powerful women. In a battle between their will and her pride, she had no chance of winning.

Accepting their offer was her only choice. It was highly unlikely anyone would be interested in her, even with the ladies' assistance. If she kept her head about her, there would be no harm in going through the motions.

"Yes, of course," Jane finally said, her voice hollow even to her own ears. "I do appreciate your wanting to help me."

"You are doing so much for my family," Lady Bledsoe said, and her voice caught. "I must do something for you."

"Just as I explained to Lady Ridgefield about our association, I am happy to help your son," Jane whispered, her thoughts turning to the sweet draw of Nicholas's unexpected kisses and the heat of his touch. She moved her gaze to a spot on the floor so Lady Bledsoe wouldn't see too much. "You do not need to repay that."

"How is my son faring?" Lady Bledsoe asked with a quick glance toward the door through which Lady Ridgefield had departed. In the hallway, the other women's voices still echoed as they said their farewells.

Jane smiled, and this time it was not forced or awkward. "He is improving with each lesson. Most of the knowledge I am imparting is nothing more than reminders of what he knew from his youth. Today we discussed dining, and though the ideas frustrated him, he did well."

"That is good, for he may need to test those skills soon. Tomorrow I will be sending him an invitation to a ball I plan to host in a few days' time."

Jane gasped as she stared at Lady Bledsoe. "But he—"

Before she could finish, Lady Ridgefield re-entered the room, beaming broadly. "Were you telling Jane of your ball? We will need to quickly arrange for some new clothing to be designed for you, my dear, but I have the perfect seamstress for the job."

Jane blinked, still reeling from the idea that Nicholas would be tested so soon. "What?"

Lady Ridgefield's smile fell. "The ball, my dear. It will be your coming out with our support."

"My coming out?" Jane pushed to her feet. When the group had said they would sponsor a Season for her, she hadn't thought they meant *immediately*.

Lady Bledsoe nodded. "Yes, but do not worry. *All* will be well. I know it will be true. Lady Ridgefield, will you escort me to the foyer? Good night, Jane."

"Good night," Jane managed to choke out.

The two ladies departed the room, and Jane sank back down into the soft settee cushions. Never had she thought Lady Bledsoe would push Nicholas into Society so quickly. Although he was making strides, he continued to remain rough around the edges. She truly didn't know if he was ready for the kind of keen observation and judgment he would endure at his mother's party.

If he failed, it would be Jane's fault. Hers for allowing distraction while they worked together.

And hers for telling Lady Bledsoe about their secret meetings.

If he succeeded . . . well, that led to other issues entirely. He was a handsome, rich man with an influential, powerful family. If he made any kind of good impression with key parties, he would be accepted.

And their association would be over.

She pushed at the harsh, hollow sting that worked through her entire being at that thought. There was no time for that now. Tonight, when she returned to his home, she would have to confess what she had done. What she had revealed to his mother. And warn him about the invitation he was about to receive. Perhaps there was a way for him to refuse it without hurting her feelings.

"Did that not go splendidly, Jane?"

She rose to her feet and turned to face Lady Ridgefield. Her employer's round cheeks were flushed pink with utter pleasure and her eyes were bright with excitement. Jane couldn't help but smile. Lady Ridgefield only meant her the very best. She could have no idea how complicated things had become.

"Yes, my lady." Jane sighed. "I do appreciate all your thought and care when it comes to me. Now, can I get you anything at all?"

Her employer stopped dead in the middle of the room and stared at Jane. Her face softened with a look so sweet and motherly, Jane almost turned away from it.

"Do you not understand? You no longer work for me."

Jane blinked. "But I—"

"If you are to be a success, you cannot be a servant any longer. I am now your guardian in a way. Responsible for reintroducing you to Society. We shall find you a fine husband. Perhaps a rich squire or a second son of a viscount or an earl."

Jane nodded slowly, still uncertain what else she could do.

"And Lady Bledsoe has high hopes that her son will be accepted back into Society that night, as well," Lady Ridgefield continued. "So we will search for a wife for him, too. If he were to marry a daughter of a duke or some other high-ranking gentleman, it would solidify his return."

Shutting her eyes, Jane ignored the pricking sensation that suddenly troubled her. Those were not tears. Just a sneeze she could suppress. Lady Ridgefield was correct. The fastest way for Nicholas to regain his position in Society was to have a good showing at his mother's party . . . and to quickly woo and wed a woman of influence.

Not a woman like her, that was certain.

"You shall see, Jane, after the party in a few days, everything will change."

She opened her eyes and forced another smile for her jubilant former employer who meant so well. "You are right about that, my lady. *Everything.*"

But she intended to enjoy every moment she had left with Nicholas before that inevitable moment.

Chapter 16

Jane stepped into one of the many parlors in Nicholas's home. She nodded her farewell to Gladwell and then looked around. She was shocked at the change to the chamber since her last visit. All the fine furniture had been moved back against the walls, leaving a vast empty space in the middle of the room. She shivered when she thought of why.

Near the fireplace, Nicholas and his friend Ronan Riley, the one he called Rage, were talking, their heads close together. Jane's shiver grew deeper, and not for any fearful reason.

Nicholas was wearing some of his older clothing. A simple pair of trousers rode low on his narrow hips and a cream-colored shirt made from a rough cotton cloth was unfastened to midchest. She allowed herself a moment to stare at him before he became aware of her presence. The simple clothing suited him, as much as she hated to admit it. It brought out the wild side of him that the fancier apparel served to oppress.

Would he ever find a balance between the truth of himself and the image Society desired?

She shook her head. It didn't signify. She would be long gone from his life by the time he resolved that matter. It was not her concern.

"Good evening," she said, her voice cracking as she tried to draw their attention.

Both men straightened up, and Nicholas smiled as he crossed the room toward her. Jane caught her breath at the sight. He was all lean muscle and casual, elegant swagger as he moved. In those moments, even with his face unshaven and his clothing inappropriate, she knew he would be accepted back into Society. He had too much magnetism to be denied. Women would swoon when he passed and men would stare at him in envy.

She wouldn't be needed anymore. Perhaps she never truly was.

"Hello, Jane," he drawled as he stopped before her.

He tilted his head to examine her face, and Jane blushed. Surely he could read her thoughts as clearly as ever. That was one skill he seemed to have from the beginning. He could invade her feelings without even trying.

"You look tired," he said softly, only for her ears.

"A gentleman never says such a thing about a lady," she chastised.

He arched a brow and simply looked at her for a long, charged moment. "I am not being a gentleman," he finally noted. "I am being your friend."

Jane jerked her gaze to him in surprise at that statement. Friends. Was that what they were? Sometimes it seemed like it. And sometimes it seemed like much more floated between them.

"It was a trying day," she finally admitted.

His frown drew down, and a dark anger entered his bright eyes. Reaching out, he briefly touched her upper arm and nodded. Then he released her and turned back to Rage.

"I would like to do a brief sparring demonstration, Rage. Then I'll work with Jane alone."

"Of course," Rage said with a knowing twinkle in his eye that made Jane's blush even hotter. "And a good evening to you, Miss Jane."

She smiled at the fighter. "Good evening, Mr. Riley."

"Why don't you sit over there," Nicholas said, motioning to a comfortable chair across the room. "I'll talk you through what we're doing." His voice elevated a fraction. "And you can watch while I put Rage here on his arse a few times."

"Only if you're lucky." Rage chuckled as he went to work stripping off his shirt and wrapping his hands with a thin strip of cloth.

Jane found herself shamefully holding her

breath as she watched Nicholas walk away. In one movement, he stripped open the final buttons on his shirt. As he tugged it away, she clenched her fingers against the armrest of her chair. There was no point in denying the absolute desire she felt for the man. It was unlike anything she had ever experienced before.

And she liked it. She liked the achy, nervous feeling low in her belly. She liked the anticipation of not *if* he would kiss her, but when. And that morning, when she found herself pinned beneath him, she liked it when he touched her so intimately.

Worse, she wanted more, even though she *knew* there was no future between them other than a few more stolen days at most.

The two men moved to the middle of the empty room, mercifully cutting off her desperate and needy thoughts. She watched as they circled each other, their hands raised up in fists close to their heads.

"I keep my hands up in order to protect myself," Nicholas called over his shoulder without looking. "If I lower them, Rage could slip in a powerful shot and knock me out before I even get to fight."

"And I have," Rage taunted good-naturedly. "Many a time."

Nicholas laughed, but didn't stop circling or lower his hands. "There are several kinds of punches, but today I'll focus on a jab for you."

Without warning, he shot his right hand out straight forward and caught Rage in the stomach. Jane gasped out her shock, but even though the other man gave him a look and grunted, the punch didn't seem to disturb Rage's good humor.

"That punch has the most power. I'll show you how to increase it later." Nicholas grinned at his friend. "Ready for the real show?"

"Whenever you are," Rage said.

Their circling suddenly increased in its urgency and Jane felt the electric tension in the air double. Nicholas no longer spoke as he moved, and Rage's grin had been replaced by a focused stare.

Without warning, the circling ended. Nicholas moved forward and threw three punches in rapid succession, a right, a left, and another right that swung around in a looping motion. Rage rocked back from the blows, but immediately countered with a quick jab to Nicholas's body.

Jane rushed to her feet as the two men ended up grappling, locked in a close clinch as they struggled for supremacy. They broke apart again, moving around each other. As the shock of watching the two friends battle wore off, Jane began to understand the basics of what they were doing.

Each man was looking for the right opening, a place where he could throw at least one punch, although the combinations of blows seemed to do the most damage. But they were not just attacking, they always had to defend as well, blocking a punch even as they threw another.

As much as it shocked her, Jane had to admit there was beauty to it, and clear intelligence.

The blows continued to be exchanged until finally Rage staggered back, catching himself with one hand on the back of a settee. Both men were panting with exertion, and Rage lifted a hand in what looked like an act of submission.

Nicholas grinned and moved up to tap knuckles with his friend. "That punch to my ribs nearly put me out." He laughed, as if they had been playing a boyish game rather than pounding on each other.

Rage shook his head. "If you'd caught me more squarely on the chin with that roundhouse, this fight would have been over far more quickly. Good sparring match."

Nicholas thumped his friend on the back and then turned toward Jane. When he saw she was on her feet, he moved toward her. "I hope we didn't frighten you."

She shook her head, shocked that she *wasn't* afraid. "I have never seen two men exchange blows like that. I admit I was taken aback, but I can appreciate why it interests you, and why others come to see it. Have you ever played chess?"

He nodded as he began to strip off the cloth that gave his knuckles some small amount of protection. "Yes."

"That is what it reminded me of," she mused, trying not to stare blatantly at his now sweaty chest. "A very violent physical chess match."

Rage tossed his own hand wraps across the back of a chair and gave the two a quick, dramatic bow. "Good evening. Miss Jane, I do hope to see you again soon."

She waved to him as he departed the room, closing the door behind him and leaving them alone.

Nicholas refocused his attention on her. "That is actually a very good comparison," he said with admiration. "In chess, one must not only look at the move before him, but think several moves ahead. It's the same in a fight. It's not just the next punch, but what combination that punch can lead to."

"And what defense," Jane pointed out.

He smiled broadly, and for a moment Jane sensed a sort of childlike pleasure that she understood his life's passion.

"Not many women would see it that way," he said as he beckoned her to the middle of the room.

She shrugged one shoulder. "Many women mince and faint because that is what they believe is expected of them. But I cannot imagine any woman not appreciating the way you moved tonight."

The instant she said the words, Jane wished

she could take them back. They had two meanings, and she had intended them both. Judging by the way Nicholas's lids grew heavy and his smile took on that feral, animal quality it sometimes possessed, he knew it.

"For now I only care if *you* appreciate my . . . moves," he drawled. Then he chuckled, and the heavy weight of the moment passed. "Allow me to show you some basic defenses."

Jane did not resist as Nicholas positioned himself behind her. One big hand slipped around to cup her hip, adjusting her stance until her legs were wider and one was situated in front of the other. His hands lingered against her body for a moment too long before they slid away.

Jane held back a sigh. She felt his body heat behind her, caressing her as surely as his touch. And she smelled him, too. That hot combination of clean sweat, sandalwood, and the spicy scent that was only Nicholas wrapped around her in a pleasant, dizzying blanket.

He moved to stand in front of her, and she blinked a few times in the hopes that her hazy desire wouldn't be completely evident.

"Now you want to raise your hands as I did," he explained.

She lifted her shaky fists and positioned them in as close a manner as she could. He adjusted her gently until she was in the right position.

"In a scenario where you're being attacked,"

he said, his voice low and gravelly, "it won't be as polite as what you saw between Rage and me."

She couldn't help but smile as she thought of the battle the two friends had just waged. But Nicholas didn't return the expression. To her surprise, he was utterly serious.

"I know what you're thinking, but there are rules in a fight like ours. I'll hurt an opponent if I must, but that isn't my main goal. A man who attacks you will not live up to those standards. So you can't fight politely, either. Kick him between the legs, gouge his eye, flatten your palm to his nose, whatever it takes to protect yourself."

Jane's smile faded as she stared up at Nicholas. The solutions he was describing would be born of dire situations, indeed. She shivered.

"I don't think my cousin would have harmed me." She turned her head. "At least, I must hope he wouldn't have. His actions shocked me, but he didn't hurt me."

Nicholas's mouth thinned to an angry line that she had never seen before. "Perhaps he would not have, but I don't want you to be in a position where you test that theory."

Slowly, she jerked out a nod. "Then how should I punch him or anyone else who dared attack me?"

"Shoot your fist out straight, twisting your hips to give the hit the most power. Try it." He flicked his fingers toward himself.

Her eyes widened. "You wish for me to hit *you*?"

He nodded with a small laugh. "You won't hurt me."

She frowned. He was so cocksure. She threw the punch. He leaned back so her fist skimmed over his chin without fully connecting. Frustrated, she threw again, trying to mimic his movements as he easily leaned away from them. Every so often, he would adjust her fist or demonstrate a proper stance. Eventually Jane was exhausted, and she leaned over to catch her breath.

"That's enough for tonight," Nicholas said with a smile. "You are a natural. You could make a mint in the underground. I'm sure men would pay to watch you fight."

Jane couldn't help but laugh at the absurd idea of fighting for a living. "But you were correct, I didn't hurt you. In fact, I hardly hit you at all. So how could I manage to hurt a man of your size who was intent on causing me harm?"

He shook his head. "I knew your attack was coming. I helped plan it. Many women don't even think to fight back when attacked. Someone who was intent on hurting you would not be ready for it. If you do land a punch, be sure to follow it up with another attack. A kick, a second punch. And then run."

Again, she shivered. "I hope I will never have to use those skills."

He cupped her chin and tilted her face toward his. Those bright blue eyes drew her in, forced her to continue staring when the intensity within made her want to pull away.

"I hope so, too," he whispered. "Now, do you have any questions?"

She shivered. "Why did you tattoo yourself?"

He froze, and his hand drifted away in surprise. "On my back?"

She nodded, a flush darkening her cheeks. But with Nicholas there was no use trying to pretend away the question.

"That was one thing I did not expect you to ask." He chuckled.

She shrugged one shoulder. "I have wondered, that is all. I've not seen anything like it."

"Have you had much occasion to gaze upon half-naked men?" he teased, but behind the playfulness his earlier intensity remained.

She turned her face. "I think you know I haven't."

"And I'm pleased by that."

He turned to show her his back and she stared at the tattoo. In the dim bedroom that morning, there hadn't been enough light to truly see the mark, and tonight while he sparred, she had been distracted and too far away. But now she saw it was a few characters that she didn't understand. It was done in black ink and was about the size of two of her fingers pressed together. She found herself reaching up and tracing the marks with her fingertip.

Nicholas sucked in his breath, a harsh, hard sound that echoed in her own nerve endings. Touching him only led to trouble and more . . . but she kept her fingers against his warm skin.

"They are Chinese characters," he explained, his breath as short as it had been during the fight. "I met a man from the Orient who taught me some different fighting skills. The word means 'stone,' which was my nickname in the underground."

Jane nodded. She had heard Rage refer to Nicholas as such a few times. "Why put it on your body in such a permanent way?"

He turned, and her fingers glided across his skin before she pulled them away, clutching them to her chest as if they had been burned. He stared at her a long moment before he replied.

"Because Stone didn't just come from my name, Stoneworth. A stone is hard, it does not bend. It has power when wielded as a weapon." He shook his head. "I did not want to forget that. I still don't."

She nodded. There was much about this man she didn't understand, but the pain that flickered in his eyes, she did.

He moved toward her, shocking her from her thoughts. There was a purpose in his movement, a swagger that always meant he was going to kiss her.

And she wanted that. But she hadn't yet done the one thing she had vowed to do when she arrived.

Tell him the truth. And before she allowed him to kiss her, before she forgot everything but sensation, she needed to do that.

"Wait," she whispered as his fingers moved into her hair.

He growled a deep, low sound of displeasure, and his fingers massaged her scalp until she moaned in response.

"I-I must tell you something," she managed to squeak out as his lips descended to find the curve of her throat.

"It can't wait?" he whispered against her skin, setting her on fire.

She choked on another moan. "No," she admitted. "Your—your mother. She knows the truth. She knows that I've been training you to be a gentleman."

Nicholas jerked back and stared at her. "What? How?"

She flushed. Now for the difficult part. "She knows because . . . because I told her."

Chapter 17

Nicholas paced restlessly, moving from one end of the room to the other and only occasionally sparing Jane a glance. She remained rooted in the spot where he had taught her to punch and then had begun a far more pleasurable exploration.

She looked utterly miserable.

"I'm sorry," she whispered. "As I explained, it was an accident. The way your mother spoke to me that day made me think she knew. And once I said something, there was no way out. Lady Bledsoe is a very clever woman."

Nicholas snorted out a sound of agreement. "Oh, that she is. Damn it. I only wish you had ignored her request and told me earlier. I feel like I've been unarmed in a battle."

She tilted her head. "Do you really consider yourself at war with your family?"

He stopped pacing and let out a long, heavy sigh that came from deep within his very soul.

"No, just with their expectations. And with my own nature."

Jane nodded slowly, and it was as if she did understand his struggle. Bit by bit, the noose of his brother's life was tightening around his neck. Soon enough, there would be nothing left of Nicholas, or at least not the *real* him.

"I hated to lie," she said softly. "But I was in a difficult position. I had to tell you tonight because she has plans for us both."

"Christ," Nicholas bit out. He sank into the closest chair. "What is in her head?"

Jane clenched and unclenched her fists at her sides, a nervous habit that betrayed her feelings, but she didn't stop looking at him. Direct and honest. Until this slip with his mother . . . which he understood, knowing the marchioness as he did . . . honest was what Jane had always been with him. Perhaps she was the only one, aside from Rage.

"Tomorrow you will receive an invitation to a ball your mother wishes to hold in your honor." She hesitated. "I tried to put her off the idea, Nicholas, but she would not be swayed, no matter how strenuously I argued."

His lips pinched. He should have seen this coming. The Season was already in full swing, and she was desperate to see him back in Society's clutches. Desperate to see him take over his brother's place.

He groaned at that idea. "Well, there will be no refusing her," he muttered.

Jane moved toward him a halting step, but then stopped. He found himself wishing she hadn't.

"But we haven't reviewed certain things nearly enough. Your clothing is perfect now, but you're still shaky on address. We haven't even covered the basics of dancing." She shook her head. "You aren't ready, Nicholas. And I apologize, for it is my fault. I have allowed too many . . . distractions."

He frowned. She said the word *distractions* like it was poison. But what she referred to were the stolen moments they had both allowed. Ones he had enjoyed immensely.

"We are both responsible for that, Jane," he murmured without betraying his thoughts on the matter. "You cannot take the blame for my actions."

He sighed and forced his mind to the matter at hand. Although he hated the idea of change, he *had* been paying attention to Jane's lessons. Society was a viper's nest, but he had certainly been in more dangerous situations.

Still, Jane was correct in some ways. He was rough and he wasn't sure he would *ever* be what his parents wanted him to be. What Anthony had been. No matter how many lessons he took, no matter how much time passed while he studied and changed.

"You said she had plans for us both," Nicholas

said, changing the worrisome subject. "What nefarious plot is she involving you in?"

Jane smiled as she let her gaze return to him. And, as always, he felt a surge of triumph that he had softened her somber expression. She had so few pleasures, he felt like a king when he was responsible for one.

"Nothing nefarious, my lord," she said with a laughing lilt to her tone, though a shadow remained in her expression. "Your mother wishes to repay me for my efforts regarding you."

"Great God," Nicholas groaned. "I can only imagine what she would consider repayment."

Jane looked past him toward the window, her expression and tone suddenly far away. "She wishes to reintroduce me to Society. I believe her ultimate goal is to marry me off as well as my current circumstance can warrant."

Nicholas's stomach jolted, a wave of nausea hitting him with unexpected force and then vanishing. He stared at Jane, standing in the middle of his parlor in her faded gown, her ruddy, dark hair mussed from his fingers, her eyes so infinitely sad. The idea of any other man seeing her vulnerability, touching her as he had, claiming her in the one way he had not . . . it aroused emotions in him he could hardly believe.

"She wants to sponsor you with a Season?" he repeated flatly.

She nodded. "It seems we will both be reintroduced to Society during her ball." She shook her head. "As you said, she is impossible to refuse."

"And why should you?" Nicholas asked, his voice hollow in his own ears. "A woman like you does not deserve to be a servant. She deserves to have beautiful gowns and dance and laugh and be frivolous. If my mother and her cohorts are successful in marrying you well, you will have all those things and more."

Jane stared at him, and for a moment he saw a flash of pain cross her face. It mimicked his own. And while it was edifying to know she felt the same way about their inevitable parting as he did, it didn't change that inevitability. Nicholas was working toward reentering Society, but he was far from a true gentleman. For Jane to regain her status, she would have to marry someone with established respectability.

The same was true for him. If his brother's legacy had been damaged by Nicholas's behavior, the strongest repairs would be done when he married a woman of rank. He knew that to be true, despite the sinking feeling it created in his stomach.

Desire was all there could ever be between them. And that desire couldn't ever be fully realized. He was enough of a gentleman to recognize that, if nothing else.

Jane folded her arms across her chest, and Nicholas was reminded of the way she had faced off with him at the beginning of their strange bargain. A warrior woman, unafraid even in the face of his aggression and ill manners. Even then, he had been moved by her.

But now, seeing her put up that armor, it cut him. She was readying herself for their ultimate break. For the moment when they would pretend they had never met. Never touched. Never been what he had called her earlier. Friends. For somehow she had become that to him. A friend.

"Marriage is not something I can consider now," she said, filling the awkward silence. "It is a frivolous endeavor when I have more important things to focus upon."

"Like your brother, you mean," he said quietly.

She nodded as she fiddled with a loose string on her sleeve. "Pleasure isn't something I can pursue until I know he's safe."

Nicholas couldn't help his mouth dropping open. "Jane—"

She shook her head to cut him off. "I know what you will say. That we don't know anything about Marcus. But we are getting close." Her words were wistful. "So close. I will indulge your mother, but there will be no marriage for me."

Nicholas hated himself when a rush of joy was his reaction to her statement.

She turned away. "I must be going now. Lady Ridgefield is having a mantua maker come tomorrow morning to fit me for a gown. But I will return in the evening for our final lesson. Dancing. I don't know how we will cover that in one night, but I'll do my best."

Nicholas opened his mouth, but then shut it just as quickly. If he said too much, Jane wouldn't return. And he found he wanted her there just one more time.

"Very well. Come close to midnight, if you can," he said. "I will be out until then."

She gave a brief glance over her shoulder and then nodded. "Yes, I will."

She began to move toward the door, but Nicholas called out to stop her. "Jane, is it not polite to say farewell to your host?"

She stopped midstep and slowly turned back. His heart sank. For whatever reason, tonight had put a distance between them. One he knew was fully necessary, and yet he hated it with a passion.

"Of course, forgive me," she said softly. Coming back to him, she held out a hand for him to shake. "Thank you for your assistance tonight, my lord."

He frowned at her formality, but took her hand. Her skin was warm and soft beneath his rougher palm. Instead of shaking it, he turned her hand over, palm up, and lifted it to his lips. Gently he pressed his mouth to her skin, breathing in the soft scent of rosewater.

"Good evening, Jane," he said softly before he let her go. "I shall see you tomorrow."

She blinked a few times, then hurried from the room without further comment or explanation. And Nicholas wondered if the ache around his heart would be the same when she was gone from his life for good.

"Jane has gone?"

Nicholas looked up from the paperwork strewn across his desk as Rage entered his office.

"Yes, an hour ago. You sound surprised."

His friend arched a brow as he threw himself into the nearest chair and stared at him. "I am. There was so much tension in the air between you, I honestly thought you might bed her."

Nicholas bunched his hands into fists on the desk as anger flooded him. It was part upset that Rage would disparage Jane, and part anger at himself for not doing exactly as his friend had expected.

"Jane Fenton is a lady," he growled. "One does not bed a lady. Not without offering her more than a tumble."

"I suppose," Rage said after a long pause.

Nicholas could feel his friend reading his every movement, his every word. It was as if they were in a fight again and Rage was determined to find the chinks in his defenses.

"All that isn't important," Nicholas said, trying to avoid further scrutiny. "I promised Jane I would find her brother. That hasn't changed. I want to go back into the underground tomorrow night."

Rage shook his head. "You don't seem to recall this, but your original plan *wasn't* to find her brother. You didn't think it was possible and I agreed. Your original plan was to make her *think* you were looking for the man, while you allowed her to train you. And your original plan wasn't to teach her to fight off the advances of her cousin, either. Or to look like someone stole your dog every time she left."

Nicholas glared at his friend. "Shut your bloody mouth, Rage. Plans change. Now that I have learned more about the situation, I think I might be able to resolve the issue with her brother for her. Why should I not do that after all Jane has sacrificed for me?"

"Yes, why not?" Rage said, sarcasm dripping from every word. "For charity purposes. Poor, *poor* Jane."

Nicholas glared at him. "Not for fucking charity, Rage."

"You're not admitting that your little mouse has gotten under your skin, are you?" Rage smiled.

"Of course not," he snapped, returning his gaze to his papers, if not his true attention. "Don't be foolish."

"Oh, I wouldn't blame you if you had," Rage said as he leaned back in his chair, his hands folded behind his neck. "The woman *is* interesting, after all. And lovely. That little sense of sadness about her is quite fetching. Makes a man want to cheer her up. If you truly do not want her, I might have a try."

His friend was goading him, of course, trying to force a response to make him reveal his weakness. Nicholas recognized the trap, but couldn't stop himself from falling into it.

"Careful now, *friend*," he said in a tone that left no doubt as to the consequences of continuing down that line.

His friend hesitated, but then a slow smile crept over his features. "You see, you are besotted."

Nicholas pushed away from his desk with a screech of wood on wood. He paced to the window. "Christ, you are annoying. You're talking out of your arse, Rage."

"Am I?" his friend said softly, without moving from his seat. "You say you have no feelings for Jane beyond an obvious desire. In the past, you wouldn't have cared if I made a play for a woman who fit that description. In fact, you used to know I would never try to 'take' any woman who was yours."

Nicholas flinched. "She's not my woman."

"No?" Rage laughed. "I must have been confused by the way you can't take your eyes off of her."

"Please." Nicholas snorted a laugh of his own.

"I have had many women who captured my attention. The only difference with Jane is that I can't follow through on that desire because of her position. She isn't some barmaid I can tup and leave behind. With Jane, there would be expectations and consequences. If I could merely take her to bed, I'm certain I would think little about her after it was over. *That* is all you sense, my friend. All there is."

At least that was what he intended to keep telling himself. That Jane was only a distraction of body.

"Hmmm." Rage frowned. "Very well, if that is what you insist upon. Then let us talk of something else. You know you will have to marry. If not this Season, then next. That is how your strange little world works. If you want acceptance, a good marriage is the way to attain it."

Nicholas spun on his friend. "I fucking realize I have to take on this mantle of responsibility that my saintly brother left behind, and part of that is producing sons as heirs and spares to carry on our fine family name. For that I need a wife."

"Have you considered Jane for that position?"

Nicholas stopped short. Occasionally, yes, he had thought of what it would be like if Jane was the woman he linked himself to forever. It hadn't been an unpleasant thought in many ways. He liked her and he knew he could depend upon her. He desired her, or at least he did for the time being. It would not be difficult to fulfill his husbandly duties with her, that was certain.

But she also knew him, far more deeply than any other woman had. The idea of sharing that kind of intimacy was . . . well, when it came to a wife, he wasn't certain he wanted that. A woman who would simply smile and not ask questions would be better.

And then there was the fact that he was no gentleman. Not really. And Jane deserved that. She deserved a man who would elevate her status, not cause more whispers. He had seen her face when she spoke of how she was dismissed. Whether she admitted it or not, Jane wanted to be part of Society again. And with him, there would be no guarantee of that happening.

"I need someone who will bring me back into the fold. So does she. It would not work," he finally murmured. "And I really don't want to discuss it further."

Rage opened his mouth as if to say more, despite Nicholas's admonishment, but then closed it. "Very well. Then tomorrow we'll go back into the underground and see what we can find. Any reason why you don't want to go tonight?"

"I'm not in the mood," he said, his tone leaving no room for further discussion. Rage finally took the hint, got to his feet, and left the room.

After his friend was gone, Nicholas straightened up. Rage could see he was dancing around his real reasons, but his friend knew him well enough not to push.

Because the fact was that Nicholas just felt too *raw* to go into the underground. Too troubled. Distraction could get him killed. And even more, he feared that if he was threatened tonight, of all nights, he might take things too far.

So instead, he would drown his emotions in a bottle of fine bourbon, then sleep off the hangover and the cause of it. By tomorrow, he was certain he would have his emotions well in hand.

He had to. Tomorrow he said farewell to Jane.

Chapter 18

J ane winced as the dressmaker jabbed her yet again with a pin.

"My apologies, miss," the woman said with a brief, nervous smile.

Jane nodded at her in the mirror's reflection. She could hardly blame the seamstress. After all, she was surrounded by the large, loud group consisting of Lady Bledsoe, Lady Ridgefield, and their friends. All of them had something to add or suggest to the beleaguered woman, and she hadn't had as much practice as Jane had at blocking out their endless chatter.

Jane stared at her reflection and marveled. Despite the pin poking, the dressmaker really was a talent. Although the gown she was designing was little more than a few draped pieces of fabric right now, Jane could see that it would likely be the most beautiful dress she had ever worn. The fabric was a lovely shade of deep blue. In a pile beside her were other silks of lighter blue and even one that was white with hand-stitched flowers scattered across it.

Shutting her eyes, Jane tried hard not to think of how expensive this gown was going to be. It was humiliating to be the adopted charity case of these women.

And yet, her heart leapt at the idea of wearing such a glorious gown. Of coming to a party not as a servant, but as a woman. To dance, which she had always adored.

When the dressmaker accidentally pinched her, Jane almost thanked the woman for dragging her out of her fantasy world. It was *wrong* to take pleasure in this endeavor. To let herself think about playing and dancing as if she hadn't a care in the world.

This party . . . it was more for the ladies who were helping her. And it was for Nicholas.

Her gaze flitted to the clock. It was nearly noon, which meant in twelve short hours she would be with him again. How she wished she could wear this gown when they met, but it wouldn't be ready.

Nor would it be appropriate. Nicholas had been kind last night, and she had felt the thrum of desire that coursed between them . . . but she had also known he was dismissing her. He had been so adamant she take his mother's assistance and find herself an appropriate husband. One that fit her station. It had been a kind set-down, but a set-down nonetheless.

As the women continued to chatter, Lady Bledsoe stepped up to Jane. From the elevated stepstool where she stood, Jane smiled down at the woman weakly.

"You do look lovely. I think you shall be divine when Miss Willows is finished with her work."

Lady Bledsoe glanced at the pretty redheaded seamstress. The woman seemed to sense an unspoken order, for she set her pins aside and said, "Excuse me while I examine this other fabric."

Once she had moved aside and the two women had some privacy, Lady Bledsoe leaned closer. "Nicholas's invitation to my ball was sent this morning, and before I left for here, he had already responded that he will be in attendance."

The other woman's eyes danced so brightly that Jane couldn't help but smile. "I only hope my lessons will be enough, my lady. He has had such a short time to become reacquainted with Society's stringent rules and regulations."

Lady Bledsoe waved off her concern. "I am certain he will do fine." Her smile fell. "Unlike his father, I do not desire that Nicholas lose all his own spark and personality. I have never wanted him to be perfect. Or to be Anthony."

Jane hesitated, uncertain of how to respond. It was not her place to wax poetic on Nicholas's perfection or the beauty of his imperfections.

"Perhaps you should tell him that, my lady,"

she finally said softly. "I am not certain he knows of your support."

Lady Bledsoe opened her mouth to respond, but before she could, Duchess Kirkwood stepped forward. "I do declare, Jane, that color makes your skin look alabaster. You shall be the belle of the ball."

Lady Abebowale nodded, her expression filled with astonishment. "I admit, I said that a woman who lowered herself to a servant could never fit back into Society, but with our help you just might do it. I'm certain we can find you a husband of rank who will be willing to overlook your fallen history."

Jane's lips pinched into a sour smile for both the woman and her reminder. After all, this entire exercise had a purpose, and it was exactly the one Lady Abebowale had been uncouth enough to point out. These women were trying to find her a husband. One who would be "willing" to stoop to her level.

One who wasn't Nicholas Stoneworth.

"Well, again I do thank you ladies for your immense kindness," Jane said, hearing the strain in her voice. "I hope I won't disappoint you in the way I conduct myself at the ball."

The dressmaker returned to her side to take up her pinning, and the women all fell back into their scattered, loud conversation, leaving Jane to return to her own thoughts.

It wasn't her behavior at the ball she really had concerns about. No, her real worries involved her behavior tonight when she met with Nicholas for their final lesson. Because when she was with him, it was harder and harder to remember that she was only a teacher and he, her student.

It was hard to remember anything except that she wanted him. And that she could never have him.

Nicholas exited his carriage behind Rage and looked around at the neighborhood. They were still in a more middle-class place, for it would be dangerous to dismount from such a fine vehicle in the midst of squalor and depravity. That was only asking for attention and trouble of the worst kind.

It was better to walk the last short distance and appear to be just two blokes. Later they could meet the carriage back in the safety of this place.

"What's the plan?" Rage asked as they set out on their way toward the bars and gambling hells and brothels of the squalid underground. It was a short walk, and they crossed the distance briskly.

"We'll split," Nicholas said.

As they passed the unspoken line between the middle-class neighborhoods and the squalor of the lower, he shifted his attention. He felt every stare of every man as they walked by, was aware of the street urchin and the lightskirt who were huddled in a doorway. *This* was living, or at least being alive. Awareness, danger, uncertainty, they all fed him.

Only tonight they felt a little less filling.

"Where are you going to go?" Rage asked as they avoided a drunk who had passed out on the cobblestones in the gutter.

"That whore who thought she knew Jane's brother mentioned something about Hannigan's," Nicholas said. "It may be nothing, but since it's the worst gambling hell in the city, I may find something there."

"And what about me?" Rage asked. "Should I follow up at the opium dens?"

"Yes, but be careful," Nicholas said with a shudder. The idea of being so out of control of one's body troubled him more than any other. "You know how desperate those fools can be. If the opium hounds think you have anything that can help them pay for another hit, they'll try to take it with no thought to the value of your life."

Rage nodded. "You be careful, too. Your face isn't unknown. There are some who would love to injure or kill the biggest pugilist in the underground. I'll see you at dawn back at the house."

Nicholas nodded, and the two men exchanged a quick glance before he turned down one street and Rage continued on his way. Although much of the action wouldn't start in the hells and bars until after eleven or twelve, Nicholas was meeting

Jane at that time, so he would depart early. Luckily he could depend on Rage to uncover information discreetly. He would just do the best he could with the time he had.

Thoughts of Jane intruded as he continued down the street. *Their* time was severely limited. Tonight was all they had left, and then they would be finished. Oh, he would see her at balls and soirees. They might even say a polite hello. But that would be the extent of their interaction.

With a shake of his head, Nicholas stopped outside Hannigan's, a seedy, run-down gambling hell that had been thrown together in the burned-out shell of an old warehouse. He gave the guard at the door a nod, and the man sized him up in an instant before he motioned him inside.

The first thing that hit Nicholas was the stench. The smell of burned wood mingled with sweat and worse. The gambling halls were called hells, and when Nicholas looked around at this one, he felt the moniker fit. Men huddled in small groups, playing rounds of various card and dice games. Many had the haunted look of opium fiends, well on their way to utter destruction.

Others still had an air of wealth around them, although by the time they descended to a place like this, most of their money and valuable property had been lost. Now they were reduced to gambling with horses, clothing . . . even the virtues of their sisters and wives and daughters.

Desperation was the word of the day here, and it turned Nicholas's stomach. He stepped a few paces inside and was immediately approached by a tall brute of a man. With a quick glance, Nicholas sized him up. The goliath had the height and reach advantage on him, but his lumbering movements were slow and sluggish. In a fight, Nicholas was reasonably certain he could get the better of him if he avoided fists with his speed.

"Two pounds to play," the monster said without preamble, his voice so deep that it reverberated in Nicholas's belly.

He dug in his pocket and drew out the fee. It was so little, but to the men in this state it was a small fortune. And most would lose even more blunt before the night was over.

"If I give you five more, perhaps you can provide me with some information," he said with an air of boredom. He didn't want to appear too eager.

The man stared at him a long moment, face placid and unemotional. "Maybe. Maybe not."

Nicholas drew out the money and slid it into the man's hand. "A man named Marcus Fenton."

The giant said nothing as he pocketed the blunt.

With a scowl, Nicholas withdrew Jane's miniature and held it out. "That's the one. Know of him? Or know someone who does?"

"Lots of blokes come in here," the man said

with a shrug of one great shoulder. "Hard to say. But Flint over there might know."

He motioned to a skinny, dirty man who was crouching on the floor, playing dice while he loudly carried on a conversation that Nicholas couldn't understand from across the room.

"Thank you," he said as he moved toward the small group where the man called Flint was playing.

As he neared them, he stopped to listen. To his horror, he realized the man wasn't talking to his companions, but to himself. His sickly, thin voice went on and on, words streaming together in a diatribe that included thoughts on the game, as well as the king, a dog that he spoke to but didn't exist, and a woman named Agnes.

"Shit," Nicholas muttered as he came closer. If this man knew anything about Marcus, it would be virtually impossible to access that information from his broken mind.

"You Flint?" he asked as he drew near.

"Flint. Flint is me," the skinny man said, rocking gently before he tossed the dice again. The other men didn't even look up or acknowledge Nicholas.

"I want to talk to you," he said, using a firm, even tone.

The man looked up at him briefly, but there was no lucidity in his gaze. He could have been looking at air for all he registered.

"Flint is me," he repeated. "Flint."

"Someone said you might know a man named Marcus Fenton. This man." Nicholas held out the miniature.

All three men glanced at the locket, and Nicholas stiffened. It was a risk, putting the silver jewelry out in public where someone might become more interested in its value than the pictures within.

"Fenty," Flint cackled. "Pretty Fenty Fenton."

Nicholas's nostrils flared at the other man's stench. Frustration clawed at him. He wasn't certain if Flint was just rambling or if there truly was a flicker of recognition when he looked at the small portrait.

"Bloke looks familiar," said one of Flint's companions, eyeing Nicholas with caution. "Wha's it worth to ya?"

Nicholas turned his attention to the other man. Although he wasn't as far gone as his mad companion, he was equally dirty and his hair was wild. Again, Nicholas wasn't certain if there was some truth to the statement that he recognized Marcus, or if it was just an attempt to get desperately needed money.

"Depends on the information," Nicholas said, cool. "Give me a little and we'll see."

" 'E used to come in here with Flint, maybe a year or so ago," the other man said with a motion in Flint's direction.

The timeline of the man's statement matched. "Have you seen him since?"

"Naw. He been gone for a long time now." The man tilted his head with expectation.

Nicholas reached into his pocket and drew out money. "That's worth five. Your friend won't be able to tell me more, will he?"

The other man chuckled, his laugh dark with smoke and sickness. "Flint's been gone in his mind a long time, but sometimes we can get 'im to remember. Hey, Flinty. Remember Fenton? Pretty Boy Fenton?"

"Fenty dead." Flint smiled up at Nicholas. "Dead, dead, dead, dead . . ."

He went on, repeating the word over and over until he was close to hysterics. His friend shrugged almost apologetically, and Nicholas tossed the man another five pounds as he turned away.

Dead. Flint might be mad, but he was also probably right. If Marcus Fenton *had* truly been frequenting a place like this and keeping company with men like these . . . it likely meant his desire for opium and gambling and God knew what other vices was out of control. Death was inevitable for men in those situations.

His stomach turned as he made his way to the door of the establishment. None of what he'd seen or heard was proof of Marcus's death, of course. The word of a crazy man and a dirty gambler weren't anything to base a final judgment upon, but it was certainly evidence that Jane's cousin had been right when he declared her brother dead.

Nicholas burst out into the dark, cool evening and sucked in several long breaths. The sooty air around him was only slightly less filthy than that inside, but it felt fresh in comparison.

He thought of Jane, so hopeful, so dedicated to finding her lost brother that she was willing to put her own life and happiness on hold. If she had been here tonight, if she had seen and heard what he had uncovered . . . he could only imagine her reaction.

It hadn't taken much of an acquaintance with her for him to realize just how bound Jane had become to her quest for Marcus. In some way, it kept her going. The idea that she wasn't all alone, that she could save her brother and somehow make things right again, was all she thought she had. She wouldn't even consider pursuing marriage or a life of her own until she had done so.

And now he was going to have to tell her that it was very likely she didn't even have that anymore. That with every bit of evidence, with every person he spoke to who had any tiny knowledge of her brother, the more Nicholas thought Marcus was gone. Dead in a gutter where he would have been buried like a rat when the street patrols found him.

Lost to her forever.

He shut his eyes briefly, trying not to imagine

Jane's pain when he told her that truth. When he opened them again, he found he was no longer alone in the street. Two men had come out of the shadows, or perhaps even followed him from the hells.

Nicholas stiffened. In his utter focus on Jane he had done the one thing he hadn't been so foolish as to do for years. He had forgotten his surroundings. And now the two grinned at him, rotten teeth exposed.

One withdrew a knife.

"'Ello guv. You know, I was tryin' to figure out who you was the whole time you was traipsin' about the hell, flashin' that pretty locket and passin' out money. And then I got it. You're that boxer they call Stone."

"That's right," Nicholas said, circling slowly in order to get a wall at his back so he couldn't be attacked from behind. "What of it?"

"Not anything," continued the man with the knife. "I just always wondered if I could beat a man like you. And I wondered if you could beat two men." He tilted the knife back and forth in a menacing fashion. "And if you could beat a blade."

Nicholas sneered. "Let's find out, shall we?"

Chapter 19

J ane climbed out of the unmarked carriage and looked up at Nicholas's house. Tonight was the last time she would come here. The last time they would be alone.

Despite herself, that thought made her stomach sink and her eyes sting with tears that she blinked back violently. She could not, *would* not allow herself to be so maudlin and foolish. Whatever else had transpired between them, she and Nicholas had made a bargain. Tonight she would complete her terms. That was all there was to it.

With a deep breath, she began to make her way toward the house, each step feeling as if it weighed a hundred stone. She reached for the door when she heard a sound behind her. A hired hack pulled up to where the carriage Nicholas arranged for her had just departed.

Jane swallowed hard and quickly looked for a place to hide. She ducked behind the nearest bush and peeked out to see who could be visiting Nicholas at this late hour.

To her surprise, when the door opened, it was Nicholas himself who exited the vehicle. Staggered out was more like it. The driver didn't even hesitate. As soon as his passenger was on the ground, he took off around the corner. The moment he was gone, Nicholas tipped forward with a grunt.

Jane came out of her hiding place and moved toward him, irritation making her spine stiff. Their last night together, the one lesson when she needed him to be balanced, and he was *drunk*.

"On your feet, then," she snapped as she came to a stop before him. "Come on, my lord."

Nicholas was still on his hands and knees and he looked up at her, his piercing blue eyes cutting right down through her anger and into her heart. He smiled.

"Well, at least I get to see angels," he muttered, more to himself than to her.

"What are you going on about?" Jane asked, irritation lingering despite his irresistible draw. "How much did you drink?"

She bent to help him up and touched wetness on his dark jacket. Lovely. She yanked her hand back and gasped in horror. In the moonlight, she saw her fingers were tainted red with blood.

"Nicholas," she cried out, dropping to her knees. "Is this your blood or someone else's?"

He grabbed for her arm and tried to get up. She braced herself and rose with him, steadying him even though he outweighed her by a great deal.

"Some of it is someone else's," he said as they began to limp toward the house. "But the lion's share is my own, I'm afraid. He cut me pretty deep. It's the blow to my head that really troubles me, though."

"Oh God," Jane breathed as she pounded on the door, leaving little bloody marks behind as a reminder.

The door opened, and Mrs. Fieldframe stood inside. She gave the two of them a bitterly disapproving look, but then the blood drained from her face and she opened the door wide.

"Great God, Miss Jane! What has happened to Lord Stoneworth?"

They got into the kitchen in a series of stumbling steps, and Nicholas collapsed into a wooden chair with another pained moan.

"Nothing to be frightened by, I assure you, ladies," he said with a little smile, but to Jane it seemed a terribly weak version. "A bit of a scuffle and someone wasn't playing fair. A cut on the shoulder and perhaps the leg. And a blow to the head."

"I'll fetch Gladwell," Mrs. Fieldframe said as she scurried from the room.

Jane stared at Nicholas, so pale and off kilter, even as he sat perfectly still on the kitchen chair.

She grabbed for a rag and moved toward him to wipe his brow. If he was cut, that wound would need to be cleaned and dressed. She leaned down and began to unbutton his coat.

"What happened, Nicholas? How on earth were you hurt?"

He shrugged and then winced as the coat shifted against his shoulder. "Just went into the underground and wasn't paying attention. It was my own foolish fault. A man with a knife and his remarkably strong little friend decided they wanted to challenge the great boxer, but they evened the score with a knife and some kind of table or chair. At least it felt wooden when it hit me."

"My God, Nicholas," Jane breathed as she peeled the jacket away and revealed a bloody shirt beneath. "You could have been killed!"

He nodded as she tugged at the buttons of his shirt and peeled that away, as well. A gash marred the perfectly rounded muscles of his shoulders.

"Indeed. But you should see the two of *them* now," he joked.

Jane didn't laugh as she pressed the cloth against his shoulder to slow the bleeding. Before she could say anything further, Gladwell and several footmen rushed into the room with Mrs. Fieldframe close behind.

When the servants saw their injured master, the room erupted in voices and calls for more help. But Gladwell's words boomed above them all.

"Martin, fetch the doctor immediately. And Humphrey, help me get His Lordship to his bed."

Nicholas got to his feet so suddenly that the room fell utterly silent. "No doctor," he belted out before he reached up to touch his head. He blinked a few times. "No doctor. A doctor could spread word around, and that would be bad for Jane and for my already tarnished reputation. Find Rage. He's still in King's Crossing."

A few of the footmen gasped as Nicholas said the neighborhood. Jane shot her gaze at him. It must be a very bad one, indeed.

"Where, sir?" one of them asked.

"The opium dens, I believe. Two or three of you should go and be armed. Bring him back, he knows how to stitch a wound." As the men ran off to do as he had ordered, Nicholas sank back down. "Mrs. Fieldframe, we'll need clean rags, both damp and dry, also brandy. And Gladwell, I *will* take your offer of help to my chamber."

Jane stood back as everyone sprang into action. She wasn't needed, but she didn't want to leave. Not while Nicholas was hurt. Not until she knew he would be all right.

As a footman and the butler helped Nicholas up the short flight of stairs that led from the kitchen, he looked at her over his shoulder.

"Aren't you coming?" he asked, his pale face still intense and handsome. "I would like you there."

Relief flooded Jane as she raced to follow the men. They moved up the stairs slowly, but Nicholas's steps were even and he seemed to hold a majority of his weight on his own, which Jane took as a good sign. Once they reached the room, she waited outside for a few moments while the male servants helped Nicholas out of his bloody trousers.

The door opened and Gladwell stepped out, holding an armload of ruined clothing. His face was pale with worry as he nodded to her briefly and then hurried off, she assumed to destroy the items. She certainly never wanted to see that thin, worn jacket ever again.

Stepping inside, she was disappointed to see a footman still moving about the room, lighting candles, moving items, almost more restlessly pacing than performing any real duties.

She turned her attention to the bed. Nicholas lay there, pale on the white sheets. His chest was bare except for the strip of linen cloth that he was holding over the wound on his shoulder. She could see blood was already beginning to seep through the fine fabric. With a shiver she moved closer. One tanned leg was out of the bedclothes as well, and she held back a cry of worry when she saw yet another gash across Nicholas's muscular thigh.

"Humphrey, will you be so kind as to help Gladwell?"

Nicholas's voice drew Jane's attention to his

face. He was speaking to the servant but watching her, and his intense scrutiny in the face of her raw emotion made her blush.

The footman nodded and rushed from the room, shutting the door behind him.

Although they had been alone dozens of times, suddenly Jane felt awkward and uncertain. She fingered the edge of the sheet restlessly, avoiding Nicholas's stare as best she could. It was difficult when the heat of it blazed on her like the roaring fire.

"Your servants adore you, you know. Despite all bad beginnings," she managed to choke out.

Nicholas chuckled. "Do they? Gladwell spent the entire time he was assisting me berating me for my foolhardy behavior."

"He was pale when he left the room. And poor Humphrey just wanted to do *something* to help you." She moved a step toward him. "As do I."

Nicholas reached out a hand and took hers, tugging her even closer. "Look at me, Jane."

She slowly did so and found, to her horror, that tears had welled up in her eyes. One made its way to her cheek, and Nicholas frowned as he wiped it away with his thumb.

"It's a scratch, darling. Nothing more."

She shook her head. "When I realized you had been hurt—when I saw you lying there—" She sniffled. "I couldn't help but think of all the people I had lost. I didn't want to lose you, too."

Surprise flowed over Nicholas's face, smoothing the harsh lines as it mingled with pleasure. His fingers slid up from her cheek and found their way into her hair. He cupped her scalp and gently urged her ever closer. She didn't resist, but melted against him and pressed her mouth to his.

So many times they had kissed and it had been a skirmish of sorts. A chess match, a war, a battle of resistance and surrender.

But this kiss was much different. There was a gentleness in his touch, a warmer, closer feeling to being in his arms.

And Jane realized in that moment that she was in love with him.

The surprise of that feeling, as it floated through her mind and overtook all other emotion, made her jolt back. He let her go instantly, watching her as she backed away. He was all but expressionless, and she tried to make herself as much.

How could she love him? How was that even possible? She had long given up on that notion, especially after her father's death and her decision to refuse her cousin's help. Love had seemed so out of reach then. So selfish.

And yet now she couldn't deny it and she didn't want to.

"Jane?" he said, his tone even.

She opened her mouth to speak, but before she could, the door to the bedchamber opened. She spun around to face the intruder, uncertain if she was pleased for the interruption or not. It was Rage Riley, and her heart pounded with relief.

"What were you thinking, taking on two men, and one with a knife?" Rage asked as he strode into the room bearing a small leather case, a pile of rags, and a bowl of warm water. "You are an ass, Stone."

Nicholas shrugged. "I didn't exactly take them on as much as I was attacked by them. But I appreciate your concern."

Rage spared her a glance. "He always was too cocky." He snapped the case open and revealed a little sewing kit. "You might not want to stay for this, Miss Jane."

She shook her head. "No, I want to help."

Rage stared at her for a long moment, then sent a brief glance toward Nicholas before he nodded. "Very well. Take this water, would you, love? And the towels, that's a girl. Just hand me what I ask for."

He moved past her to examine both the wounds Nicholas had received. "Not but a scratch, either one. I'll be finished in a moment."

Nicholas sent Jane a glance over Rage's shoulder as if to say, *I told you so,* but remained silent. Jane moved closer, handing Rage any item he required, from thread to a cloth to the bandages he bound over the stitching when he was finished.

"There, good as new, with only a couple new scars for your future." Rage put his kit away.

"I'll be certain to tell everyone I got them in a mighty battle, not just a foolish encounter in an alley that I should have been more ready for," Nicholas said as he moved his injured shoulder with a wince.

"You know better than to not pay attention to your surroundings, especially there," Rage scolded, sounding more like a worried mother than a dangerous pugilist. Jane couldn't help but smile at the banter between the two. "They said you hit your head."

Nicholas nodded. "Had something broken over it, actually. I was dizzy as hell for the first half hour or so, but I've been better since I got into the bed."

"Still," Rage said as he moved toward the door. "Best try to stay awake for the night if you can. To be safe."

"I'm sure I can find something to do," Nicholas said, his gaze moving to Jane.

She shifted, a flutter of intense awareness and desire awakening in her lower belly. He was teasing, or at least teasing in part, but his implication that she would stay with him hit her hard. She loved this man. Now that the shock had worn off, she couldn't deny the truth of it. And tonight might very well be the last they had together. They would each return to their own worlds and be parted.

So if tonight was all she had, wasn't she foolish

if she threw it away? Wouldn't she regret it if she left without taking every moment she could? And God knew, she had enough regrets about the past as it was. She didn't need any more.

"I'm sure you will," Rage said with a quick nod to Jane before he departed, shutting the door firmly behind him.

She moved to Nicholas's side, perching herself on the high edge of the big bed. Without asking leave, she took his hand and laced her fingers through his.

"Why do you need to stay awake all night?" she asked softly, watching how his rough fingers engulfed her own, feeling the strength and warmth in his palms. She wanted to memorize every scar and line of them.

He seemed mesmerized by the sight of their entangled fingers as well, for he watched them as intently as she did.

"A serious head injury can be deadly if you sleep too soon," he explained. "I don't think I have one, nor does Rage or he would have stayed, but it's best to be safe."

Jane shook her head as she lifted her gaze to his face. "You say these things so matter-of-factly. You lived in quite a world."

He nodded. "I did. There was danger and uncertainty there, but it made me feel alive."

"And could have killed you at any moment," Jane pointed out, smoothing her fingers against his skin as she spoke. "You should find something else to make you feel alive."

He sat up until they were nose to nose. "What do you suggest, Jane?"

She didn't pause to think or ponder the consequences. Instead, she tilted her head and kissed him. His arms came around her, flattening her breasts to his chest, and they both moaned in unison.

The kiss rapidly spun out of control as her hands met around his broad back and her fingers dug into the smooth flesh. She was hungry for him, and desperate to assure herself that he was unharmed.

And in some way, she wanted to express her love for him. Not in words, for that would only complicate the situation, but in her touch. In her surrender.

It might be the only chance she got.

If he sensed her desperation, Nicholas made no attempt to pull away from it. In fact, he maneuvered closer, forcing her further onto the bed, almost into his lap. He devoured her mouth, sucking her in and holding her captive with the sensual stroke of his rough tongue on hers.

Just when she thought she could die from the pleasure of the kiss, he went further. His mouth glided away from hers, moving down her throat as he urged her up on her knees, straddling his prone form beneath the sheets, her skirts bunched between them.

His mouth continued down, heating the delicate skin of her throat to her collarbone and finally to the edge of her scoop-necked gown where the swell of her breasts just peeked over the top. He cupped each one, lifting them as he blew hot air through the inexpensive fabric to heat the sensitive nipples beneath.

Jane's hips bucked forward, pressing into his chest, as pleasure unlike any she had ever known careened through her, as wildly out of control as the beating of her heart.

"I'm sorry," she panted. "I don't want to hurt you."

He looked up at her as he slid his mouth away from her breast. "Hurt me? Angel, trust me when I say that there is no pain."

He found the buttons around the back of her gown as he spoke, and suddenly the fabric gaped around her waist and tangled at her wrists. He didn't allow her to pull free before he returned his hot mouth to its place against her breast. This time, though, there was no heavy fabric to separate them. Her chemise was thin, a worn silk left over from before her father's death.

The wet heat of his tongue cut through it, and suddenly she felt every moment, every breath. Any lingering sense of hesitation left her. Whatever happened tonight, whatever happened afterward, it would be worth it.

She shrugged away from the loose arms of her gown, freeing her hands so that she could glide them along Nicholas's bare chest. He hissed in a harsh breath when she did that, his eyes shutting and his head dipping back over his shoulders for a brief moment.

"Careful," he admonished softly. "You don't know what you're inviting."

"I know *exactly* what I'm inviting," she murmured back as she pressed her mouth to the curve of his throat. "And I don't want to be careful. Not anymore. Not with you."

His eyes came open and he stared at her, unblinking, for what felt like an eternity. She could feel him fighting a war between desire and the very gentlemanly hesitations she herself had instilled in him. For the first time, she prayed her lessons hadn't stuck.

She smiled when he glided his fingertips up her bare arms and slipped her chemise straps away, baring her breasts. She shimmied and got the dress and undergarments out from under her, kicking them away so that she was naked before him except for her stockings and little worn kid boots.

"My God, you are more beautiful than I could have ever imagined," he whispered, his voice dark and husky. "And trust me, I have an exquisite imagination."

She blushed as his warm hands cupped her naked breasts. He kneaded the tender flesh there, strummed his rough thumbs over her nipples until they tingled and ached with pleasure.

"Normally I would be a bit more in charge of this," he continued before he leaned forward and stroked his tongue over her nipple lazily. "But with my injuries, I'm afraid I'm at your mercy."

She almost laughed at the idea of Nicholas being at *anyone's* mercy, but he cut off her giggle with another sucking taste of her flesh.

"Tell me what to do," she whispered. "And I will."

Chapter 20

~~~~~ ⌒⌒ ~~~~~

Nicholas's eyes widened. Jane had absolutely no idea just how many fantasies she was unlocking with those innocent words. And he had to remember that they *were* innocent, despite the fact that her goddess body was calling out to him.

She might think she wanted this, but if he took her maidenhead it would make her life infinitely more complicated. And his. So he had to keep some control.

Something he would have been fully capable of with any other woman. But tonight it was going to take far more effort than ever before.

Still, he couldn't deny himself a taste of her, a moment with her. He needed it too much now. It was practically in his blood.

"Take off the rest," he managed past dry lips.

She nodded before she slid down from his bed. He nearly strangled on his moan as she put a foot up on the edge of the nearest chair and unlaced her boots. Damn, but she had no idea what a pretty picture she made, her naked body curved over in profile.

The stockings went next, rolling down creamy thighs until she was utterly naked and his cock was throbbing with anticipation of pleasure he couldn't allow.

"Come into bed with me," he said softly, pulling the covers back.

Her eyes widened as he revealed himself to her. She had the same expression she'd had the last time she saw him naked. In this very bed. When he had made her come with just his fingers.

God, how he was going to enjoy doing that again tonight. None of his wounds hurt him in the slightest anymore, nothing else in the world mattered. Just Jane.

She came up into the bed, covering his body with her own for a brief moment before she began to slide over to the other side. He caught her hips, holding her still with her legs entangled in his, her breasts rubbing his chest, her red-brown hair tumbling over his skin like a silken waterfall.

"Stay," he managed with difficulty. "Stay here."

She nodded and shifted her weight so that she could lie fully against him. He groaned with pleasure as she settled against his chest and he felt the full, soft length of her body.

"I promise you," he whispered against her hair. "That I will not take you, no matter how much I may want to. I promise to give you pleasure, but I won't take away your innocence."

Jane lifted up to look at him and her face was filled with surprise, desire, and something even deeper. An emotion he couldn't read, even though she had always been an open book to him.

"Don't you know what I want, Nicholas?" she whispered, touching his face gently. "Don't you know I am offering my innocence to you with no qualms, no hesitation? Don't you know that I want you to be the one to take it, tonight?"

He shook his head. A little more temptation and he wouldn't be able to maintain whatever thin thread of gentlemanly fabric she had instilled in him.

"I can't do that—" he began.

She covered his lips with her fingertips to hush his refusal. "Tonight is the last one we will have together. I don't want to waste it. Not after seeing you injured. I have wasted so much time in my life already. I refuse to regret *you*."

She lifted herself and her legs came open, straddling his lap until his erection nudged the sweet slickness of her body. He gripped his fingers into fists against the sheets as hot pleasure cut through him.

"Please," she whispered, close to his ear. "Please, Nicholas."

"Yes," he finally said, his resolve broken under her innocent, yet powerful, seduction. "But not yet. Not until you are so ready that you are begging me."

Her eyes first widened, then fluttered shut when he placed his palm between her breasts and slowly slid downward. Over the flat plane of her belly, then lower still until his fingers found the wet heat of her body. He stroked his fingers through the folds, eliciting a sigh of pleasure from her parted lips.

"Did you like it when I touched you here?" he murmured, finding it hard to formulate words.

She nodded, pink darkening her cheeks. "I thought of that morning so many times since then. I dreamed of it."

"So did I," he admitted as he teased the hard bud of nerves hidden within the silky softness. "And I thought of something more. I wanted to taste you then, Jane."

Her eyes flew open in surprise. "T-taste?"

He nodded. "Let me."

"I would let you do anything right now," she whispered, her voice cracking with desire and sweet anticipation.

He urged her forward as he slid down farther on the pillows. Finally the juncture of her thighs was close enough and he spread her open again and pressed his mouth to her.

Jane clutched at the headboard, her eyes widening as she finally understood what Nicholas meant by *taste*. Only *taste* didn't fully describe what he was doing with his wicked mouth. He teased. He tormented. He explored. He awoke every part of her that she hadn't even known existed. He made her a wanton.

Soon her hips rocked in time with the slide of his tongue and her body clenched. He cupped her backside, holding her steady as he tortured her with pure and exquisite pleasure. And then he slipped a finger into her empty body, added a thumb to the place where she tingled and trembled most, and she was lost.

Her body was no longer her own to control. Nicholas had stolen her breath, her pleasure, and her heart. She cried out, her voice wild and husky in the quiet room, and she no longer cared if anyone heard her. For the first time in a long time, nothing else in the world mattered.

Her body trembled as the pleasure faded and she slowly made her way back down the length of his body, being careful not to jar his injuries any more than had already been done. Back on his lap, straddling the hard length of his erection, she caught her breath. Now was the moment. Now he would claim her.

Only he held back. He was positioned perfectly. Just the slightest lift of his hips and he would be inside her. But he only stared up at her, lips glistening from her pleasure, eyes bright with his own desire.

"If I do this, it might hurt you. In more ways than one."

"I don't care," she whispered, and she meant it. Then she took the choice away from him by positioning herself a little differently and gliding down.

Her body accepted him slowly, stretching to accommodate his hardness and size. It was not painful, it was not unpleasant, only strange. Strange to think that they were joined as one body now. That he was hers as much as she was his.

"Here it is, sweet," he groaned, his neck straining as he entered her. "Hold on to me."

She did as he ordered, clinging to his forearms as he thrust up and filled her completely. The pain burst, causing her to gasp out a reaction. But as Nicholas held steady, watching her, waiting, it began to fade.

"I'm sorry," he murmured, shaking his head. "I'm sorry."

She cupped his cheeks and leaned down to press her mouth to his. He returned the kiss with passion just as powerful as they had shared before. More powerful.

"I wanted this," she said when they broke apart. "I still do."

"Then let me make it good for you," he said, and slowly eased himself into a seated position.

The covers that had been wrapped around them fell away, but Jane wasn't cold as Nicholas began to lift his hips, thrusting himself in and out of her body with slow, steady movements. She found herself grinding down in response, rubbing herself against him with no shame, reveling in the feel of his body deep inside her own.

The pain was gone. The world outside the room was gone. The only thing she saw or felt or acknowledged was the way they touched. The pleasure as he rocked into her. The feeling of wrapping her legs around his back, of lifting herself to grasp for even more pleasure. And when it came, it tore her even further from reality, making her body shake and arch while she called out his name again and again and again.

And as he called out hers in response, they fell back onto the pillows and all was still.

Nicholas had never been much for holding a woman after he took his pleasure. Women had spent the night in his bed, of course, but he had almost always slipped into immediate sleep and not bothered to wrap himself around them and talk.

With Jane, as with everything else, it was different. As she settled her head into the crook of his good shoulder, he let out a contented sigh. He could easily stay in this fantasy world forever. It wasn't possible, but it was a lovely dream nonetheless.

Jane smoothed her hand along the muscles of his belly, absently tracing a pattern against the skin there.

"Tonight when you were hurt, you were looking for information on my brother, weren't you?"

Nicholas looked down at her. The light in the room was dimming as the fire died, but he could still see the crease of her frown.

"I was in a bad neighborhood," he said, not lying, but avoiding her question.

While he was injured and while Jane writhed in his arms, he had allowed himself to forget what he had uncovered about Marcus. Now he wasn't willing to share it and ruin this bliss.

"But Rage was in the opium dens," she said, glancing up and spearing him with a gaze filled with trust. "And that is where Marcus might have been."

He hesitated, but then nodded.

Her frown grew deeper. "I'm sorry you were hurt because of my request of you."

He cupped her chin and tilted her face so she had to look into his eyes. "I was hurt because I was foolishly distracted."

"By what?"

He dropped his hand away. "What do you mean by what?"

"Well, Rage was right. You've been in that underground world for so long. I cannot imagine you being so distracted as to not look for an attack. What was on your mind that would so trouble you?"

Nicholas bit his tongue. He couldn't tell her he'd been thinking about breaking her heart. It would only feed her guilt and ruin their remarkable evening.

Plus it would lead to more questions. And ultimately he would have to confess what he'd heard from the gambling opium fiend. And what his ramblings suggested about Marcus's whereabouts would break this amazing, unexpected woman. Until he had more proof, Nicholas wasn't prepared to do that.

Jane seemed to sense his hesitance and tilted her head to the side. "Very well, you do not have to tell me what was on your mind. But while in the underground, did you at least discover anything about my brother?"

Again, Nicholas was speechless. Did he lie outright or tell the truth?

"No," he finally said, making the easier choice and hating himself for it. "I did not."

She settled her head back on his shoulder. "I want you to know I will understand if your dedication to the project changes after tonight. After your injury, and with your—"

"Stop." He cut her off with the one word, and

she glanced up at him again. "I said I would help you and I will."

"I have faith in that," she whispered.

Faith. He almost laughed. He hadn't had faith in anyone, nor had anyone trust in him, for so long he could hardly recall it. And now Jane offered him faith and trust even while he lied to her.

"You deserve to be happy," he said softly, brushing hair away from her face. He longed to change the subject. "Are you ready for my mother's ball?"

Jane frowned, but it was a far less troubled expression than it had been when they spoke of her brother. "Almost. Tomorrow I have my last fitting for my gown. But I am more worried about you, Nicholas. Tonight we were to train so you could dance at her ball."

"Well, that will not happen," he said with a sigh. "I much prefer what we *did* do, at any rate."

She laughed and he bathed in it, letting it clean his soul after the troubling night he had endured.

"You are a cad, sir," she said with a little pinch against his stomach.

He laughed with her, swatting her hand away playfully until he finally caught her chin and brought her in for a kiss that took her laughter and his breath away.

When they parted, she immediately turned her face. He frowned. There was a sense of sadness in her tonight. A feeling that she was pulling away from him, even though they had been as intimate as two people could be.

"Why do you move away from me?" he whispered, pulling her closer. "Why do you turn your face?"

She shrugged. "In two days, you will debut at the ball, and if all goes well, you will be accepted."

He nodded, still uncertain as to why that fact would trouble her. He knew his own reasons for the dread that made him nauseous when he thought of it, but not hers.

"Our training, our bargain, it ends tonight." She touched his face. "There is nothing else I can do for you."

He threaded his fingers into her hair, watching as the light played off her face. She was correct, of course. By the terms of their agreement, once he made that entrance back into Society, they would never meet in secret again.

His heart sank at the idea.

"I can think of a few more things you can do for me," he said, pushing away the emotions she inspired, but allowing the desire to come forward.

"What are they?" she asked, but he could see by the sparkle in her eyes that she already knew. And welcomed his touch.

"Let's start with this and see what happens," he murmured before he leaned down and kissed her.

Chapter 21

Jane shifted restlessly from one foot to the other as she looked around the crowded ballroom. When she nervously smoothed her hands over her gown, she felt silk instead of serviceable muslin, and that put her even more on edge.

For the first time in nearly a year, she was at a ball as a guest, not a servant.

Lady Ridgefield patted her arm and leaned closer. "Once again, my dear, I must say how lovely you look."

Jane blushed. "Thank you, my lady. It is all your doing and the others."

"No." Lady Ridgefield turned toward her and looked at her head on. "It is more than the dress or the style of your hair. There is something different about you tonight, actually it has been there for a few days now. A light from within you. A sparkle in your eyes. Like you have some kind of delightful secret."

Jane sucked in a breath and tried to keep her

face placid. If she had been lit from the inside as of late, it was because she *did* have a secret. And wonderful memories of the night she had spent in Nicholas's arms. Those memories were with her all the time now, vivid and wonderful.

She hoped they never lost their freshness since that night could never be repeated.

Lady Ridgefield turned away. "I want to apologize to you, my dear."

Jane was pulled from her fantasies in an instant. Lady Ridgefield was so flighty and silly it was rare for her to ever sound serious. But now she sounded dejected.

"Apologize? Whatever for?"

Her employer . . . *former* employer gave her a sheepish side glance. "I never even thought of bringing you out into Society until Lady Bledsoe brought the subject up. I merely kept you as my companion because I thought it was right, that I was helping you. But seeing you so happy as you make your return . . . it makes me realize just how selfish I was."

"My dearest Lady Ridgefield, how can you say that?" Jane caught her hand and drew the other woman away from the crowd. "You have been the kindest, most wonderful friend and employer I ever could have dreamed of having. I came to you with no references, no experience, and you took me on with naught but faith to go upon. I came to *you*." Jane blinked as tears stung her eyes.

Lady Ridgefield shifted, almost as if she were uncomfortable. "Yes. But you were not unhappy with me?"

"Of course not." Jane squeezed her hands. "And I never expected anyone to help me return to Society. I was not pining for it. I promise you."

That seemed to brighten the other woman, for she smiled. "Good. I admit that has been weighing on me the past few days. But now we are here and I vow you will be the center of all attention before this night is through. Or at least until Lord Stoneworth appears and takes it all."

Jane stiffened at the mention of Nicholas's name. They had not spoken since she slipped from his bed early the morning before. And yet he had been on her mind ever since. As the ball grew nearer, so did her anticipation. She would see him again. He had not yet arrived, but she was counting the moments.

"Will he be here tonight?" she asked, doing her best to appear innocent when she was desperate for any word of him.

Lady Ridgefield nodded. "I can only hope this reintroduction into Society will go better than the last. But his dear mother seems to think it will be well."

Before Jane could dig for more information, a voice cut through the crowed. "Why, is that Jane Fenton?"

She looked up to see Georgiana Mortimer

making her way through the groups of people toward her. They had come out into Society the same year and had even been friends. But Georgiana had not spoken, nor even looked at Jane since her father died. And now she was Countess St. James, married to a powerful and much older man.

Jane braced herself for the encounter.

"My dear, don't you look lovely? It is so nice to see you back at these events," her former friend said before she leaned forward and pressed a kiss to each of Jane's cheeks.

Jane stood in stunned silence for a moment, then briefly pondered reminding Georgiana that she *had* been at virtually every event the other woman had attended during the past year, but held her tongue.

Her silence didn't seem to affect Georgiana in the least, for she was already greeting Lady Ridgefield and babbling on about gowns or something equally frivolous.

"Do you remember Elizabeth and Hermione from our old group?" Georgiana continued, squeezing Jane's hands gently.

"Y-yes," she finally stammered.

Georgiana flashed a brilliant grin. "They are here tonight, as well. Elizabeth married a duke, you know. Or . . . he will be a duke once his father is dead. Poor Hermione is still unmarried, but I hear Marquis Waterbury is interested in her, though I seem to recall he danced with *you* a few times when we all came out. At any rate, we would love if you would come and talk to us. We're just over by the terrace doors there."

She motioned across the room to indicate where the other girls stood. Jane smiled, and the two waved simultaneously.

"I . . ." She hesitated.

Lady Ridgefield smiled. "Of course she will. What a wonderful chance to reacquaint yourselves."

"Excellent. I'll see you in just a moment, Jane. And good evening, Lady Ridgefield," Georgiana said before she swept off into the crowd.

Jane stared after her. When the young woman was out of earshot, she turned back to Lady Ridgefield in astonishment.

"None of them have even looked at me since . . . I cannot remember when. In fact, I think Hermione may have given me the cut direct right after my brother was declared dead and I told my cousin I would not take his money. Why would they—"

"You have powerful friends now," Lady Ridgefield said with a smile. "Lady Bledsoe, especially, has been praising you to the heavens. She is paving your way, my dear. And you should accept her help, for she has far more influence than I. Now go be with your friends and enjoy yourself. I shall come and do my chaperone duties later."

Jane nodded as her former employer gave

her a little shove toward the women across the room. As Jane dutifully made her way to them, her mind spun. It was somewhat humiliating that her acceptance was born from the praise of other women. And as she looked around the room, acknowledging unexpected hellos and smiles from those around her, Jane was surprised to find that she didn't feel like she belonged here anymore.

She didn't belong in either the servant world or the one she had been raised in. Just like Nicholas. He said over and over that he didn't belong in this world, although he had been willing to sacrifice everything he enjoyed and held dear to make the effort to fit in.

"There she is," Georgiana said, motioning Jane into her group. "You remember everyone, don't you?"

Jane nodded as the other women said hello and exchanged awkward hugs. Even though they were welcoming her, she couldn't help but feel a distance from them. After all, these women had all but forgotten she existed when she fell onto harder times. None had reached out to her or even given her common courtesy. Even now, she could see their friendliness was only caused by a desire to impress Jane's influential sponsors.

"I believe that is the prettiest dress in the room," Elizabeth, now Lady Comnouck, said with a smile that was almost sincere. "That color complements your eyes very nicely. But you were always one of the prettier girls in our set."

Jane glanced down at the dark blue dress she wore. Although she would never admit it, she had spent a good deal of time staring at herself in the mirror tonight after she had been dressed. It was like looking at a stranger. A princess.

"Thank you," she said with a blush. "It is a lovely gown."

"Indeed," Hermione said with a quick glance up and down Jane's frame. "I suppose Lady Ridgefield and Lady Bledsoe's money *can* do wonders."

Jane frowned at the catty remark and the other women quickly changed the subject as Hermione sipped her drink and stared off into the crowd with disinterest. Again their talk turned to frivolous things. Clothing and who was marrying whom. Jane had begun to allow her mind to drift off when a buzz in the crowd drew her attention.

"There he is," Elizabeth whispered, though her tone was anything but soft. "Is it a wager?"

"Who?" Jane asked, but already she knew why the crowd had begun to shift and move. An electric energy had entered the air, an awareness throughout her every pore that could only signal the arrival of one person.

Nicholas.

She craned her neck to see, and suddenly the crowd parted and there he was. She smiled as she thought of how much this was like the first time she saw him. And how little.

That night he had been feral, dark, dangerous. And he was still all those things, but he was dressed impeccably, he was shaved neatly, and his dangerous nature was tamed to the extent that most people would not even notice it because they were drawn to his other good qualities.

"It's Nicholas Stoneworth, your patron's son," Hermione provided with a sour expression. "We've been wagering over his failure tonight. I say he will make a spectacle of himself within the first hour. Elizabeth says two, and Georgiana here is very kind. She believes he'll last to midnight before he reveals his true nature."

Jane turned on the women with a gasp. Standing together, their necks craned to see over the crowd, their faces filled with joy at the potential for someone else's pain, they reminded her of a nest of vipers.

"What about it, Jane," Georgiana said with a giggle. "Will you throw in a pound?"

"She might not have a pound, Georgie," Hermione said, her cruel gaze falling on Jane.

"I have the money," Jane said softly. "But I wouldn't place a bet on his failure. In fact, I will bet you all *twenty* pounds that he succeeds beyond anyone's wildest imaginings. I will wager thirty that Hermione here is leaning on his arm, trying to catch his eye before the Season is over."

With that, she spun on her heel and left the gaping women behind. The moment her back was turned, she regretted her outburst. Making enemies was tantamount to spitting in the faces of Lady Bledsoe and Lady Ridgefield. But worse, it might cause talk about her relationship with Nicholas. Defending him so passionately was only bound to cause trouble.

Except that she couldn't let their nastiness stand. Not after he had worked so hard and long. Not after they had both sacrificed so much for his success.

She stopped at the edge of the dance floor and watched Nicholas surreptitiously. He was gliding into the room with grace, but now she recognized his movements as the calculations they were. He had the same subtle stance that he did the night he sparred with Rage. Waiting for an attack, planning a counter to it. Only this time, they were not physical battles.

He looked impeccable. He was wearing the waistcoat she had once complimented when she saw his newly designed clothing. The one that brought out the startling contrast of his bright, intense eyes. His jacket fit perfectly across broad shoulders. She watched closely to see if he was feeling any remnants of the attack on him earlier in the week, but he didn't so much as flinch as he stepped into the room and shook the hands of those around him.

And there were plenty of hands to shake. Jane smiled as man after man approached him, taking a moment to say their hellos. Nicholas's expression was perfect. Cool, detached, but not unfriendly. A far cry from the growling, half-drunk barbarian she had first seen across a room just like this one.

Lady Bledsoe stepped up to her son with a smile and said something. He laughed in response, and Jane found herself smiling along with him. He almost looked like he was enjoying this, though she knew his true feelings on gatherings of this kind.

Then his mother motioned to someone behind her, and a small group of young women stepped forward. Jane's heart sank as Nicholas kissed their hands and smiled as they were introduced. By the twittering giggles of the women and their blushes, it seemed that he would have no trouble in *that* realm, either.

Jane turned away, no longer as pleased by his triumphant return to Society as she had been. In fact, she felt . . . She wasn't sure what it was. It wasn't anger, and it wasn't jealousy. Well, perhaps a small bit of jealousy, but that wasn't the main thrust of the painful emotions that clouded her mind.

It was sadness.

She should have been happy for him. Their training had clearly been successful, at least at first blush. And she had no doubt Nicholas would continue to work toward respectability, if only to protect his brother's reputation. But she wasn't happy. For this night, this success he was finding here, it signaled the true end of the nights they had shared. The reality of the situation was becoming very clear to her. He would marry some woman just like those his mother had introduced him to a moment ago.

And Jane would become a footnote in his past. Another woman who had shared his bed for a brief night. At some point, he might not even recall her name.

She swallowed hard.

"I beg your pardon?"

With a start, Jane turned toward the male voice that had interrupted her reverie. A young man stood at her side, dark eyes friendly and open.

"I'm sorry, I suppose I was woolgathering," Jane said, remembering her manners.

"You are Jane Fenton, are you not?" the gentleman said. When Jane nodded, he continued, "I have been looking for your chaperone to be properly introduced, but I cannot wait a moment longer. I am Bertram Eggertan. I wondered if you would be willing to dance the next with me?"

Jane hesitated. Her heart was certainly not in the mood for dancing. She glanced one last time at

Nicholas. He was surrounded by ladies now and seemed quite engrossed by their conversation.

She straightened her shoulders. She and Nicholas Stoneworth were on very different paths now. It was how it had to be.

"Yes, Mister Eggertan. I would be most pleased to dance the next with you," she said as she held out her hand.

"Your party is quite a success," Nicholas said, taking a sip of his drink.

"As are you, my dear," his mother said with a smile.

Nicholas hesitated before he answered because his attention was drawn, just as it had been all night, to Jane. She was spinning across the dance floor in the arms of yet another gentleman. She looked to be having a good time, too. Which set his teeth on edge.

"Thank you," he finally managed to say, returning his attention to his mother. He forced a smile. "I am far from perfect. I think I offended Lord Glenamara when I mispronounced his name. And I'm certain I cursed in front of Lady Wilkshire."

His mother shrugged one shoulder. "You cannot be expected to know all over night. These things take time."

"As you well know." He winked at her. "Jane told me you have been aware of my doings all this time. Smart of you to keep her from telling me."

"Ah, Jane," Lady Bledsoe said on a sigh as her gaze slipped to the woman in question.

Which forced Nicholas to do the same. Thankfully she was finished with her latest conquest and was now standing with a small group of women, chatting quietly. He was pleased until two men approached with punch for her. He sighed.

"She is a dear girl," his mother said softly, but he felt her attention on him even as she continued to look at Jane. "I hope my influence can help her retain some position in Society. What do you think of her? You spent a great deal of time with her over the past few weeks, did you not?"

Nicholas stiffened as every moment of the time he'd spent with Jane flashed through his mind, but especially that last night when she had given him her body so sweetly.

"I have never known anyone like her in my life," he said softly. "She is a lady in every sense of the word. And a great friend to have."

"It sounds as though you were lucky to have her," his mother mused as she turned her stare back to him. "You know, she seems to be doing quite well in Society tonight. She has gained some acceptance and is catching the attention of a few men in the lower gentry."

"Good." He choked on the word. "She deserves every happiness."

"Indeed," his mother said softly. Then her smile brightened her face. "Now, you have not danced tonight and you must. Look, Jane has no partner and the waltz is to be played next."

Nicholas stared at his mother. She wasn't being particularly subtle about the fact that she was pushing him in Jane's direction. It surprised him. Surely she knew that Jane would need a respectable man to be fully accepted. And he would need a powerful woman for the same reasons.

"She is surrounded by admirers, Mama," he said.

"She is. But I'm certain if you pressed your suit, she would abandon them for you." His mother arched a brow and then turned to walk away.

Nicholas watched her go. She was right, of course. If he went and demanded a dance from Jane, none of those untitled ninnies holding court around her would stop him. But was that right? He was no gentleman, not in his heart. And they were.

Except he wanted to dance with Jane. He wanted his *first* dance to be with her. He found himself moving toward her, almost as if he were drawn to her by some unspoken power.

"Excuse me, gentlemen," he said as he shouldered his way into the group around her. They parted immediately, as did Jane's lips. And he saw all his own desire, all his own longing, mirrored in her eyes. "I believe this dance is mine."

Chapter 22

Jane's hand shook as she placed it in Nicholas's and they waited for the music to start. When he had asked . . . actually *demanded* that she dance with him, there had been no polite way to refuse. If a woman of *her* rank turned him down, it would cause no end of trouble for them both.

Of course, a large portion of her agreement wasn't because she wanted to protect either of their reputations. It was because she *wanted* to be here with him. And as the first strains of the waltz began, she let herself forget everything else and just feel what it was like to be in his arms.

"You have certainly been popular tonight, Jane," Nicholas said softly as they began to move to the music.

She blushed. "Not popular. I have only danced three times."

"Four," he corrected quietly. "I was counting. And you have been brought punch by five different men on four occasions."

Jane swallowed hard with the realization that he had been tracking her movements so closely.

"You have been popular yourself," she countered when she remembered how to speak. "There has scarce been a time when you were not surrounded by admiring women."

"I don't remember any of their names."

Nicholas suddenly executed a graceful movement, maneuvering them around another couple with ease. Jane's eyes widened.

"You are a wonderful dancer," she said in astonishment, for certainly *she* had not taught him the surety and grace he was displaying now. With a quick glance, she saw those around the edge of the dance floor watching them with approval.

"I am," he said with a cockiness that made her laugh. She thrilled at the fact that Nicholas retained some part of his true personality, despite all pressures for him to transform away from it.

"I am beginning to believe you did not need gentleman lessons after all," she said.

"Oh, but you are wrong," he said, pulling her just a fraction closer and quickening her heart in the process. "I did need them. I am afraid I still do. You see, when I am holding you, I have remarkably ungentlemanly thoughts."

Jane licked her suddenly dry lips, which elicited a small growl from Nicholas. Her body felt very heavy now. And it tingled madly in all the very worst places.

"Do you?" she squeaked.

He nodded slowly, his gaze never leaving hers. "I think I need some refresher courses. Will you meet me in the parlor off the second hallway in half an hour?"

Jane bit back a gasp. Utter temptation had just been laid at her feet, and yet she could not take it. Could she?

"My lord—" she began.

He shook his head. "I promise you, Jane, I just want to be near you." He paused with a sheepish smile. "And kiss you."

Jane flashed to all the wicked places he had kissed her a few nights ago. "Where?"

He laughed full-on this time, drawing even more attention to them. "Meet me," he said, his voice growing quiet again. "Please."

She nodded. She couldn't help herself. This man was too compelling to deny. Too tempting to refuse.

And what was the harm in one kiss?

Nicholas folded his arms as he stared across the parlor at his father. Hugh Stoneworth, Marquis Bledsoe was pacing the room, his handsome face dark with anger and disappointment. It was a common occurrence when they were together; Nicholas had come to expect it.

What he hadn't expected was how much it hurt him this time. He'd worked so hard to come up to his father's standards, and still it wasn't enough.

Nicholas tossed a quick glance at his mother and Lucinda, who had followed his father to the parlor when they saw him slip from the ballroom a few moments before. He hadn't even realized Lucinda was at the ball, but she had explained, before all hell broke loose, that she had merely been watching.

Checking up on him, was what she really meant. It would have stung if she hadn't then smiled at him with approval. At least one person in the room had some little faith in him. And his mother seemed to be leaning more toward approval than disapproval.

Of course all three of them would have been railing at him if they knew his true reason for escaping the crowd and finding refuge in this small, little-used chamber.

He'd been so anxious to meet with Jane that he had come early, and thank God. If the family had burst in when he was alone with her, it only would have made things worse.

"And what do you have to say for yourself?" his father snapped, rapping his knuckles on the side table near him.

Nicholas sighed as he dug in his pocket for a cigar. As he bit off the end and spit it toward the fire, he shrugged. "Tell me what you want to hear and I'm happy to say it."

"Oh, Nicholas," his sister-in-law breathed with a shake of her head. His mouth pinched at her drawn frown and the way his mother's eyes widened.

"You see, Marianne," his father said, turning to his wife with exasperation. "That is exactly what I mean. You may tell me all you like that the zebra has changed his stripes, but he is still a damned zebra."

"As opposed to the prize racehorse that your favorite son was?" Nicholas asked bitterly.

His father turned back on him, pain lighting in his eyes as strongly as anger. "Yes. That's right. You may dress better or tidy yourself up or even pretend at being polite, but you are still wild beneath it all. I've heard several reports of your behavior tonight that were enough to tell me you haven't changed. You still aren't—"

"Anthony?" Nicholas asked, low and dangerous. He met his father's stare full-on and saw the answer even before his father said it.

"Nicholas, Hugh!" his mother pleaded, a tear running down her face. "This will only become more bitter if you do not stop it now."

"But I never was, was I?" Nicholas asked, ignoring her interruption as he moved toward his father. "Never good enough. Never close to being what he was, no matter how I tried. So I stopped trying, Father. I became everything he wasn't. And it was glorious."

"Then why did you bother coming back?" his father snapped as he turned away. "If your life was so bloody perfect in that underground hell-hole where you think you were a god, why bother to come up to the surface?"

"Stop it!"

At first Nicholas was so wrapped up in the showdown with his father that he thought the feminine voice was his mother's. But once it registered, he realized it wasn't.

He was shocked to realize that it was Jane who had spoken.

Slowly, he turned to the door to find her standing inside. He nearly stumbled back with surprise. He assumed if she came to the room and saw it was occupied, she would have the sense to protect her reputation and slip away.

Instead, she stood before all four of them as if she had every right to be there. Her face was pale, especially against the dark silk of her gown. Her hands were fisted at her sides, trembling wildly, as were her full lips. She looked angry and pained and so deliciously beautiful that it took Nicholas's breath away.

"Who are you?" Hugh Stoneworth asked in that haughty tone only one of his rank could master. The one Nicholas had despised as long as he could remember. "That little girl my wife has taken under her wing? Be gone, this is none of your affair."

He dismissed her with a wave of his hand that would have made any other woman run. But not Jane. Nicholas watched in wonder as she denied his father's order and slammed the door behind her.

"It *is* my affair," she snapped, her tone as cold and regal as a queen's. "You asked your son why he came back here, and I would like to edify you with the answer he is too proud and too good to give you."

His father stepped back. Nicholas could have swallowed his tongue with the shock. His great and powerful father had actually stepped *back* from a woman who barely came to his shoulder and yet was controlling the room like a general.

"Nicholas came here because he loved his brother. He loved Anthony with a power you will probably never fully fathom."

Nicholas couldn't help the strangled groan that escaped his lips at those words. They were ones he hadn't said out loud to anyone in his family. Hadn't said out loud to anyone at all in a very long time. So hearing them from Jane, feeling their truth . . . was like a punch. And Jane seemed to understand that, for she shot him a briefly apologetic glance before she refocused on his father.

"Perhaps he behaved poorly at first. In our grief, we can do many things we later come to regret. But once he realized his actions would reflect poorly on his brother's wife and his children and his good name . . . *your* good name, Lord Bledsoe, he did his damnedest to change."

Now it was Lucinda who stiffened. Her pale face grew even more ghostly white and her eyes filled with tears. But when she looked at Nicholas, she smiled, and he could see that she was recalling their conversation that night so many days ago. Lucinda had set him on this path. Set him to finding Jane.

Another reason to be eternally grateful to her.

"Did his damnedest?" his father barked, and then gave a humorless laugh. "What would you know of that, girl?"

Jane clenched her fists at her sides. "More than you will ever know. He fought, long and hard, and surrendered so much of himself, and all in order to make *you* happy. But I can see just from watching you for five minutes that you shall *never* be happy no matter what he does. Because you aren't angry or disappointed with Nicholas. You are angry and disappointed that Anthony died."

Every person in the room gasped at her candor. Nicholas stepped forward, ready to come between the now purple marquis and the amazing woman who looked ready to go to battle right there in the parlor.

Her voice grew softer now, but lost none of its power. "I understand loss, my lord, God knows I do. And it is so easy to turn to anger and hatred when we are broken." She swiped at a tear. "But you have a son, Lord Bledsoe. You have a son right here who is alive and healthy, despite all recent events. Do not throw him away because you grieve the one you lost. All it will do is make you lose them both."

It seemed all of Jane's bluster and bravado went out of her in the instant she said the final words. As if she had woken from a dream, she shook her head and then stared up at the marquis with a sudden flicker of fear in her brown eyes.

But his father was simply staring at her, mouth agape, stunned into silence for the first time that Nicholas could recall. His mother was all but sobbing now, tears streaming silently down her face as she looked from father to son.

Finally, it was Lucinda who came forward, taking slow steps. The stark black of her mourning gown and the far-reaching sadness that seemed to permeate her very being was a harsh reminder of everything the family had lost.

She stopped in front of Jane and extended a hand.

"We have not met. I am Lucinda Stoneworth, Anthony's wife."

Jane swallowed hard before she held out a trembling hand. "A pleasure to meet you, my lady." As they shook, she said, "I hope I did not offend you."

Lucinda smiled. "To the contrary, I think you said what I have been thinking for six months."

She turned to Nicholas's father and gave him a sad smile as she reached up to pat his cheek with great affection. "Miss Fenton's passionate words were correct, my lord."

Lord Bledsoe stiffened further, but Lucinda caught his hand and squeezed. Nicholas stared in wonder, for in that moment he saw the utter grief on every line of his father's face. Somehow he hadn't fully recognized it before. In his own pain, in his own frustration, he sometimes forgot that his father had lost a son. One whom he had been closest to for so many reasons.

He felt a powerful empathy for the man. And a new understanding.

"No one will ever replace my husband," Lucinda said softly. "Or the father of my children. Or your son. But it isn't fair to punish Nicholas for that simply because he and Anthony have a similar face."

She turned and smiled at him again. "Nicholas is himself. And Anthony loved him for it."

The last words were choked out, and Lucinda lifted her hand to her mouth to cover a quiet sob. Then she nodded to each person in the room and hurried out.

Nicholas stood stiffly, waiting for his father to renew his tirades. But instead, the older man turned and speared his son with a look. But it wasn't one of censure, not this time. It was just a stare. As if he hadn't seen Nicholas for a long time and was finally doing so.

He opened his mouth and shut it a few times before he choked out, "Marianne, we should see about Lucinda."

Then he turned on his heel and left the room in a jerky clip. Nicholas's mother hesitated for a moment before she rushed after him, leaving Jane and Nicholas alone.

As soon as the others had gone, Jane turned to him. Her face was pasty pale and tear-streaked from the emotional encounter.

"I-I'm sorry," she whispered, her voice breaking.

Nicholas shut the door quietly and then moved toward her. "Do you know what you did?"

Her chin dropped and began to wobble. "I never should have interfered, but when I heard him speaking to you in that manner—"

"Hush," he soothed, wrapping his arms around her and drawing her close.

He dropped his mouth to hers for a kiss. Jane was stiff with surprise for a moment, but then her arms came around his neck and she clung to him as if she feared they would never kiss again. Part of him understood that fear. Shared it.

Finally, he drew back and looked down at her. "No one has spoken up for me like that in an age. No one since—"

He stopped abruptly, unable to complete the sentence after everything that had just transpired. Jane's face softened, and he saw she understood without his having to say another word. She knew he was referring to Anthony.

Still silent, she lifted up on her tiptoes and kissed him. It was a gentle kiss, something meant for comfort, but the moment their lips touched a second time, he realized he wasn't going to be able to let it stop there. He wanted her.

Actually, it went deeper than that. He *needed* her. Needed her to forget the ugliness with his father. Needed her to make the dull ache of grief for his brother fade.

Slowly, he backed her toward the door. He leaned her against it, pressing himself fully to her frame as he reached around to turn the key in the lock.

"Nicholas?" she whispered, her tone a question as she looked up at him.

He didn't answer with words, but with another searing kiss. She moaned, a muffled sound against his mouth, and made no protest when he began to hike her silky skirt up around her hips. He cupped her gently, and his erection grew even harder when he found she was already wet and hot, ready for him. She arched against his fingers, her head tilting back and her eyes shutting with an expression of pleasure.

"We don't have much time," he panted as he wrestled with the fastenings on his trousers.

She nodded as she helped him, freeing his hard cock with her soft fingers and stroking him just once, gently. He growled with the pleasure of her touch.

He cupped her backside, stroking the silky skin of her hips as he lifted her up against the door. She groaned when he slid the tip of his erection over the slick heat of her body, and then he glided forward.

She was wet enough that he fitted to the hilt inside her in one long stroke, and they both sighed in unison. She gripped her legs around his back, her fingers digging into the heavy fabric of his coat as he began to move.

Although he fought for finesse, his emotions were so wild and wired that it was a losing battle. Soon his hips jerked out of control, his pelvis ground against hers without any rhythm except that of his overpowering desire.

But his lack of control didn't seem to diminish her pleasure. She arched, biting back little cries as she thrust back against him, creating a delicious friction that had him right on the edge of release within moments.

Finally, she stiffened and her sheath began to pulse wildly around him as a powerful orgasm washed over her. The feel of her body at the height of pleasure, the look of pure release on her face stole any remaining control he had left, and he let himself be lost, pouring his essence into her as he braced on the door and choked back a wild cry.

For a long time, they remained joined, foreheads touching, panting breaths finally slowing until their chests rose and fell in time. Gently, Nicholas helped Jane slide away from him, parting their bodies with a little groan of displeasure. She touched his cheek before she slipped her tangled chemise and gown back around her and reached up to right her hair as best she could.

"I must go back," she said, glancing at the door where they had just coupled so wildly. Her expression had a wistful quality, and Nicholas knew she would much rather stay here with him.

"I know." He sighed as he fastened his trousers. "And I should find my family. I want to be certain Lucinda and my mother are well. And I suppose it is past time that I have a talk with my father."

Jane nodded, but he saw the twisted emotions that darkened her expression. She shook her head.

"I am sorry my outburst upset them. Your mother, especially, has been nothing but kind to me, and I'm certain I hurt her and made her regret ever taking me under her wing."

She caught his hands in hers and held them against her heart as she looked up at him. In the soft light of the room, she almost looked like an angel. His angel.

"But Nicholas, I meant every word I said to them. I tried to change you when I taught you those rules of Society. I tried to make you fit into some kind of mold, but that was wrong. You are *you*, Nicholas. With both flaws and wonderful qualities. Don't lose them. Not for anyone."

He stared at her in wonder, struck dumb by the power of what she was saying. No one had ever given him such unconditional acceptance before. Even his twin had wished for him to change.

She leaned up and pressed a soft, almost chaste kiss against his cheek.

"Goodbye, Nicholas," she whispered before she slipped from the room.

He stood in the same place where she had left him for a long time after she was gone, running over in his mind everything that had happened. And it took him almost that long to realize Jane had not said good night, but goodbye.

Chapter 23

❧❧

"It's no wonder you have a headache," Lady Ridgefield said as she patted Jane's hand while they waited in the foyer for her carriage to be brought around. "What a night you have had."

Jane gave a weak, bemused smile. If only her former employer knew the half of it. But perhaps it was best she didn't. Jane had already made enough enemies tonight. And lost so much.

But she didn't regret what she had done. Nicholas deserved every defense she had made of him. And her reward . . . that last beautiful moment in the parlor when they made love, well, that would remain in her memory forever. It was a perfect farewell.

"Oh, my dear, your eyes are filled with tears," Lady Ridgefield said with a frown. "You must be in such pain, allow me to go out and see what is taking that footman so long!"

Jane nodded, too worried she would burst into tears to say anything. As she stood in the foyer, she drew in a few breaths to calm herself. And then she felt another person's presence behind her.

She turned to find Lady Bledsoe standing in the hallway.

"I'm glad to catch you alone," the other woman said as she entered the small entryway.

Jane swallowed hard as her heart rate increased tenfold. "M-my lady," she stammered. "I—"

"Everything you said tonight was right, Jane," Lady Bledsoe said. In the bright light, Jane could see she had been crying. "It hadn't been said before, probably because I was too tangled in my own grief to do it. But it wasn't fair to Nicholas. And I'm glad he has someone who loves him enough to defend him."

Jane's lips parted in surprise. Were her feelings so clear to this woman? She moved forward.

"My lady, I know Nicholas must marry someone of more elevated status than my own. When he does, it will ensure his position in Society and make people forget his past. I don't want you to think that I would ever endanger that for him, no matter my own feelings."

Lady Bledsoe reached out and caught her hand in a tight squeeze. The sudden passion in the other woman's eyes was so shocking that Jane could not react, only stare.

"I know better than most that life is very short, Jane. All I ever wanted for my sons was happiness. Anthony had his with Lucinda, who he loved with all his heart. I would not be so unfair as to ask my other son to accept less. Why do you think I helped introduce you back into Society? Did you really think it was only as repayment for what you'd done for Nicholas?" She shook her head. "It wasn't. You did well tonight. A few more nights like this and a marriage to you would not hurt my son in the least. And if anyone had anything to say about it, they could contend with *me*."

Jane realized she had been holding her breath and let it all out in a loud exhalation that echoed in the silent hall around them. She opened her mouth to speak, but no words would come. This all had to be a dream, didn't it? Lady Bledsoe *wanted* her to marry Nicholas?

Suddenly Lady Ridgefield was at her elbow, patting her arm with clumsy affection.

"Ah, Lady Bledsoe, I'm so glad you have found us. Dear Jane has a touch of headache and I am going to take her home. But I think our night was a great success, don't you?"

Lady Bledsoe held Jane's gaze evenly. "A great success, indeed. Jane, I hope you will think of all I've said. Good evening, my dear, Lady Ridgefield."

With a nod, the other woman turned away. And all Jane could do was stare after her.

"I'm going to marry Jane."

Rage choked on his drink, the liquid nearly propelling across the room as Nicholas's friend stared at him. "I beg your pardon?"

Nicholas nodded. "You know what happened tonight."

Rage shrugged. Nicholas had been telling him the entire story for the hour he'd been home.

"You said it yourself that since I must marry, I might as well marry someone I actually like. Someone I desire."

"It couldn't hurt," Rage said with a chuckle. "But what happened to marrying someone of higher rank in order to garner more acceptance from Society?"

Nicholas hesitated. That had been the original plan, but now it seemed untenable. Jane's passionate defense of him tonight had been a stark reminder that he couldn't truly live his brother's life. He had to find some way to remain true to himself even while he continued to honor Anthony.

Jane seemed a damn fine beginning.

"Society can rot," he growled, eliciting a grin from Rage. "I'll play by some of their rules, but I won't be miserable for them. Besides, when I marry Jane I may not elevate her status, but I can give her a great deal." He pictured the way she had lit up in her beautiful gown. "She deserves to wear pretty clothes like she did tonight. To be able to look any of those biddies in the eye without shame."

"It sounds like you have it all worked out," Rage said with a sip of his drink.

Nicholas frowned. His friend sounded a bit . . . sarcastic.

"You're the one who first suggested this, but now you don't seem to approve. Do you not like Jane?"

"On the contrary, I like her a great deal," Rage said, but offered no further explanation for his cryptic remark. "So when do you intend to ask for her hand?"

Nicholas shrugged. "I want her to have more time out in Society before I do so. My mother is working hard so that everyone will forget that she was forced to become a paid companion. If I allow Jane to become more accepted, it's far less likely anyone will say anything impertinent about her later. A few weeks, perhaps."

Rage tilted his head. There was question in his friend's stare, but before he could voice it, the parlor door opened and Gladwell stepped inside.

"I beg your pardon, my lord, but you have a guest."

"Jane?" Nicholas found himself saying as he stepped forward in anticipation. He missed their stolen nights together. Even more after tonight's passionate encounter.

"No. It is Viscount Patrick Fenton, my lord, and he is quite insistent that he see you right away, despite the late hour." Gladwell gave a sniff of disapproval that demonstrated just how *insistent* Jane's cousin must have been.

Nicholas set his drink down with a loud, heavy clunk and stared at the butler.

"Patrick Fenton has the audacity to come *here*?" he said in disbelief.

Of course the man could have no idea of Nicholas's hatred of him. This man had been the cause of Jane's grief in so many ways. And he had dared put his hands on her. Which made Nicholas want to tear him apart piece by piece. Slowly.

"Send him in," he said, low and harsh.

As the butler went to fetch his uninvited guest, Rage turned on him. "Hold on, mate. You can't kill the man. They'll put you away."

"I'm not going to kill him," Nicholas said with great difficulty. "At least, that isn't my intention. In fact, I'm very interested in what he has to say."

"Viscount Patrick Fenton, my lord," Gladwell announced before he stepped back and allowed the gentleman to enter.

Nicholas had never seen Fenton before and was surprised by his appearance. He'd imagined some wrinkled old man, rubbing his hands together like a villain from a gothic story. The person who stood before him was far younger than Nicholas had pictured. In fact, they were likely of an age. And Fenton didn't look nefarious, but young and handsome, rather like Jane's brother. They shared the same dark hair. The same sharp green eyes.

"What can I do for you, *Lord Fenton*?" he asked, cold even though his rage was boiling hot below the surface.

"Good evening, Lord Stoneworth. Thank you for seeing me despite the late hour. I realize you did not expect me, but I would like to speak to you alone." The other man looked at him, then glanced pointedly at Rage. "We have business of a very private nature."

Rage cocked an eyebrow in Nicholas's direction. It was a look that asked Nicholas what he wanted. He nodded toward the door silently, and his friend left without a word.

Once they were alone, Nicholas leaned back against the desk, folded his arms, and glared at Fenton. "Why don't we dispense with pleasantries and you just tell me what the hell you want?"

"I had no doubt that Jane told you of all my horrible deeds," Fenton said with a sad laugh. "I assume that is part of how she obtained your assistance."

Nicholas straightened up. It seemed Fenton knew a great deal, but Nicholas had no intention of verifying any of his guesses.

"I don't know what you're going on about."

Fenton arched a brow. "Let's not play silly games, my lord. I'm not the kind of man who delights in them, and I somehow doubt you are, either. I know that you have been assisting my cousin Jane on her endless search for her brother.

When she came to my home earlier this week, she mentioned someone was helping her."

Nicholas's eyes went wide. Jane had told him she said something to upset Patrick, but she hadn't confessed *that*. It seemed her temper had gotten the best of her and loosened her tongue.

"When I saw the two of you together tonight at your mother's ball, it didn't take much to put the pieces together," Fenton continued. "After all, you *do* have connections in the underground."

Nicholas couldn't help but be impressed. The man was intelligent, that was certain. That didn't mean Nicholas liked him.

"When you refer to earlier in the week, do you mean the day you accosted her?" Nicholas asked mildly, although the idea of this bastard putting a mere finger on Jane inspired his rage.

To his surprise, Fenton's chin dropped and his cheeks brightened with high color. "I will admit, I lost my temper. I did grab Jane's arms. I frightened her and I hate myself for that. But you must understand, Stoneworth, I have been forced to endure her contempt, her hatred, her tirades, for nearly a year now. When she implied I might have had a hand in her brother's disappearance . . ." He frowned, and a flash of frustrated anger lit up his expression. "Well, that was the last straw."

Nicholas moved so swiftly that he was in front of Fenton before the man had a chance to react.

He took pleasure in how his eyes widened in fear and surprise.

"You had no right to touch her," he growled. "And if you ever repeat that mistake, I will make you wish you had never been born, the consequences be damned."

There was a long moment of silence that hung heavy in the air between them, and then Fenton nodded.

"I understand you perfectly, Stoneworth."

Nicholas raised his hands to demonstrate he had no intention of doing so tonight and backed away a few steps.

This man was confusing. Jane had described him in such terrible terms, and yet the person standing before him was very calm, even in the face of threats. He was afraid, which was sensible considering Nicholas's reputation. But he was also composed. He didn't back away or cower.

In short, Nicholas couldn't read him. Which was an uncommon occurrence.

"What *do* you want, Fenton?" he asked.

"First, I came here because I sensed . . ." Fenton cleared his throat. "*Something* between you and my cousin. As her only living relative, I must tell you that I will not allow her to be compromised."

"I intend to marry her," Nicholas bit out, short.

Fenton's eyes widened ever so slightly, and before he could cover the emotion, a flash of regret passed over his handsome features.

"I see," he finally said.

And so did Nicholas. This man was in love with Jane. She didn't know it, but he saw it as clearly as if Patrick had written it across the walls in bright red paint.

Patrick straightened his shoulders, and all his emotions were gone as if they had never existed. Nicholas had a grudging respect for his ability to do that.

"If that is your intent, then it is even more imperative that you know what I have come here to share."

"And what is that?" Nicholas asked, folding his arms.

Patrick reached into his inside coat pocket and withdrew a packet of folded paper, bound with a red ribbon. Nicholas's name had been printed neatly on the outside of the bundle.

"*This* is the proof that Jane has been searching for so desperately," her cousin said matter-of-factly.

Nicholas wrinkled his brow in confusion, but he took the package. As he carefully opened the sheets, Patrick paced away.

"As much as it pains me to say it, Marcus Fenton *is* dead." The other man stopped at the window and looked outside at the inky black night. "He died over a year ago, probably in an opium den, though we will never know for certain. When Jane's father got the proof from the letter you have there, he fell into a sadness and illness that killed him. But even in his devastated state, he made me promise I wouldn't tell Jane. He feared she could not bear it after all the other loss and pain in her life."

Nicholas's eyes narrowed. "You and her father thought very little of her, then. She is stronger than you imagine."

The other man turned slowly and looked Nicholas up and down. "Perhaps that is true. I *did* argue with her father that I could not hide the truth from her forever. But my uncle Samuel was always stubborn." He smiled, and his affection for the man he spoke of was as clear as his frustration had been. "He insisted I wait until she was calm. Until she was ready to hear the truth. As you know, that moment has yet to come. She has fully convinced herself that I employed trickery to have Marcus declared dead, when in reality it was the second letter in the bundle there that convinced the courts."

Nicholas turned to the second sheet. "This is from her father, a declaration of his son's death and confirmation that you are the true heir."

Patrick nodded slowly.

"But these letters speak of proof. Of a ring." Nicholas held up the sheets.

Patrick dug into his pocket and withdrew a signet ring. He held it out and Nicholas took it, examining the shining gold carefully. An ornate "F" decorated the front.

"That was my cousin's. It was a family heirloom. Even in his darkest hour, Marcus did not sell it. Jane doesn't know this, but my uncle *was* in contact with him before his death. He saw Marcus about a month before he vanished permanently and he had it still. Someone stripped it from his body, and the investigator who uncovered the truth somehow found it in the trade shops and paid a pretty penny to return it. When he brought it to my uncle, dried blood still stained it."

Nicholas shut his eyes. These letters, the ring her brother had protected even in his most mad state, coupled with the information Nicholas had garnered from the poor, crazed man in the hells would surely be enough to prove the truth for Jane.

"And why did you bring these things to me?" Nicholas asked, his tone flat as he held the items out to Patrick.

The other man shook his head in refusal. "For so long, I have tried to allow my cousin to forgive me. I allowed her to leave my protection even when I could have forced her to stay. I helped arrange for her to be hired by Lady Ridgefield."

Nicholas's eyebrows went up in surprise.

"Oh yes. If you do not believe me, ask the lady

herself. She was in no need for a companion until I asked her to grant me the favor. She grew to love and depend upon Jane, but she never would have sought her out."

"If you cared for Jane so much, why did you not allow her to remove her father's letters?" Nicholas asked, remembering how much pain had been in Jane's voice when she spoke of those precious items.

Patrick sighed heavily. "If she was not forced to return to her father's home to go over his papers and effects, she never would have come at all. It was the only way I could keep watch over her. To see for myself that she was well and not in need of anything. If you do, indeed, marry her, I will happily turn over any and all papers to you. They are her legacy, along with a healthy sum of money she has always refused. I would be happy to offer that to you as her dowry, if you will agree to make sure she receives it."

Fenton ran a hand through his hair restlessly. "You asked me why I brought you this proof tonight. It is because I have finally accepted that Jane will never see me as anything but a villain who stole what was rightfully Marcus's. Someone who is plotting against her at every turn. She will *never* reach a point where she will believe any evidence I present to her. But she seems to trust you. Perhaps more than just trust, judging from her smile with you tonight."

Patrick turned away, but not before Nicholas saw his sour frown. "It is not an expression I have seen in a very long time. So perhaps, if the word comes from you, she *will* believe the truth. That Marcus is gone."

Nicholas stared at the papers in his hands and then looked at Patrick. "Can I verify these things are true?"

The other man nodded. "I will put you in touch with the barrister who witnessed her father's signature on that letter. And the investigator he used will happily provide you with more details on what he found."

Nicholas turned away. He would follow up on Patrick's proof, of course, but he had always trusted his gut. And it was telling him that this man wasn't lying. About any of it.

"This will break Jane's heart. Her spirit. Her hope for her brother is all she has left," he murmured, more to himself than anything else.

Fenton cleared his throat, a raw sound that drew Nicholas's attention. The other man looked as sick as he felt. If they had nothing else in common, they shared a distaste for bringing Jane pain.

"I know it will," Fenton said softly. "That was part of why I allowed this charade to go on for so long. But I've always thought that keeping her hopes alive indefinitely, making her watch and wait forever for a brother who will never come home . . . was a greater cruelty. But I leave it to you to decide what is best. And since it is so late and you did not invite me here, I will take my leave."

Shoulders slumped, Patrick Fenton began to make his way to the door.

"Wait," Nicholas called out, moving toward him.

Jane's cousin stopped, turning back with wariness in his eyes. But the wariness faded when Nicholas held out his hand wordlessly. As they shook, a world of understanding went between them. Nicholas could certainly appreciate how difficult keeping this secret had been for Fenton.

Once the other man had gone, he sat down to read and reread the letters. When the door opened a short time later and Rage entered the room, he quietly folded them and put them away.

"What did he want?" his friend asked.

Nicholas glanced up at Rage. He would share any of his own secrets with this man. They were as close as brothers, Nicholas could trust him with his very life. But this secret wasn't his. It was Jane's. And *she* would be the first person he told, not someone who was a veritable stranger to her.

"Nothing of consequence," he lied. "Just wanted to make certain I wasn't ruining his cousin."

Rage laughed. "And what did you tell him?"

"That I intend to make her my wife," he said.

Rage nodded. They spoke for a few moments more, and then his friend departed.

When he was alone, Nicholas withdrew the

ring from his pocket once more. It wasn't heavy, but it felt like a huge weight in his palm. A burden Patrick Fenton had passed on to him.

The burden of breaking Jane's heart.

How in God's name was he going to do it?

For so long, she had kept herself from happiness out of some misguided loyalty to her brother. As if punishing herself would bring him home. Or that being happy would prevent him from being found.

But tonight . . . Tonight she had been in high spirits. He'd seen it as she found acceptance from her former friends and peers. He'd watched it in the way she held herself in that beautiful gown.

The moment he told her the truth, all that happiness would vanish, and it wouldn't return for a long time. She would mourn Marcus, just as he had mourned Anthony, for many months to come. A piece of her would never be the same.

And the worst part of it was that if he told her now, tonight or tomorrow, she would suffer all that grief alone. Lady Ridgefield was sweet, but she wouldn't know what to do with Jane's pain. She wouldn't hold her through the night as she cried. She wouldn't know when to allow her anger, or when to let her sob, or when to make her smile.

But *he* would. Once they were married, he could reveal the truth to her. Gently. And he would be there for her night and day as she came to terms with it.

But only if he waited.

Just a few more weeks of lies. Secrets. As soon as he asked for her hand, they could start reading the banns and be married at the earliest time. A few days to celebrate, and then he could sit Jane down and give her the truth she had sought for so long. A bitter gift to begin their marriage, but a gift nonetheless.

And in the meantime, she would have a little of the joy she had more than earned.

He set the ring on the table and stared at it.

"Soon Jane," he murmured. "Soon you will have everything you deserve. Including the truth. As much as it will break your heart."

Chapter 24

Jane let her brush move through her hair in long, even strokes, watching her reflection in the mirror as she did so and marveling at how much in her life had changed just in the last few weeks.

Despite her outburst at the Lady Bledsoe's ball, Nicholas's mother had continued her kindness. And her sponsorship, with the support of the other women in their circle, had led to Jane being accepted back into Society. She was not treated with the same recognition she had been given when she debuted before, but slowly more and more people spoke to her. Smiled at her. Acknowledged her existence.

The men had all but forgotten her once lowered status. Since Nicholas had danced with her, she had never been without a partner or admirer.

With the women, it was harder. Her harsh words to Georgiana and her cronies had caused a setback. Most of her former friends still held up their noses. But she had found new friends. Women who had been a bit older or a bit younger than she when she debuted. There was a small circle whose company she actually enjoyed. Kind women who treated her as one of their own.

And though she was changed, and she would never be the girl who had once frivolously prayed for a sparkling debut, she could admit that she liked being accepted again.

But it was none of those things that made her cheeks flush as she set her brush down and began to plait her hair into a braid before she got into bed. It was Nicholas.

Since the ball a few weeks ago, he had been . . . well, she could call it nothing less than courting her. At every event, he insisted on dancing at least three times with her. He found ways to stand near her. Touch her. Talk to her. No matter how she tried to discourage him, turn him toward women who could make a more successful match, he ignored that.

Others were beginning to notice, as well. The men who danced with her now no longer flirted. They were friendly and attentive, but everyone knew that the recently reformed Lord Stoneworth was staking his claim. And they respected that as much as they were beginning to respect him.

She smiled, her heart lighter than it had been in ages. She didn't dare hope for too much, but she was beginning to believe that she could be happy again. Better still, she was starting to think that Marcus would want that for her. After all, Nicholas was continuing his search for her brother. He was vague about the details when she asked, but she felt certain he wouldn't give up, no matter what the future held for them.

A light rap on her door drew her thoughts back to the present, and she turned to face her guest. "Yes?"

One of the housemaids stepped inside, looking a bit furtive and uncertain.

"I'm sorry to bother you, Miss Jane, but you had a letter delivered to the back. I was told to bring it straight to you."

Jane wrinkled her brow. A letter, this time of night? She got to her feet and held out her hand to take the missive. The housemaid curtsied her way from the room, closing the door.

She stared at the handwriting on the address, but did not recognize it. It wasn't her cousin's, for which she was grateful. Patrick had actually sent word to her that he was leaving London three weeks ago, and she had not been forced to endure his presence since.

Shrugging, she broke the seal and unfolded the pages. The moment she read the first line, she sank into the chair she had vacated moments ago, her entire body tingling. It was from Nicholas.

Dear Jane:

I must see you alone, not on a dance floor or a parlor where I cannot express myself freely. Please come to me tonight, if you can. I will send a carriage to wait behind Lady Ridgefield's garden. What I have to say to you is not for Society to hear, or for anyone else to be a part of. It is between you and me.

N

She shivered as she read and reread the words. It was wrong to go to him, of course. Now that she no longer had the excuse of being his teacher, it was improper. But she didn't care. She wanted to be with Nicholas. To see him. Touch him. Be free to say what she wished without worrying that someone would interrupt or overhear.

Hurrying to the window, she looked outside. Her room overlooked the garden, and sure enough, there was a dark carriage parked just over the wall. If she waited another hour or so, the household would be quiet and she could slip away, just as she had all those other nights.

With a laugh she couldn't stifle, Jane rushed to her wardrobe and began to ready herself.

Nicholas fingered the letters he had been carrying with him every day since Patrick Fenton had given them to him. The proof that Jane's brother was truly dead had sat in his pocket like a weight. A heavy reminder that even as he watched Jane blossom and lighten with happiness, even as he grew more and more anxious to have her as his wife . . . he also held the keys to her utter heartbreak.

Tonight he had sent for her. Tonight he would ask her to be his bride. Once the marriage was performed, he could tell her the truth and be there for her in the aftermath.

"Nicholas?"

He turned and caught his breath as Jane stepped into the parlor and pulled the door closed behind her. Every time he saw her, she seemed to become more beautiful. It was as if a candle had been lit inside her when she returned to Society, and with each passing day it burned brighter, making her luminescent.

She smiled as she moved toward him. "I have missed you," she admitted as she wrapped her arms around him and hugged him.

"You have seen me at least a few times a week for the past three weeks," he teased, even as his arms came around her and he reveled in her soft warmth and light scent.

"It isn't the same," she said as she drew back. "And you know it, for you wrote it in your letter to me."

She reached into the reticule that dangled from her wrist and withdrew the short missive he had written to her that evening. She held it out as if it proved everything, and he couldn't deny that it did. They both knew that their time alone here was very different from the stuffy ballrooms where they had to play as if they'd never touched, never kissed. Where they could be close, but not too close.

"And what is that?" She laughed, motioning toward his hand. "More letters for me?"

Nicholas froze. He had all but forgotten he still held her cousin's proof in his hand. When Jane was near him, he seemed to forget *everything* but her.

"No," he said his tone sharper than he had intended. "They are nothing."

Her brow wrinkled, but her smile remained. "So determined that I not see them. I hope they are not love letters from some other lady. I would hate to have to fight a duel over you."

He opened his coat and began to put them in his pocket, with Jane tilting her head to read the address all the while.

"They do not look like love letters, though. The address is so formal. Viscount Nicholas Stonewor—" she stopped midsentence as Nicholas let his coat fall back into place.

"These are not important, Jane," he said, forcing a smile.

She slowly straightened, and to his horror, all the frivolity and joy had left her face. Her cheeks were pale and her lips thin as she stared at him.

"Perhaps I am wrong," she said softly. "Perhaps I am simply looking for trouble, but the hand that addressed the letter you so desperately hid from me looks very much like that of my cousin, Patrick Fenton. Am I mistaken?"

Nicholas stared at her, locked in a war with himself. If Jane were any other woman, he would have simply lied to her and kissed her until she forgot everything else but him. It was tempting to do that now, but he found he couldn't. For she *was* Jane. The woman who had changed him, in more ways than one. The woman he intended to marry.

"They *are* from Patrick," she whispered, her tone filled with hurt disbelief and confusion. "That is why you hid them from me."

Nicholas cleared his throat and slowly nodded. "Yes, they are from Patrick."

She held out a hand, pale and trembling. "I want to see what he sent you."

Nicholas clasped her hand in both of his. "Jane, this isn't why I brought you here tonight. I had the packet out and was examining it and I meant to put it away before you came. But when I saw you, I was so captivated by you that I didn't. But I never meant for you to see—"

"To see letters from the man I hate more than anyone else in this world?" Jane interrupted, snatching her hand away and clutching it in a fist against her chest. "If he has written to you, the subject can only be me. And I have a right to know what he is saying. Is he lying to you about me? Is he telling you things? Is he—"

"It isn't about you, Jane," Nicholas said, trying to keep his tone low and calm when his heart was beating so fast he feared he would lose consciousness.

"Don't lie to me," she whispered, and her voice broke. "Of all the people in the world, *you* cannot lie to me."

Nicholas shut his eyes. She could have said many things, but that was the one he couldn't ignore or argue against. He hated that he was going to have to reveal the truth to her this way. Tonight, when he had meant to give her nothing but happiness and a bright future.

Instead, he would crush her and make her face the past.

But there was nothing else to be done. He took out the evidence Patrick had given him and held it out. She took the packet, her eyes brimming with tears, but before she could do anything else, he held up a hand to stop her. Reaching into another pocket, he withdrew her brother's signet ring and placed it on top of the letter gently.

She stared at the ring, all remaining color bleeding away from her face. She stood there so long, so quietly that Nicholas almost said something to her.

"No." She drew out the sound of the word, long and harsh like a wail. It was the worst thing he had ever heard in his life. "No. No. No. No."

She said it so many times that it flooded the room.

"I'm sorry, Jane," he whispered as he moved to her.

He wrapped his arms around her as the weight of the truth she had probably always known, but never faced, hit her. Jane went limp in his arms, sobs racking her even as she continued to scream "no" again and again and again.

Jane sat on the parlor floor, half in Nicholas's lap. She had been crying for nearly an hour, and now it seemed as if there were no tears left. No sorrow left. She was all but numb.

Her brother was dead.

Seeing the ring, seeing Nicholas's ashen face when he presented it to her . . . that was all the proof she needed. Marcus was dead and she was alone in the world.

Or at least that was what she had always believed. If Marcus was gone, she would be alone. Except right now a man's strong arms were around her, silently allowing her grief as he held her, rocked her.

She blew her nose and wiped her eyes before she straightened up slowly and looked at Nicholas.

"I-I'm sorry," she gasped, her voice still hiccup-y and choked.

"Never apologize for your feelings." He shook his head. "Of all things, Jane, *this* I understand."

She stared at him in wonder. "Yes. You do, don't you?"

He nodded wordlessly.

Her fingers ached as she opened them from the tight grip she had made around the letters and ring when she realized what they meant. The ring had cut a circle into her palm, and it throbbed gently. Quietly she slipped the ring on her thumb, for it was far too large to fit on any other finger.

Then she stared at the letters.

"Patrick gave these to you?" she said softly.

Nicholas pushed a lock of tangled hair from her eyes and nodded. "Yes."

A little flicker of hope swelled in her chest. "He's a liar, Nicholas. What if he isn't—"

He cut her off quickly. "Angel, I checked every-thing. Your cousin didn't interfere."

Her chin dipped down as the last hope died.

Nicholas cupped her face and tilted it back up. "Why don't you read them? I think you'll under-stand more when you do."

Dread overtook her as she stared at the packet in her hand. Such a big part of her didn't want to read them. Didn't want to see. Didn't want the truth to be final.

But she couldn't be a coward. This was what she had been searching for. And she owed it to her brother to see her search through to the end, no matter how much she hated it.

Slowly, she nodded and untied the ribbon that bound the papers. The first letter was from an investigator and detailed the search for her brother. Eyes dry, but only because she was out of tears, she read the cold, businesslike recitation of a very lengthy search. She read about the ring, which she squeezed gently. Her brother had kept this, even when he was lost to opium. She would never take it off.

When she reached the final sheet, her breath caught and she let the others flutter to the ground. There was her father's hand. And it was dated just a few days before his death. It validated her cousin. It admitted he knew his son was gone. And it was addressed to the very solicitors who had named Patrick heir just a few weeks later.

The tears she had thought were over flowed again.

"He knew?" she whispered, fighting against the tide of anger that mingled with her pain. "My father *knew* Marcus was dead?"

"He solicited the search that found the evidence," Nicholas explained softly. "He had known for many months, apparently."

"Why didn't he tell me?" she said, pushing away from his arms and getting up to pace around the room. "He let me believe my brother could still be alive? In fact, he told me on his deathbed never to give up hope for Marcus. Why? Why did he do that?"

She was saying it more to herself than Nicholas, but he answered nonetheless. "He felt you were not strong enough to deal with so much grief at once. He asked your cousin to wait until you were stronger. Until you were ready to hear it."

"And Patrick was happy to keep the secret," she spat as she swiped at the tears, forcing them away to focus on her anger.

Nicholas got to his feet, watching her pace. "No. He wasn't. I realize you have put every angry and bitter emotion into hating your cousin, but I spoke to him, Jane. I believed what he said, and the evidence supports his words. He tried to convince your father to tell you the truth before he died. And ever since, Patrick has been waiting for you to get to a place where you would actually *hear* him."

She stopped. In her mind, she played through all the exchanges she'd had with Patrick over the past year. Not all of them had been pleasant, but he had always remained calm. Polite. The only time he ever lost his temper was the last time they met, when she implied that he might have had some part in Marcus's death.

She shook her head. Could she have been so wrong about her cousin? Had she simply transferred all her anger over the pain in her life onto him . . . unfairly? And pushed away the one remaining family member she had?

Just as she had accused Nicholas's father of doing weeks ago.

"Oh God," she whispered, covering her mouth as she stared at him. "If this is true . . . can it be true?"

He nodded. "As I said, I spoke to him and I do believe he is sincere."

She covered her eyes. There was so much horrible information hitting her that she could scarcely process all of it. But slowly, layer by layer, it sank in.

"Wait," she said softly, reaching for the stack of papers that had fallen to the floor when she staggered up. She turned them over and reread the address. All that was written on the back of the papers was Nicholas's name. No street, no neighborhood.

"Did my cousin deliver these to you, himself?"

Nicholas wrinkled his brow as if he didn't understand why she asked the question. "Yes."

Her lips parted in surprise. "But—but Patrick has been out of London since the day after your mother's ball. That was three weeks ago, Nicholas. How long have you known that my brother was dead and not told me?"

Chapter 25

For more than an hour, Nicholas had watched helplessly as Jane waded through the painful emotions of loss and grief. His heart had hurt and burned to make it better, but he knew from very personal experience that there was nothing he could do for her but hold her. And allow her the pain. She had certainly earned it.

But now, as she stood holding out the letters, staring at him in disbelief and anger, he desperately wanted to fix things. Fix what he had done, for he could see that she saw it as a great betrayal.

And it was. He had done it with every good intention, but he could see now how wrong he had been.

He moved a step closer, trying desperately to find some words that would explain the unexplainable.

"How long, Nicholas?" she repeated, her tone elevating. Her hand shook, making the papers rustle.

"Your cousin gave those items to me the night before he departed London," he admitted softly. And since he realized that his honesty was all he could give her now, he added, "And I had found other evidence, myself, that led me to believe your brother was dead before that."

A strangled sound of pain echoed from her lips as she backed away from him, staggering around furniture as she put as much distance between them as was possible in the small room.

"You knew for nearly a month and you said *nothing*? I asked you how your investigation was progressing and you *lied*. You made love to me, even as you knew the most important secret of my life." She shook her head. "How could you? How could you?"

He held his hands up helplessly. Every time he moved toward her, she darted farther away. Her hands were balled up as fists and he could see she wanted desperately to use the skills in fighting he had taught her against him. Perhaps he deserved it.

"At first it was because I couldn't fully prove what I had uncovered," he explained, though every word seemed hollow. "And later it was because you were so happy."

She shook her head in disbelief. "You thought I would rather have the frivolity of a few balls than know the truth about my brother?"

"Of course not," he said, feeling the weight of

her accusation. "I knew you would want to know, that you *deserved* to know—"

"And yet you did not tell me."

He held up his hands in a gesture of surrender. "You have tried to control and smash your joy for so long. I knew once the truth came out that you would find none for a long time. I wanted you to have a little time, Jane, that is all. A little enjoyment before the bitterness."

She stared at him, her blank expression censuring him silently.

"And when did you intend to tell me?" she asked, low. "For it certainly wasn't tonight. You hid the letters from me and tried to keep me from uncovering the truth. So when did you plan to share this knowledge?"

He drew a long, harsh breath, and this time he moved toward her until she had backed herself into the wall and had nowhere else to go.

"I wanted to wait until after we were married," he said softly.

She opened her mouth to retort, but then she stopped.

"M-married?" she finally repeated.

He nodded. God, he hoped she would hear him past her emotional fog. He *needed* her to hear him.

"I brought you here tonight, not to tell you about your brother, but because I intended to ask you to marry me."

He dug into his pocket and pulled out a small jewelry case. When he opened it, he revealed the delicate golden ring within. A dark blue sapphire decorated it, surrounded by two diamonds that twinkled in the candlelight.

Jane seemed stunned into silence. All she could do was stare from the ring to him and back again.

He took advantage of the rare silence to continue, "You have been the most important friend and partner of my life, Jane. I know we could be happy together, despite what has happened tonight. Please, say you will be my wife."

She shook her head slowly as she lifted her gaze back to his face. "How long after we married would you have told me about Marcus?"

"Jane—" he began, still holding out the ring.

"How long?" she repeated, her tone icy cold. It cut through him like a dagger.

He snapped the jewelry case shut. "Not long. When the time was right, I would have found a way."

The words sounded so foolish, and she gave a derisive snort.

"After I discover you have been lying to me for a month, you want me to enter into a lifelong bond with you? How am I to know you aren't lying about other things? How am I to know that you won't continue to lie? How can I ever trust you again?"

"People make mistakes, Jane," he said softly as he edged toward her. Reaching out, he stroked her face with the back of his hand, brushing her hair away. He had a little hope when her eyes fluttered shut. "Your father lied to you out of love. Your cousin out of the same."

She shook her head in disbelief. "So you are trying to excuse your behavior because others who I loved betrayed me, as well?"

He drew a breath. "No, I—"

Her eyes snapped fire as she ignored him. "You see, the key difference is that I never thought *you* would lie to me. After everything we went through, after everything I saw, I believed in you. I loved you so much for all I thought you were. And I trusted that you wouldn't lie to me. But you did. And I don't know if I can forgive that. Perhaps from anyone else, but not from you."

"Jane," he whispered.

"No," she said, pushing past him and making her way to the door. "I'm going home, Nicholas. I don't know if I'll want to see you again. Please don't pursue me."

"Don't do this, Jane," he said, moving toward her.

But before he could reach her, she was out the door, slamming it behind her and leaving him alone.

"Fuck!" he bellowed, and threw the ring box

with all his might. It bounced off the wall and skittered across the floor.

That was it. She was gone. And it was only in that horrible moment that Nicholas realized that Jane had said she once loved him.

And that he had lost that, too.

Jane didn't actually have a plan when she staggered up the stairway to her cousin's London home. All she knew was that she had to see Patrick, even if that meant following after him to the countryside.

She pounded on the door, trying to find some semblance of calm as she did. The last thing she wanted was to appear hysterical in front of her former servants. Of course, as the door finally opened to reveal the butler in his dressing gown, she realized it was probably too late for that.

"Miss Jane?" her old butler said, concern plain in every word. "Dear heavens, come inside, child. Is everything well? Are you hurt?"

"No, Jenkins," she said with as much brightness as she could. "I'm sorry to call so late, but I must find Patrick. Please, will you tell me where he has gone?"

"I'm here, Jane."

She looked up the staircase at the end of the foyer to find her cousin himself, coming down the stairs at a rapid pace. He, too, was in a dressing gown, and his hair was mussed from sleep. Of course it was three in the morning, so she wasn't entirely surprised.

"I only returned a few hours ago," he explained. "What has happened?"

"I—" she began and then stopped.

How in the world could she even start? She still wasn't sure she trusted Patrick, yet if she had been wrong about him all this time she owed him so many apologies. And then there was the issue of Nicholas.

"Please," he said as he touched her elbow and turned her toward a parlor. "Come sit. Jenkins, go back to bed, it is all right."

The butler gave Jane a quick glance. "I do hope you are well, miss," he said before he scurried back up the stairs toward the servants' quarters.

Jane allowed Patrick to take her into a parlor where the fire was still embers from the night before. He threw a few logs on to warm the room and quickly poured brandy into a glass.

"Drink this," he ordered. "And then tell me what has happened. It is the middle of the night and you are distraught. I must know."

She nodded. "I'm sorry to come so late. But I—"

Still struggling for words, she finally reached into her reticule and withdrew the papers she had received from Nicholas. When she held them out, Patrick stiffened.

"I see," he said softly. "Tell me."

So she did. Slowly, she poured out the entire story of going to meet with Nicholas and his revelation of her brother's fate, and her father's and Patrick's part in keeping the truth from her.

The only thing she left out was how much more betrayed she felt by the man she loved. That her father and Patrick would lie stung her, there was no denying that. But that Nicholas would do so ... well, it was so painful she could hardly breathe.

"Oh, Jane, I am sorry. I hoped Lord Stoneworth would find a better way to reveal the truth," Patrick said softly. "But I am glad you know. I am truly sorry for your loss."

She nodded. "And I am for yours, Patrick. I know you loved my brother like he was your own. And I-I, oh, I am so sorry for ever implying you could have hurt him. I didn't want to believe he was dead. My father's final words encouraged me to do so. I behaved reprehensively toward you."

Patrick shrugged as if she had only tugged his hair or stuck out her tongue, rather than treated him like a pariah for more than a year.

"There were many things that happened during that time. We cannot change them now, so do not worry yourself. We will start anew."

She nodded. "I will try."

"But as your last living relative, there is something else I must discuss with you," he said, and his tone was very serious.

"What is it?" she asked, dread tightening her

chest at the thought that there might be more secrets.

He cleared his throat. "You said that you went to Nicholas's house tonight and that is when you discovered this."

She nodded before the full recognition of what she had confessed hit her.

"So you snuck to his home in the middle of the night," her cousin continued. "Without a chaperone. Jane, you are ruined. Even if nothing happened tonight, I doubt I am wrong in thinking that it has before."

She turned away with a blush and remained silent.

"My dear, you must marry him," he said. "Or marry *someone*."

"But no one knows but you," she said, shaking her head. "And it will not happen again."

Because every time she thought of the fact that Nicholas had withheld the truth from her for a month, it hurt more and more. The idea of marrying him, which would have made her joyful a few hours before, was now an impossibility. She loved him, yet she didn't trust him. How could that be overcome?

"But *I* know, Jane," Patrick said. "And you know, as does he. I cannot forget that. He told me he intended to marry you. Has he not asked you?"

She swallowed hard as she thought of the beautiful ring Nicholas offered her. She had to force the steel back into her heart before she whispered, "Yes."

"Then we must go back to him tomorrow and you will tell him that you accept," Patrick said. There was a tightness around his mouth, and Jane wasn't certain if it was annoyance or something else that caused it.

She shook her head. "But he knew about this for so long and he didn't tell me, Patrick. He lied to me. How can I ever trust him again? I love him, but that makes it worse in some ways. I feel betrayed. I feel embarrassed. I feel hurt."

Patrick shut his eyes. "But you are compromised. You *must* marry."

Jane shook her head. Everything was so overwhelming right now, she could hardly think straight.

"You cannot ask me to go back and look at him," she pleaded, running a shaking hand through her hair.

"But you care for him, you love him. You said you did," her cousin reasoned.

"Patrick, I have spent the past few *years* being lied to by everyone I loved. Knowing that makes me sick to my stomach." She clenched a fist against her chest. "I cannot bear the thought of going forward with the rest of my life being lied to as well. I cannot."

"I don't know what to do." He sighed. "In good conscience, I cannot let you continue on without a marriage. But you refuse to go back to him, and after all these years of hating me, I don't want to force you. How will you have me handle this?"

Jane shook her head. Her cousin had always been a stickler for propriety. Even if no one in the world would ever know, he wasn't going to let the subject drop.

She covered her face with her hands. "Oh, Patrick," she groaned. "How did everything become so tangled and destroyed?"

He smiled sadly. "With good intentions. Isn't that what they say the road to hell is paved with?"

She looked at him through her fingers. To her horror, tears slid hot against her skin. Her cousin's face softened.

"Jane," he breathed on a heavy sigh. He took her hands and held them gently. "This has been a very emotional and trying day for you. Perhaps I am wrong in demanding an answer from you immediately. Why don't we give this a few days' rest? We can discuss it again then."

Jane nodded, though in her heart she couldn't imagine she would feel any different in a week or in a year. Marcus would still be dead. And the one man she had trusted more than any other, the one man she loved . . . he would still be a liar.

Chapter 26

Nicholas was wide awake when Gladwell came to his chamber door, despite the early hour. He had been awake all night, staring up at the canopy above his bed, thinking about Jane.

And hating himself.

"I'm sorry to disturb you, sir, but Lord Fenton has returned," his butler said, almost gently.

Nicholas sat up and stared. "Fenton is here?"

Gladwell nodded. "Yes. And he refuses to leave until he has an audience. He seems very upset, my lord."

"He should get in line," Nicholas said, snorting out a humorless laugh.

He swung his legs over the edge of the bed. He was still fully clothed in the shirt and trousers he'd been wearing when Jane stormed out of his life and his home . . . probably for good. The scent of her perfume clung to them, and he was loath to remove them and lose that final part of her.

If Gladwell was surprised that he was lying

abed fully clothed, he said nothing about it. Instead, he murmured, "I will tell him you will be down in a moment, my lord, and put him in the south parlor."

"Thank you."

He expected his servant to go, but instead, Gladwell hesitated at the door.

"What is it?" Nicholas asked, his nerves frayed to a near breaking point.

"Sir, the servants all love Miss Jane," Gladwell offered. "Henderson was her driver last night and noticed she was quite upset when she departed here. Is there anything any of us can do for her . . . or for you?"

Nicholas stared at the man. Jane told him the gruff, judgmental man loved him, but he hadn't believed her. Now Gladwell was looking at Nicholas with pity and understanding.

"I'm afraid not, my friend," Nicholas said softly, bracing his arms on the dressing table and examining his haggerd face in the mirror. "There is nothing that can be done, I don't think."

"I've never approved of fisticuffs . . . especially in my sitting rooms, but it seems that you are a fighter, sir, in more ways than one. Perhaps one thing you could do is fight."

Nicholas jolted at his servant's observation and turned his gaze on Gladwell. He stared back evenly and nodded before he stepped into the hallway and left Nicholas alone.

As he quickly tidied his hair and girded himself in preparation for facing off with an apparently angry Patrick Fenton, he thought of what the butler had said. When it came to the fisticuffs his servant didn't approve of, Nicholas was prepared. As he was for cards or knife fights or any other kind of illicit activity that required cunning and skill.

But when it came to Jane, he was uncertain. Robbed of his normal weapons. Left bereft.

He strode downstairs and drew a deep breath before he entered the parlor. Patrick Fenton was standing at the window as he entered, his broad back stiff with anger as he stared out over the street below. Nicholas sighed and closed the door behind him.

The second the click of the latch echoed in the room, Fenton turned. He glared at Nicholas, then made his way across the room in several long strides. Nicholas could tell the other man was going to hit him. He knew the signs after so many fights. He could have blocked it, dodged it, even thrown his own punch first.

But he didn't. He stood stock-still and let the man swing.

The punch connected squarely with his eye and he staggered back, but kept his feet.

"Impressive," he said as he lifted his hand to his blurry eye. That was going to blacken later, even if he got ice.

Fenton stepped back. It didn't seem as if he was going to swing again, and Nicholas found himself a little disappointed. At least the throbbing physical pain made him forget, even for a second, the circumstances that brought Jane's cousin here.

"You bastard," the other man said with a disgusted shake of his head. "You were supposed to tell her gently."

"Like you and her father did, you mean?" Nicholas snapped. "How did you find out?"

Patrick paced away and flopped into the nearest cushioned chair. "She came to me at three in the morning, practically hysterical. She choked out the whole story."

Nicholas pursed his lips as he took his own seat across from Fenton. Somehow he didn't like it that Jane had gone to this man after she left him.

"It wasn't meant to happen this way," he explained.

Fenton shook his head. "I assume not. But she's brokenhearted nonetheless. Not only does she have to face her brother's death, but she is twisting herself in knots over the fact that the man she loves lied to her."

"Loved," Nicholas corrected as he shot to his feet and made for the liquor cabinet. It didn't matter that it was the ungodly hour of seven in the morning. He needed whiskey. "She told me last night that she 'loved' me. Not loves me."

"Pour me one of those and stop being an idiot,"

Fenton said. "She loves you. Present tense. But she's so jumbled and hurt right now that she is willing to do anything to push that feeling away."

Nicholas handed him the drink, and Fenton glared at him.

"I told her that since she has been compromised, probably *many* times, that she must marry. But she is very resistant."

Those words were like a vise around Nicholas's heart.

Fenton frowned. "Do you love her?"

Nicholas set his drink down. That was the question he'd been trying to avoid. Love wasn't something he had envisioned for himself. It was a luxury he hadn't been able to afford in the dangerous underground. And when he returned to Society he hadn't been able to imagine himself *liking*, let alone loving the kind of women he saw flirting behind fans and playing coquettish games.

But Jane was different. In every way. She had been his teacher, his friend, his lover, his partner. When he closed his eyes, it was easy to imagine a future with her. A family with her.

"If it takes you this long to answer," Fenton said coldly, "then perhaps that says it all. She deserves someone who will love her, Stoneworth. And if that isn't you, then I will offer my hand to her again."

Nicholas sucked in a breath. "What?"

"Someone *must* marry her," the other man said.

"In case there is a child. And at least I know I shall treat her well. I shall love her if you cannot."

"If there is a child, then it is mine to protect. Mine to legitimize," Nicholas snapped, unable to stop himself from picturing Jane holding a baby in her arms. His baby.

Fenton shook his head. "But do you love her?"

Nicholas swallowed hard. The idea of losing Jane was akin to pulling his heart from his chest. The idea of her marrying another man was even worse.

Did he love her? Did thinking of her every day, wishing to be near her, wanting to talk to her, equal *love*?

It did. He realized it in a flash, but then perhaps he had always known it but denied it. He loved Jane. He loved her passionate and brave nature. He loved her acceptance and defense of him, with all his flaws. He loved her laughter. He loved her touch, her taste, her smell.

And he didn't want to lose that. He *wouldn't* lose that. Gladwell had been right. This was the fight of Nicholas's life. And he had no intention of losing.

"I love Jane," he said. "More than my life. But winning her, especially in the state she is in currently, isn't going to be easy. But nothing worth having ever is."

"Indeed. And if that is the case, then I think I know a way to help you."

Fenton looked away, and Nicholas pitied and respected him. He was willing to give Jane up in order to ensure her happiness. Nicholas couldn't imagine the loss and hoped he wouldn't have to face it himself before this was through.

Clearing his throat, Nicholas said, "What is your plan?"

Jane sat in Lady Ridgefield's parlor, staring at the fire as it slowly ate away at a log. Around her, Lady Ridgefield and a few of her companions were chatting, but Jane hardly heard their talk. She was too wrapped up in her own thoughts, her own memories, her own tangled emotions.

"Jane?" Lady Ridgefield said so that no one else would hear. She set a hand over hers and gave it a gentle squeeze. "Are you well, dear? You have been so quiet."

Jane shook off her tangled emotions and smiled. "I'm so sorry, my lady. I am woolgathering. I'm afraid I did not get much sleep last night and I am tired."

And that was utterly true. By the time she snuck back into the house it had been almost dawn. And then she had lain in her bed, thinking about Marcus, thinking about Patrick . . . and thinking about Nicholas. So much about Nicholas and his proposal and the fact that he had lied to her when she had believed, so strongly, that he never would.

She sighed.

"You do look tired, my dear," Lady Ridgefield said. "Perhaps when your cousin arrives, we should send him away, rather than have you go riding with him."

"My cousin?" Jane said, wrinkling her brow. "Patrick is coming today?"

"Yes, my dear. I mentioned it at breakfast, did you not hear me?"

Jane dipped her chin with embarrassment. At breakfast she had been completely in her own world as she fingered her late brother's ring beneath the table and thought of the one Nicholas had offered her. She couldn't remember anything about the meal. She might have agreed to invade Spain, for all she knew.

"I'm so sorry," she whispered. "I will be more attentive."

Lady Ridgefield laughed softly. "My goodness, Jane, you never have need to apologize to me. But yes, your cousin is coming today, in fact he should be arriving any moment. I must say I am very happy to hear that you two have repaired the breach between you. Families should be together."

Jane bit her lip. She and Patrick *were* on their way to repairing the rift that had developed between them. She owed him a great many apologies for her deplorable treatment of him. And he owed her the same for keeping her father's secrets. But they would forgive each other.

So why couldn't she forgive Nicholas, too?

Jane squeezed her eyes shut, ignoring the little voice that kept asking her that question. She was too raw to answer it.

"The air might do me good," she said, giving Lady Ridgefield a smile. "I think I shall go riding with my cousin when he comes, after all."

She was certain Patrick had an agenda in mind for their outing. Probably further insistence that she marry someone to solve the problem of her ruination.

Marry Nicholas. That was the thought that kept echoing in her mind. And it was getting harder and harder to silence it.

Lady Ridgefield's butler stepped into the parlor and cleared his throat. "My lady, Lord Fenton has arrived."

The feminine sounds of pleasure that filled the room made Jane look at the women in her company. Two of them were close in age to her, and they were blushing and giggling like girls at the thought of seeing Patrick. She smiled. He *was* handsome, of course. She had just never really considered him as a *man*.

Obviously, these women did.

"Send him in," Lady Ridgefield said as everyone in the party got to her feet, including Jane.

She forced another smile and hoped she would not blush as her cousin stepped into the room. He did not look any worse for wear after their long night, though when his green gaze fell on hers, she felt his lingering concern move through her. She was both embarrassed by and appreciative of it.

"Good afternoon, ladies," Patrick said with a smile and a bow for the room. "How fine to find such a lovely group here."

The ladies twittered, and for a brief moment there was conversation and flirtation. Jane smiled through it all, but her thoughts wandered again, only to be brought back when her cousin said, "Well, Jane. Would you care to come riding with me? We could go to Hyde Park and take a turn around the lake."

She nodded. "Of course, Patrick."

Saying her farewells to the ladies in her company, including the very disappointed younger ones, she took her cousin's extended arm and allowed him to lead her out the front door. As they moved to the drive, she frowned.

"You brought your carriage, rather than your phaeton?" she asked as she looked at the enclosed boxy vehicle parked on the crunchy gravel.

He shrugged as he moved to open the door. "It could rain."

As she stepped inside, Jane was about to point out the cloudless sky, but before she could, her cousin abruptly shut the door to the vehicle and rapped on the wall outside. The carriage began to move.

Jane moved to grab the door handle, but before she could grasp it, a hand darted out of the darkness in the corner of the seat and caught her wrist.

She cried out in surprise as she looked down at the imprisoning hand. Before she even peered through the dark, she knew who her companion was. After so many days and nights, she recognized the scarred, pronounced knuckles.

"Nicholas," she hissed as her eyes finally adjusted and she could see him.

He smiled, but the expression was tight. "Hello, Jane."

Although she couldn't deny how much she liked the brush of his skin on hers, Jane still tried to shake his fingers from her wrist. He held fast.

"Why don't you sit back?" he asked, his voice low and calm. "We're driving quickly now. I wouldn't want you to be hurt."

She frowned. It would be childish to hurtle herself from the moving vehicle, even if she wanted to do such a thing. And she had no thought in her head that Nicholas would try to harm her.

At least not with his body. His words, though. His explanations and excuses . . . those were another story entirely.

"I am not ready to see you," she said as she moved to the seat opposite his and settled back. "I wish you hadn't come."

A sudden thought entered her head and she

stared at him. "How ever did you convince my cousin to assist you?"

"Very simply. Patrick Fenton truly has your best interest at heart. He says you love me, even though you want to say that my lies killed that emotion. And he thinks that marrying a man you love would make you happy."

Nicholas leaned forward, and she caught a heady whiff of his masculine scent. She fought with every breath in her not to draw closer to it and to him.

"Is your cousin right, Jane?" he said softly. "Do you love me? Despite your own objections?"

She stiffened her spine. The last thing she wanted to do was admit that. She had regretted saying she loved him last night, even if she had softened it by implying that emotion was in the past. Now he could use her vulnerability against her to get what he wanted. Whatever that was.

"I don't want to talk to you about this."

He shrugged one shoulder. "That is fair enough. Perhaps I don't deserve to hear you declare your feelings. But I think I do deserve to say my piece."

"Defend yourself, you mean?" she said with a shake of her head. "Make excuses for your actions?"

He shook his head. "No. There is no excuse for my actions. You were absolutely right in everything you said to me last night. I lied to you when you put your faith in me. I withheld information that you deserved to know for far too long. I thought it would be best to wait until we were married and I could be there for you in your grief. But I was wrong. Very wrong."

Jane was speechless. Those words were the last she had ever expected to hear from him, and now she had no idea how to respond.

"However, that isn't what I want to say," he continued.

She felt her hands begin to shake, and she shoved them in her lap so that he wouldn't see her weakening to him. "What do you want to say?"

He nodded. "I wanted to express to you that I am deeply, passionately, and completely in love with you."

She caught her breath as a burst of unstoppable joy rushed through her being. But then the doubt crept in behind it.

"Don't say such a thing to me in order to obtain what you desire," she whispered. "Don't say it so that I'll agree to forgive you or marry you or whatever it is you want from me."

He reached out and took her hand gently. She allowed it, for the brush of his thumb across her skin was just too good to deny.

"I would never say that in order to manipulate you. Once, perhaps, I would have, but you changed me, Jane. Not because you helped me relearn the ways of a good gentleman, but because you reminded me what it was like to be a good *man*. You believed that is what I could be, and it made me want to try. To make you smile. To make you laugh. To make myself worthy of you."

Jane could only suck her breath in loudly. He couldn't be saying this. He couldn't be pouring his heart out and making her believe again. Have faith again. Love him even more than she had before she saw his face in the darkness.

"Sweetest, loveliest Jane," he whispered, and now he moved to sit beside her. Close in the darkness, his breath stirred her face and his warmth wrapped around her body. "I do love you. I love you enough to let you go, if that is truly what you desire. If I have irrevocably broken your trust, then you should push me out of your life forever. Love someone else. Find whatever happiness you so richly deserve."

He stroked a finger down her cheek.

"But if you can forgive me. If you can see some way, today or in the future, that you could release your anger and love me again . . . then I want you to marry me. I want you to be my wife and the mother of my children. And my constant teacher in behavior and deportment and *love* and life. Give me the chance to prove that the faith you once put in me was well placed."

He leaned down and brushed his lips, feather light, over hers. She shut her eyes with a quiet sob as he did so. But he didn't take the kiss further. He simply released her and moved to the other side of the carriage.

"*That* is what I wanted to say, Jane."

She stared at him. He was quietly sitting, muscular arms folded, awaiting her reply, but not demanding it. But for once she could read him as he always read her. In the dim light, she saw how nervous he was. How anxious. It was in the lines around his mouth, in the expression in his bright eyes. In every fiber of his being.

He was desperate for her reply. Desperate to hear her say that she would forgive him.

And that realization, the idea that she had brought a strong and powerful man to such a level of need, broke her final resistance.

"Do you think I'm strong?" she whispered.

He nodded. "The strongest woman I have ever known. Unlike your father and your cousin, I didn't keep this secret because I thought you were weak."

"But you believed I needed you through my grief," she whispered. In her heart, she knew he was likely right. The truth that Marcus was gone cut through her like a saber. She *wanted* Nicholas's arms around her. She wanted his soothing words of comfort.

But she didn't want to marry a man who believed her to be weak. Too many men in her life had thought that of her.

"Great God, Jane, to lose your brother is a thing

one should never endure alone." He blinked, and she was shocked to see tears glistening in his bright eyes. "I know that better than most. How I wish I had had you by my side those first few months after Anthony died. To lean on. To talk to. To simply be with so that I could feel whole in some way. But I don't think having support from one you love makes you weak. It just makes you human."

She shut her eyes. That was what she needed to hear.

"I do love you," she said, letting her eyes come open. "I have probably loved you since the first moment I came into your home and you terrified me."

He smiled, and she did the same through her tears before she continued, "And though I do not like what you did, I don't want to lose you. Because I-I do need you, Nicholas. And I want to share all my grief and sadness and all my joy and triumph with you, as you share yours with me."

"Then you will marry me?" he asked, his voice all but trembling with emotion.

She nodded, and his grin was her reward. Wide and full of hope for their future and unwavering love for her.

Now it was she who moved across the carriage toward him. She wrapped her arms around his neck and smiled up at him. "And you can spend at least the first ten years of our marriage making up for the fact that you lied."

He pulled her closer. "I shall start now."

She pushed at his chest playfully, her joy overriding her sadness, at least for the moment. And she recognized that was what he had clumsily tried to give her by keeping the truth from her. Not as a betrayal, but as a gift.

And she loved him more for it.

"Nicholas! We are going to Hyde Park," she protested. "I wouldn't want to be mussed, people will talk. Do you remember nothing of my lessons?"

He shook his head. "Oh no, my dear. We are not heading for Hyde Park. You and I are off to Scotland. Gretna Green, to be precise."

Her mouth dropped open and she stared at him, flabbergasted. "Gretna Green! But—but what if I had refused to hear you?"

"Then I would have had a very long trip to beg," he said, his fingers trailing to the buttons along the back of her gown. "But I much prefer using the days ahead of us for more pleasurable activity."

Jane sighed as his lips found her throat and his skilled fingers made short work of her buttons.

"So do I, my love. So do I."

At Avon Books, we know your passion for romance—once you finish one of our novels, you find yourself wanting more.

May we tempt you with . . .

- **Excerpts** from our upcoming releases.

- Entertaining **extras**, including authors' personal photo albums and book lists.

- Behind-the-scenes **scoop** on your favorite characters and series.

- **Sweepstakes** for the chance to win free books, romantic getaways, and other fun prizes.

- Writing **tips** from our authors and editors.

- **Blog** with our authors and find out why they love to write romance.

- **Exclusive content** that's not contained within the pages of our novels.

Join us at
www.avonbooks.com